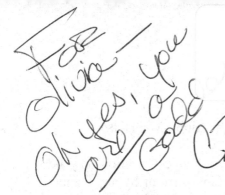

# CRONES AMONG US

## A City Slickers For
## Menopausal Women

### A Novel By
# Lindy Michaels

Printed in the United States of America


ISBN: 978-0692540961

This book is a work of fiction. All names, characters, places and descriptions are a product of the author's imagination. Any resemblance to actual persons, living or dead is entirely coincidental.


Cover Design Artwork by Tiffany Miller/
TifanyMillerMosaics.com

## Dedicated To:

To my amazing daughters, Erin and Shani and, of course, my fantastic grandchildren, Ethan, Mia, Cierra and Zoë Rose.

To women, everywhere, who might not like the idea of aging. It is time to celebrate...where you started and what you've become. It is time to celebrate your lives!

A special thanks to Tiffany Miller, my 'third daughter,' for her incredible mosaic artwork that graces this cover.

A special thanks to Karin Buchak for doing all the techno book stuff I would have had no idea how to do!

# CHAPTER ONE

## (Early 1990's)

Sara stood naked in front of the full length mirror in her bedroom, backwards. She looked into a hand mirror, forwards, thus seeing her backside in the full length mirror. And she stared. And stared. Why, she wondered, did she keep doing this destructive ritual day after day? Why? Was she some sort of glutton for punishment? Would she peek out, one eye squinted, one day and miraculously see the calves, the thighs, the ass of the sixteen year old she once was? She considered herself to be an intelligent woman. How about the body of the twenty-four year old she once was? The thirty-two year old? The forty-one year old?

Could she have self-worth as a human being and still despise her now somewhat cellulited body? If a man loved her mind, could he accept her dimpled lower limbs? In her idealistic soul she hoped so, but then that theory, or better, that reality hadn't been tested since, well, since her legs were only almost dimpled. Had it been so long or had her body changed, aged, over night... over too many months of nights?

Crap, she said to herself! She hated the thought of being one of those women who continually looked back on their lives and their asses, longingly, wishing they had the power to turn back the clock. So? What was her excuse? And why was she doing it, looking in that mirror, backwards, forwards, so much more obsessively, ashamed to admit, so many times a day?

Was it because every time she saw her reflection the facts were right in front and/or in back of her face? Not to mention now also on her face? Wrinkles. Lines. Crows-feet. Bag. Sags. Droops. Yuck!

I'm cheered up now, she thought, trying to laugh inside her head where there were no wrinkles. I am not my thighs! I am not my augmented ass! I'm me! Still me! Will someone be able to look past all this extra flesh and see the real me? Love the real me?

Suddenly, she felt a possessed need to go on Oprah and discuss the subject at great length. Then she uncontrollably laughed out loud and the moment passed.

Noting her own weird thought process, Sara wondered if it were possible that she was just a tad dysfunctional, in her mind, at least. Why not her? Just about everyone else in the country seemed to be about one thing or another. Dysfunctional. Does that mean one 'disses' functionality? Dis. Was that DIS- pise? DIS-approve? DIS-dain? DIS-respect? Yeah, that was it. Baggy-pant teens whipped out sawed-off shot guns and aimed if dissed. Could an almost fifty year old woman, solid citizen, be dissed, though? Damn tootin'! Absolutely! After half a century of waking up each morning, one would think that should earn one some respect. Think again. So Sara thought again. And thought turned to anger. She knew the truth. Two strikes and you're almost out. Oldness. Womaness. Still the plague of American society. And that's not even counting the other 'ness.' Aloneness. Two and a half strikes.

Sara was getting increasingly depressed now and it was only eight forty-five in the morning, as she stood naked, holding her hand mirror. But she wouldn't let it go.

To add insult to depression was the fact that Rebecca, Sara's soon to be nuptialed daughter was doing, thinking and feeling things that Sara figured she should still be doing, thinking and feeling. Being in love. Getting married. Birthing children. Having sex. Sex? What was that?

Life wasn't supposed to end up like this, was it? Alone? Not her life, anyway. Thirteen, fourteen months before, had her life gone smoothly, the way life never seems to, Sara would have had an arm to lean on, a body to merge close to while dancing and warm lips to kiss after Rebecca's champagne wedding toast. But not now. Now she would have to settle for David, her ex-husband to, well, maybe, dance the parents-of-the-bride dance with, while his too young, too thin present wife would give them dirty looks from the sidelines of the dance floor. That is, if Sara and David were even speaking to each other by the time the big day arrived. That possibility was getting slimmer by the day, as they hassled over everything from the number of guests, to the food, to the music, to the cost, much to Rebecca's chagrin.

Twenty-six, twenty-seven months before, Sara had become committed to and committed, with a lovely man, adultery. Well, he was lovely then. Never in her wildest imagination could she have ever believed she would indulge in this kind of anti-social, immoral, sinful, bad, bad, bad behavior. True, she had never been what one might label Molly Moral, Gloria Goody-Two Shoes, Vicki Virtuous, Renee Righteous... okay she'd been around the block a couple of times in her youth, but the Big A? Never! Never!! Oh, maybe just this once.

Thirty-one, thirty-two years before, Sara wasn't in the mood to figure out how many months that would have been, she and Peter were in love. Ah, first love. Best love. Love that you could taste like those yummy cheese burgers and french fries and cherry cokes you voraciously consumed at the local hang after the double feature at the drive-in late at night, that never put even an ounce on your slender, nimble bod. It was back then that the eighteen, nineteen year old Sara lost her not-so-sacred virginity to the lean and muscular Peter, a hunk long before the Chippendale dancer's mother's pinned diapers on their newborn son's, later to be, sculptured tushes.

But young lovers eventually grow up and grow apart and marry others and divorce those others and marry even others... and one divorced a second time, while the other did not.

After David, a second short marriage, a longer live-in lover, Sara found herself alone for more years than she could have dreamed when she painted textured pictures of an idyllic future at sleep-overs with giggling girlfriends, on those too short high school week-ends. But as the alone years went by, she learned to like herself, really like herself and found out she was okay. And she hoped to hell that you were too. She savored her time alone, raised her daughter and worked hard at her bookshop, Book, Nook and Crannies. She walked on the Santa Monica beach at dawn and many days believed she didn't need or want a man in her life. She was woman, she was strong, she was invincible, even though some days she was so damn weary at always doing everything by herself and for herself. The some days reluctant feminist.

Then one day, Peter, a grayer, paunchier Peter, reappeared in her life. A ghost lives. A dream revisits. Within the first half hour of this casual encounter he confessed, professed a love for her, a love that indeed had never died for him. A love that had lasted inside his heart for more than three decades and two marriages, the last of which was still... well, still. Eons before she had broken that heart and try as it might, the pulsating ruby organ wedged between his ribs had continued to bleed, to weep red, for her. That is what he told her. "I love you. I still love you. I have always loved you."

Captivated, blown away by the mere issuance of his words and needy in places she didn't remember she still had needs, she kissed him hard and kissed him soft and eventually, yes, eventually did the only thing she could... unzipped his pants.

For one year they loved and lusted. And lied. He lied to his wife. And she lied to herself. But for that one emotional year, she no longer had to long for love. And then on an unseasonably cold and rainy Los Angeles February morn, the phone rang early at her bookshop.

"Good morning, Book, Nook and Crannies," she said quickly, then holding her breath, always that, hoping, anticipating his rapturous, devoted voice.

And it was he. Her white knight. Her prince. He who promised over and over again that they would spend the rest of their years on this earth, together. But even still, she so often wondered that if they had been married, as he told her was his one wish in life, instead of experiencing this year of tumultuous love filled with secrecy and hidden bliss, if her heart would still beat at such an erratic, erotic pace each time her phone rang, at the sound of all his, "I adore you's?" Would this re-found love still have had that desperate immediacy to it? Would there, could there really be a 'happily ever after,' a 'forever and a day,' for them?

"Listen," he quickly said. There was not only desperation in his voice, but did she also detect panic? "I only have a minute, Sara." He indulged in a pause which was long and uncomfortable for each of them to listen to. "I... I'm not going to be able to see you for a while. Something has changed."

Sara's heart began to pound. "What is it, Honey?" she questioned. "What's wrong? You sound terrible. Are you sick? And what's all that noise I hear in the background?"

"I can't tell you about it now. She's watching my every move. You can't believe what it's been like. I had to sneak away just to make this call."

The fact was, Peter was in a phone booth on a busy street corner, his eyes darting back and forth, as if waiting to be caught by the cops after a big bank heist. Guilty. Shaking. In the rain.

Sara's once expectant and stolen heart dropped past her uterus. She tried to remain calm, thinking, hoping, praying this wasn't what she thought it might be, what she'd nightmared might happen for so many months, truly believing it never would. Not to her. Not to them. And yet, somewhere deep inside, knowing it was inevitable.

"What's going on, Peter?" No answer. "Peter? Talk to me." Could a voice get any higher? Tighter?

He took a long, deep, endless breath, then again began to speak far too quickly for her liking.

"This whole thing has been so hard for me."

"I know, Peter. It hasn't been easy for me, either."

"But… I… I've decided to stay… with my wife. I can't see you anymore." A death pause followed. And then, "It's over, Sara."

Could she even begin to digest his words? Her lips couldn't formulate the nouns, verbs and adjectives that her mind couldn't deliberate fast enough for the time she knew she didn't have.

"Just like that?" she managed.

Oh, yeah. That would give him pause. That would make him reconsider his rash actions.

She tried again. "But, what about us?"

Could she get any more profound? Her mind was racing, thinking… you schmuck! This is how you tell me, after all this time, after all our love, after all your promises to me, after all our plans, after a year of my life!? With no explanation?

Too late.

"Please don't ask me anything about it. That's all I can say. I gotta go, Sara."

No, no, no! Let me just say something, she wanted to scream at him. Let me just hear something I can understand.

How, she wondered, can you actually expect something, considering the situation, for so long, but when it finally happens it still comes as such a shock, because the truth is, you never really believed it would happen. Her body was shaking, now. She was outraged, injured beyond belief.

"Wait a minute!. Wait!" she yelled at him. She was suddenly filled with a despair that cut deep into her soul. "You can't do that! Just call me up and say it's over, just like that! You were leaving her. You told me, remember, just the other day. Finally, you were leaving her! What about not being able to live without me? That's what you've told me for a year!" Sara felt hot tears surfacing, governed by emotions beyond her control.

"Don't, Sara. I gotta go before she finds out I'm not there."

"But you love me. I know you love me. And you know it, too. How are you going to live this way... without me? How are you going to do that, Peter?"

There was no response on Peter's end and for a moment Sara, in a panic, wondered if he was still there. If he was still there, she could reason with him. She could. She knew she could.

"Peter? Please talk to me... " was all Sara was now allowed.

"I gotta go," he said.

And the line went dead.

# CHAPTER TWO

Carol's vaginal walls were drying up. It wasn't something she was aware of on an average day... but it was night. And Dan, her husband of twenty-seven years, happened to be thrusting, driving, plunging, ramming, jabbing... well, at least he was trying his damnedest to. It's rather hard to keep so, when your wife is moaning, not in pleasure, with the outcome gratification, but in obvious suffering.

Suddenly, Carol's chest, neck, face, then finally her scalp broke out into a profuse sweat. She rolled her eyes upwards to the hostile heavens. Dan rolled off her, pissed. Her lower lip jutted out, Carol began to blow air out of her mouth, forcefully. If she angled it just right, the stale ventilation hit the tip of her nose, fanning out in facial aerodynamics, the coolness grazing her eyebrows and beyond. She moaned a non-sexual moan, again.

Dan watched this scenario, shook his head, then flopped it down on his pillow, frustrated.

"Great," he could only come up with.

Carol picked up a half-read book that lay on her bed stand and furiously fanned herself. "So, what do you want me to do?" she said, helplessly.

Unfortunately, Dan was no longer the mellow guy he once had been, back in the sixties.

"I don't know! Why the hell can't your damn doctor give you something for it?"

Carol wanted to cream him and his sensitivity, or lack thereof. Instead, she screamed in a controlled voice, only because their should-be-adult-already son of almost twenty-three, who should have left home by now, slept comfortably down the hall in his old childhood room.

"Ya know, Dan, the only time you seem to care about my symptoms is when you want sex!"

"That's bull and you know it!" Dan said, he in fact not knowing it and certainly knowing Carol didn't know it.

The truth was, when Carol had started going through menopause two years earlier, Dan had been thrilled. Now, he made it clear, he wouldn't have to hear her complain about her monthly menses, with its bloating and cramping and mood swings. Little did he know what was up the road. True, her mood no long swung, swayed or swaggered once every twenty-eight days. No. Now it violently sashayed at any given moment, day in and day out and day in and day out.

For their whole long life together sex had been one of the most important parts, one of the best parts. At least for him. Carol had always been the good wife. The dutiful wife. And yes, she had fleeting, fond remembrances of a time when she, too, had enjoyed it. Those were the days. But not these days.

Carol was angry and emotional. "You couldn't deal with ten minutes of what I've been going through for the last few years, Dan!" She figured she was giving him another chance to be sympathetic.

Unfortunately, he wasn't up for the challenge. "Believe me," he answered with a sarcastic edge, "I thank God every day that I'm a man."

She glared at him, got out of their marriage bed and ran out of the room for the solace of her bathroom. But not before whipping out of her mouth, "Oh, I bet you do!"

Theirs had been a love affair in a time gone by, dating back to college. Sweethearts. Made for each other, although back then, too young to know exactly what they were made of in the first place. They married after graduation. Within a year, from their tiny apartment, she wrote him devotedly everyday, while he served a short tour of duty in

Viet Nam. She worked fourteen hours a day to make ends meet. Rosie the Riveter. Carol the nurse.

He came home early, luckily with only minor wounds. And she healed him. They drove across the country. A carefree, happy, hippy existence. They smoked grass and laughed a lot. Then she had Jonas and things got serious. After all, kids are nothing to laugh about.

Carol admitted, perhaps, just perhaps there was the slimmest chance she was a little too over-protective, a little too nervous, a little too paranoid as a first-time mother. Okay, she was a walking neurosis, but golly, she held in her strong hands and up to her swollen breast, a life, a mind and endless dirty diapers, whose if 'dirty' was the wrong color meant a near-hysterical call to her pediatrician. She was a nurse, after all. She knew what a wrong-colored 'dirty' might mean.

But Carol also knew she was succeeding as a mother, a giver of life, when Jonas grew, sat, crawled, walked and talked on time, time judged by her now dog-eared copy of Dr. Spock's Baby Care Book. So, she loosened up a bit and by the time her son was three, she hardly noticed what the hell color his 'dirty' was, even when the little tyke proudly brought it over for her inspection, as she ate her morning croissant.

"Carol!" Dan yelled, disapprovingly. "That's disgusting. Why do you let him do that?"

"He shouldn't be embarrassed by his bodily functions," she lectured her husband.

It was the very early seventies and mothers all over the country were following new guidelines on how not to raise a neurotic child, not knowing that's exactly what they were going to end up with.

"Well, at this rate he sure won't be anal." Dan whizzed by her, chuckling out loud at his pun, ignoring the dirty look she gave him.

And so life went on for Carol and Dan, through the heated LA summers and mild LA winters. But it didn't matter to Carol what season it was now. She was hot all the time.

Jonas, who no longer showed anyone his 'dirty,' was about as sympathetic to his mother's temperature as was his father.

"Why don't you take a nice cold shower, Mom," he often innocently suggested, when she would grab anything around, at arm's length, to cool herself down with.

Why don't you go and get a job, get your own apartment and take your shit with you, thought Carol, while giving him the ultimate dirty look, then, of course, feeling horribly guilty about what she was thinking.

And so Carol continued to fan, Dan continued to fume and Jonas continued leaving his dirty laundry on the floor of his room for his mother to pick up.

# CHAPTER THREE

After Peter, Sara tried hard to get on with her life. And she did. Slowly. Eventually. She had always hated how the wondrous times passed by like a blink of an eye, while the painful times crept along slower than a snail.

It had taken her so many months just to accept the reality that Peter would not again enter her life. Enter her. Period. Initially had come pain with hope. And when that was spent, came the awful, inevitable pain without hope. She knew she should let go of him and of what she had perceived would be a rich and wonderful future with him. But dreams die hard. For so long a while she was seemingly addicted to her pain. Wallowing in it.

Using it as an excuse to do nothing. To think nothing. She felt her last chance for happiness in this life had been cruelly abducted from her. And in an unhealthy way, she savored her anger and her sadness.

But as Rebecca's wedding day approached, Sara was finally beginning to peer out from her fourteen month long self-imposed mental and physical womb... sad, soft, protected, alone, floating, in the clouded amniotic fluid of her misery.

Somehow though, through these months, she had functioned most of the time with no one the wiser. She had put on a good front to the outside world. Only a few chosen friends even knew of her affair with a married man. But she could hardly have asked for their sympathy, considering what a sinner she was, considering how they, at one time or another during the affair had warned her of the smallest percentage of it ending, as she had hoped, happily ever after.

The night after she had first again slept with Peter, she dreamt she was a harlot, a daughter of joy, if you will, going from house to house, helping to break all the vows of marriage of the good townsfolk. All the sweet, innocent wives gathered together under the great bell in the town square, to think of ways to punish this wench, this trollop, this seducer of their fine men. No, of course, they couldn't and wouldn't ever think to blame their wonderful husbands, who obviously through some kind of witchcraft had been put under her evil spell.

And so they plotted and planned how to rid themselves of this devious she-devil. Then, the nicest, sweetest, most wonderful wife of them all, Peter's wife, of course, began the witch hunt. Sara was found and put into an iron belt of chastity, then nailed up on a giant "A" in the town square for all to see and ridicule, as the great bell tolled.

After that, Sara tired desperately to dream as little as possible.

A few days before her daughter's momentous hour, Sara tried on her mother-of-the-bride dress. She thought the hyphenated word sounded so ancient, conjuring up images of a short, perfectly coifed, partially gray-haired little lady wearing a yellow and burnt orange, calf-length dress with a clutch bag and silk pumps dyed to match.

Looking forward into the mirror, Sara surveyed her reflection, a vision in cream beige lace. With girdle and control-top pantyhose doing their job, she thought she looked rather... smooth. Pretty damn good, even with, at that moment, her hair stuffed under a baseball cap.

Feeling pretty in the dress and new heels that hadn't as of yet started to pinch her toes, she turned on her favorite oldie station and began to 'jerk,' 'pony,' and 'watusi' to "Louie, Louie," just to see if she still could. She could. By the time the song ended, she was breaking a fine sweat. It wasn't until then she realized how ridiculous she must look, an almost fifty year old woman jumping around to a thirty year old song, wearing a lace dress and baseball cap that stated, "Bad Hair Day."

The big day finally dawned and Sara awoke and looked across her king-sized bed to the still sleeping Rebecca. Although the early twenties child lived with her dearly intended, tradition weighed heavily and not wanting to tempt any bad luck, she had opted not to show her no longer virginal face or body to him until their moment of truth. Sara smiled lovingly at her sleeping angel. Her only born.

For one brief moment, though, she did wish it was the not so dearly long-departed Peter who was sleeping next to her, ready to share with her this happiest of days.

A few hours later at the hotel, amid curling irons and giddy bridesmaids and nervous stomachs that nibbled and barely digested complimentary shrimp, fresh veggies and fruit, the wedding party women finished their preparations. Then, after hours of tending to her excited and slightly nauseous daughter, Sara checked in with Thomas, the groom, who was as white and stiff as a cloroxed sheet in his black tux.

This led Sara to remember her own wedding day to David. The very old, little rabbi, trying to add a dab of humor into the serious vows, said in his heavy ethnic accent, "… for better or for worse, in sickness and in health, 'til death do you part or… whenever!" It was actually a good thing he had added that "whenever," since it arrived much sooner than the other.

But the mother-of-the-bride had high hopes for this union, this merging of souls and bank accounts, as she, David and the beautiful bride-to-be waited for the strains of the Wedding March to begin, cueing their walk down the rose-petaled strewn white aisle toward the flower laden Gazebo and the nervous soon-to-be groom. Less than twenty minutes later, Sara hadn't lost a daughter at all, as she knew she wouldn't, but had gained a son-in-law whom she actually liked.

At the reception that followed, Sara greeted guests, smiled widely and gladly accepted compliments of, "You don't look old enough to have a married daughter, Sara!" She did end up dancing one dance with David, as his young, too-thin wife did shoot daggers at them through the festive air.

She also danced with Thomas, that is until his blushing bride cut in to claim her man, "my husband," as Rebecca continually repeated over and over again throughout the evening, joyously testing out the luscious sound of it. And suddenly Sara was left standing in the middle of the crowded dance floor, feeling lost and alone.

Everywhere she looked were couples. Old ones, young ones, middle ones. Smiling, happy-looking couples. She knew the odds were that more than half of these duos were most likely not all that happy, putting on their party faces for the camera. But as the music played on, it seemed little consolation to Sara.

Later, stealing a private moment with her daughter, the new bride continued to glow and glow.

"Oh, Mama, can you believe I'm married? I'm really, really, definitely married! Me! Your very own child. The person you gave birth to!"

Sara laughed at her beaming offspring. "Yes, yes, Dear. From my loins you came."

"I am so happy, Mom. Wasn't it beautiful? It was perfect, wasn't it? It was just exactly how I pictured it would be. Wasn't it just perfect?"

Sara gave her daughter a very large hug. "Yes, Honey. It couldn't have been lovelier." Sara couldn't take her eyes off her Becca, so full of hope for a life of wonderment and joy and love.

"All I want for you, my Darling, is to always be this happy. And you know what? I have this feeling the two of you will be." Sara stopped and thought a moment. "Well, let's be realistic. Maybe not always, I mean not every day, but at least one third to one half of the time!"

Rebecca's face started to drop.

"No need to worry, Becca, "Sara went on, "odds are for sure one third of the time!" Sara's eyes twinkled as Rebecca feigned a pout.

"C'mon, Ma. This is no time to joke around, considering how much this wedding cost you."

At least the kid had inherited her mother's sense of humor. But then David didn't have much sense or humor.

Rebecca went on. "But don't you worry, Mama, 'cause I'm going to have much better luck than you did. You'll see. I learned from your mistakes."

Joke over.

Sara allowed herself another moment's thought. Rebecca realizing she might have crossed the line, added, "Come on, Mother, you can change your luck. You just have to get out there. Enough with never going out, never meeting anyone new. Which reminds me, did Thomas introduce you to his Uncle Harvey, yet?"

"Gee, no, Becca, but I sure look forward to it." Sara held back the overwhelming desire to run as far away as she could from wherever Uncle Harvey might be lurking.

Later in the evening, when the DJ played "Louie, Louie" and youngsters and oldsters alike, bumped and grinded, Sara joined them with the husband of an old friend and overheard a mouth in the crowd say, "Sara still has it, doesn't she? Certainly doesn't look old enough to have a married daughter, does she?"

But she was. And she did.

# CHAPTER FOUR

Out of the sheer boredom of constantly feeling lousy, Carol decided to try and better herself, if not physically, then at least intellectually. She had long since given up walking the ugly, faded lime green hospital hallways, tending to the sick and dying. But she remained always the nurturer, basing her self-worth on how others fared, especially her husband and her son. It used to be good enough for her, tending to others. But suddenly it wasn't any longer, although she knew not why.

Once Jonas was out of high school, Carol kept meaning to go back to nursing, but things kept coming up. Or staying there, as the case seemed to be. Mainly, Jonas. Always a needy child, those needs did not end as he struggled toward manhood. So Carol martyred any inking of a life of her own for her offspring, enabling him to continue to need her. Dan, a successful contractor, didn't see this as a problem. But then Dan didn't see a lot of things, problems or not, working long hours, too busy putting things into and onto his house, rather than seeing what was happening inside of it.

They had been together for so long, much was taken for granted in the relationship, actually taken for granted from day one, especially on Dan's part. Carol had her job, the job she was born and bred to do, as far as Dan was concerned... taking care of home and hearth, himself and Jonas and dinner.

He was the man of the house, ruling his domain. What more had to be said? It was beyond their control. It was the way it was supposed to be. He, man. She, wife. For they had been born into that generation, that well taught generation.

Carol, a late bloomer, had been too busy in the Seventies to pay attention to the female uprising, then full-fledged revolution. Her roots deeply planted in the South, she tried to maintain a genteel image and proudly so, while so many of her sisters fought for their independence, by burning their bras.

It had never occurred to her that the very derivation of the words that described her gender included her counterparts: Wo-MEN. Fe-MALE. It never crossed her docile mind that they even included themselves into the word that told of the pain and agony she now found herself going through. MEN-opause. Could it possibly be that it was the male species that made up definitions to begin with? That they used this particular word to describe how they had to take an unwanted "pause" from fun and frolic, while their lesser half went through this change of life? They even had the gall to interject their gender root into the word MEN-struation. My goodness! Couldn't they even let the fair and weaker sex 'struate' without having to get into the act?

But things like that never crossed Carol's mind, back then and honestly she wasn't thinking of them now. All she knew was for a while now, she found herself creeping toward exploding in frustration and anger, overcome by a feeling of worthlessness and finally, the out of her own control emotions that her life was passing by without her in tow. Something was looming inside of her now continually hot and bloated body.

She felt incased in some kind of cocoon. Claustrophobic. Desperately wanting to crawl out, bust free and fly. But to what and to where, she did not know. And she never questioned at the time how she got there or who put her there in the first place. Instead, she blamed herself for this vague, but building sensation of non-fulfillment and discontent that was becoming more concrete in her mind, day by day.

And so it came to pass that one day, not being able to stand herself, any longer, she began going on a quest for some kind of enlightenment, some answer to a question she could not yet verbalize. Starting off, tentatively at first, she left her perfectly lovely house on occasion and volunteered at Children's Hospital, caring for the small, innocent victims of AIDS. Certainly not a job for the faint of heart, she quickly realized. Babies died in her arms, until she had to run from this harsh new reality of life.

She then gave her time at a home for battered women. These weren't the kinds of activities one jumped out of bed in the morning with anticipation for a happy days work ahead. But talking with these women affected her deeply. Had she lived such a sheltered life, always safe, always taken care of, that it seemed impossible that men could do such things, commit such violent crimes against her very own sex?

It was then that she became obsessed with the injustices hurled at women. Suddenly, she saw them everywhere she turned. She even saw them in her own life, beginning with the medical office, a place in which she had always felt so comfortable. Her very own doctor dismissed her, ignoring her truths, considering her to be a whiner and a complainer when she regaled him with her physical and mental maladies attached to her menopause. Why had she never taken notice of this before, she wondered?

Perhaps, because as a nurse, she had been taught to worship the ground the male doctors that she worked with walked on. She had followed their orders, administered medications they prescribed, watched their handy work in awe as they fixed the problems of life, trying to ward off death. And she looked on as they patched up, especially women's bodies and minds with operations and medications perhaps not always needed.

And so it was that now when her own gynecologist wrote on his all important pad for her, his scribbled signature, unintelligible, possibly never to be identified in case of a question of ethics, pills of Valium and Prozac to calm her frayed nerves to keep her psyche on an even keel, to help her cope with the inevitable transition into old age... for the first time in her life, she balked.

"But Doctor Williams, I'd rather not be on that kind of medication."

"Oh, Carol, believe me," her doctor patronizingly replied, "it will help calm you down, take the edge off. I know how depressing it is for you to realize your womanhood is coming to an end."

Carol almost spit at him, suddenly wanting to call him by his first name, Arnold, as he always did to her. How the hell would you know anything about how a woman feels, she wanted to scream at him, but didn't. Instead, she took the prescription from him, then angrily crumpled it into a ball after he left her alone in the sterile room minutes later, her feet still in the cold stirrups, her body exposed to her male god.

And with that straw, the camel's back broke for her. And she blew! And she seethed! And she was more outraged then she had ever been in her life. And she had to wonder just why it had taken forty-eight years to happen.

As she closed her legs, trying to regain some sense of her dignity, as always happened after her yearly exams, she made a mental note never to enter this doctor's office ever again. No, she would find herself a female doctor who would obviously know better how the mind and body of another woman works.

Carol's wrath stayed with her, soon taking her on what was to become a brand new direction in her quest. Uncharted territory for this up-until-now passive wife and good mother who was quite afraid if she didn't do something soon, would descend into, what, complete invisibility? What then, according to the good Doctor Arnold, did a woman become after menopause and before death... a complete non-entity?

That night at dinner, Dan and Jonas annoyed Carol even more than usual. She definitely had not left her outrage at the doctor's office. Not by a long shot.

"This meat's a little tough, Sweetie," Dan complained, chewing hard to make his point.

"Yeah, Mom. It's killing my jaws," added the father's son.

"Let 'em die," Carol mumbled under her breath, as she picked at her salad.

"What'd you say, Hon?' said Dan, cutting another piece of meat in an exaggerated manner.

"So, what'd your doctor say? You saw him, today, I hope, didn't you? Did he finally give you something new to help with your problems?"

"Menopause is not a problem, Dan." She felt herself beginning to seethe, again, her heat rising.

"Maybe not for you, but it's driving me nuts," laughed Dan, innocently thinking he was making a funny.

"Yeah, Mom. When are you going to be yourself, again?" added Jonas.

Carol glared at the two men in her life. "This is me!" she yelled. Then she got up abruptly and left the room.

The men looked at each other and shrugged, hardly wondering what in God's name could have caused this emotional outburst.

"Come on, Honey," Dan half-pleaded, with not enough sincerity to bring her back. "We were only kidding. Where's your sense of humor, these days? ... Honey?"

# CHAPTER FIVE

Book, Nook and Crannies was situated in an old fashioned plaza, self contained and quaint. Tourists and locals, alike, strolled amongst its shops and cafes, one such being a wonderful eatery, specializing in fine pastas.

Taking her lunch break there, at an outside table over which was a yellow and white striped umbrella, sat Sara with her old friend, Bonnie. Neither had ordered the specialty. While Sara nibbled on greens, Bonnie stared at her mound of cottage cheese surrounded by fresh fruit.

They had been friends dating back to high school, but they had most definitely grown apart. The years and their differing philosophical views of the worlds they now inhabited had taken their toll, but even with this, they continued to remain once-a-month-or-so pals. Quite the opposite from the more earthy and natural looking Sara, never able to completely give up her old hippie-type way of dressing, who on this day was draped in a colorful, ethnic shirt over faded blue jeans, Bonnie was dressed to the nines, wearing linen pants, a silk shirt and matching heels. Her face was perfectly and heavily made-up. With every strand of her shocking red hair in place, her manicured, square-shaped nails painted fire engine red, her figure slim, but now curvy, what with her huge breast enhancement, she daintily dipped her fork into her unappealing, low-cal lunch.

Putting a taste of this tasteless lunch to her lips, she looked over to Sara. "You're picking, Sara."

Foodless fork in hand, Sara was staring out at the plaza, where children frolicked in the near-by play area, seeing nothing.

"Sara... Hello... Where are you?" Bonnie asked, elongating each of the word's syllables.

Soon enough Sara returned to the living. "I'm sorry, Bonnie. I'm here. Somewhere."

You know, I'm really starting to worry about you, Sar. What's wrong? I know we haven't seen each other much, lately, but, I don't know, you don't seem to be yourself, lately."

"Who've I been, then?" Sara smiled, weakly.

"You got me, Honey, but you're definitely not a lot of fun these days."

Fun? What's fun, thought Sara. "Please, Bonnie. You know what a rough year or so it's been for me."

Sara took a small bite of her salad, while Bonnie continued to stare at her.

"Okay, okay. So I've been a little... off, since Becca got married. I heard that happens to lots of mothers. Mm, but she's so happy, I feel guilty feeling it."

"Well, maybe it is normal," said Bonnie, leaning over the table just a little. "You see her life as much more exciting than your own. I can understand that. But let's be honest here. I don't think what you're feeling has that much to do with Rebecca, at all. I think you've taken a vacation from life since Peter. That's what I think!"

"Do you, now?" Sara sounded annoyed.

"Now don't get all pissy about it, but it's true, Sara. And I hate seeing you this way when it doesn't have to be. Why can't I convince you to start going out, again? Have some fun, girl. I'm telling you, what you need is a good orgasm!"

Sara rolled her eyes and shook her head. Now she remembered why she didn't like spending too much time around Bonnie. The woman had a one-track mind. Well, maybe three-tracked. Men, preferable young and rich ones. Sex. And looking as young as was humanly, make that medically possible.

Bonnie tried one more time. "Okay, I have another suggestion. Why don't you treat yourself to a face lift. A little freshening up! A little suck here and there. I'm telling you, Sara, a little spruce up would do you a world of good."

Sara figured she would rather go to a forest and look up at some spruces than have some doctor reassemble her face. No, she did not believe that was the answer to women's problems. On the other hand, she thought, what was?

"Afraid not, Bonnie. You're barking up the wrong woman, here. It's not about Peter. It's not about sex. And it's definitely not about a little extra skin on my face." Maybe my wrinkled ass and legs, Sara thought, but my face, not so much. Continuing on, Sara fessed up. "Oh, I don't know. Maybe, maybe it's more about… things inside of me. My thoughts. Maybe thinking about getting older. I never really thought that much about it, before."

Bonnie looked hard at Sara's face, this time really focusing on more than her fine lines and wrinkles. "Oh my God," she said quite loudly, "I nearly forgot. You're going to be fifty this year, aren't you?"

"Don't remind me, please" said Sara, shaking her head, again. The thought seemed absolutely impossible to fathom.

"Ooh, sorry," Bonnie almost whispered. "Well, see, that's an even better reason to get some work done on yourself. Give yourself a birthday present! And I have the best doctor in the business. I mean, look what he did for me!"

Sara looked at Bonnie's smooth, way too tight skin which made her look like a forty-eight year old who had had a lot of plastic surgery.

"Don't get me wrong, you look... great, but it's just not for me."

"So, what are you going to do? Continue to be depressed? I'm telling you, you'll feel like a new woman." Bonnie wasn't giving up.

"Actually, I'm thinking of going away for a week. Just getting out of here for a little break.

This got Bonnie very excited. "Really? Where to? A cruise? How 'bout skiing in Aspen? There's still snow there. Hey, I'll join you in that."

"No, I was thinking of going on this retreat up in Washington. You know, nature, hiking, breathing some clean air for a change."

Bonnie's tight face fell in disappointment, as much as it could. "Oh. Well, that's not my style. I know, let's go to one of those all purpose spas, where we're the purpose! Doesn't a week of pampering sound marvelous?" Bonnie swooned.

The chasm of thought that divided these two women had become too deep, too wide for Sara. And she was too tired, not to mention not really interested in trying to close the gap. No, Sara wasn't looking to go to a spa or a glamorous vacation of any sort. She was looking for an experience filled with deep meaning, something much more than skin deep. But maybe her friend was right about one thing.

Maybe she had to get out among the living more. As hard as she worked, she had isolated herself. Thinking, always thinking. And if not that, then reading. Alone.

As much as she kept Rebecca in her thoughts, her welfare and happiness, the married child no longer allowed Sara to be her main concern. Raising a daughter, for the most part alone, the two had become so close. Perhaps too close. But it went both ways. As her daughter grew, their roles sometimes got reversed, especially during her illicit involvement with Peter. As the affair deepened, Rebecca, taking on the mother role, came to lecture Sara on more than one occasion.

"Mom, if he really loved you, then he'd leave his wife," the daughter often told the mother. "But the way it is now, he's having his cake and eating it too. He should shit or get off the pot!"

And later she had said, "How can you stand it, Mom? He sneaks up to your bedroom during the day, then goes home to his wife every night. He's using you!"

And it came to pass, the daughter was right. Damn it!

But now, although they talked everyday, Rebecca's priorities were with her husband, as well they should be. And Sara felt the loss. Her nest was empty. She was proud that she had raised such a loving, independent child, one so bright and talented and aware of the world around her. One who stood up for her convictions. But, oh, how she missed her.

She was obviously still there, only now changed by real adulthood, not needing her mother as she once had, soon ready to leap from maiden into motherhood, herself.

And so Sara buried herself even more deeply into her work at her bookshop. Only it suddenly wasn't as fulfilling as it once had been. What was it she was searching for? What was the answer? What the hell was the question?

Sara had worked her whole life. In the seventies she once dated a man who loved to introduce her as, "You know MS Magazine? Well, here she is! A single mother, owns her own business! Isn't she great? She doesn't need anybody." Then he went off and married 'Susie Homemaker.' Screw him! Didn't he know that she did need someone? Didn't he see that she also craved love and caring?

But that was a long time ago. So what now of the rest of her life? She longed for a new direction, now that she was totally free, now that Rebecca had someone else to comfort her when she was sad. Now, when so many of her friends, like Bonnie, were more concerned with how they looked, then who they were... who could she turn to now?

Married friends were leaving the big city in droves, retiring to places like Arizona, Idaho, New Mexico. Retire? Sara didn't want to retire. She didn't want to move. What then would she possible do for the rest of her life? She craved something she couldn't verbalize. A meeting of the minds. But whose? And where? And how? There must be others, such as herself. There must. Maybe she would find it on this retreat, this thing she was looking for. Maybe she just needed to get away and get some kind of perspective.

No, she hadn't been completely honest with Bonnie. She was going to be fifty years old and the truth was she didn't like it at all. She wanted to feel young, again. And free. And passionate about living. She wanted to feel like she once had, bubbling to over-flowing with all the possibilities that life had to offer. Was it too late, she sadly wondered?

# CHAPTER SIX

Carol thirsted for knowledge and hungered to dabble and explore. But where to begin? She felt it was a new morning of her life and if ever a mind could quiver with excitement, hers did. She began by roaming local book stores, not the Crowns, nor the BookStars, those new mega-book stores, but the few, small, cozier mom and pop operations that held on to their retail by a thin thread. No, for Carol there could be no discount for the mission of learning she was about to embark on. She sought out shops that had extensive sections on women, starving for information pertaining to her sex. She felt she had a lifetime of make-up work to do.

She took a few courses and attended a lecture on Women In The New Millennium, but truthfully didn't like what she heard about women continuing to struggle up a man's corporate ladder, dressing in severe suits, emulating the males toward whom they secretly had hate, while trying to make it in their world. Their world.

Then there were these new kind of so-called feminists, ones with huge silicone breasts who now were becoming rich by exploiting themselves, instead of being exploited by the Hugh Hefners of the world, in their own naked calendars. Exploitation is exploitation, thought Carol. She heard on the radio young men rapping about violence toward "their bitches." She had read how a number of women were now producing movies, were even heads of studios, finally breaking that glass ceiling, but were they making movies pertaining to women, especially aging women, whom they were by now, too? No they were all making men's movies, filled with action and destruction. These women had finally gotten the power, but were squandering it, in her estimation. The sad truth she was learning was that in all these years, not much had changed for her sex. It was almost the mid nineties, for crying out loud, and it was still a man's world and in so many ways women were still merely renters on this earth, paying monthly dues to their male landlords. After all this time did women even have a real identity of their own on this planet Earth? They were given a man's name, their father's, then their husbands, given choices that really only men gave to them. Carol had to look no further than her own home to know this was true.

Why had Carol never thought of these things before? Why hadn't she ever realized how enslaved she really was? All of a sudden, her harmless quest for enlightenment was turning into more of a crusade to find the woman inside of her, not related to the male species. To Dan. Was that even a possibility, she wondered?

On one inspired evening she sat captivated, listening to Maya Angelo recite black women's poetry and heard of the black sister's struggles and strife. Excitement filled her, where before there had been emptiness. Suddenly, she no longer felt quite so alone.

And she learned more about the movement that had passed her by, twenty years before, when she was washing diapers and dishes and living life to please her husband. She desperately wanted to turn back time and march together with those braless broads who fought for the rights of their own bodies. How very sad it was that she ended up not being too late, after all, since good Christian folk were still killing abortion doctors as they fought for "the right to life." Whose life?

True, some things had changed, but the majority of men still fought the female sex tooth and nail to have things their way, the man's way. And layers of anger bubbled and brewed inside of Carol at all the still injustices hurled against those humans unlucky enough in this society to have been born without a penis. Who were these women? And were they her?

Carol's friend Andi really couldn't identify with all Carol was feeling. But Carol forgave her. How could she not? Andi was only in her early thirties, had as yet to marry, made a good living writing romance novels and struggled not. She was, Carol perceived, one of the lucky ones.

Andi told her that she loved to write these kinds of fantasies since, at least, in her books the men were sensitive, intelligent and romantic. Unfortunately, she admitted, she had yet to meet such a man in her real life. Like her heroines, Andi was a strong, don't mess with me, kind of woman. The women in her books didn't settle for less and Andi didn't intend to either. Of course, they got to have much more sex than Andi did, which annoyed the crap out of her. It was why her books were so popular. It gave the average woman a dream, a fantasy, before they went into the kitchen to cook up some hash for their beer guzzling, sports watching man.

In her heart of hearts, Carol knew all men weren't demons from hell. Not even Dan. What really interested her was how women came to be in the place they were in, still in, for the most part, and more importantly, how they could get out. Especially her.

41

Carol had met Andi when they ended up one afternoon on the same museum tour of women's artists. They began talking and instantly clicked. Dan considered all of his wife's new activities, including her new friend as harmless, just a silly phase his wife was going through. As long as it didn't interfere with her real responsibilities, him being the foremost, he wasn't all that concerned. In fact, he was not that interested in any of his wife's new interests. Since Carol seemed a little happier of late, then whatever she was doing was fine with him.

And so it was that on a mild and sunny morning, Carol and Andi drove north on the beautiful Pacific Coast Highway towards Malibu. It had been some years since the great fire had ravaged the area and now the hills were again thick with grass and wild flowers. Spring was in the air and no matter how devastating were the multiple natural disasters that seemed to constantly attack Southern California, a whiff of the ocean air, that first view of the historic coast and one no longer need wonder what made people continue to settle here, or what kept the already settled defiant to stay put.

A while later found Carol and Andi immersed in the large women's section, entitled, "Yes, My Women, Life Is Tough," in the bookshop, Book Nook and Crannies. When Carol saw this shop, saw the shelves crammed with books she knew would be of utmost interest to her, she felt she was home.

As she inspected the books, most of which she one day hoped to make her own, both physically and philosophically, she jotted down titles and authors on a large yellow legal pad she had brought with her. Would she live long enough to read all there was to read, she wondered, learn all there was to learn? And then, live all there was to live?

She loved this book shop and thanked Andi for bringing her here. Looking around, she gazed at aisle after aisle of books packed to the ceiling with great literature. In one corner was on old-fashioned wood-burning stove, surrounded by comfy chairs and couches, inviting one to curl up and read. A winding staircase led to an attic area filled with children's books, where story hours were held. A bohemian looking young woman sat on a high stool behind the cash register near the front door, tending to the needs of customers, of which there were many, while soft classical music filtered throughout the shop. Carol instantly wanted to become partners with whoever owned such a wonderful place, whose vision allowed her to step into this lovely literary world.

At that same moment, a hassled Sara sat at her desk in her open-spaced office, dealing with the harsh realities of owning one's own business. Piled high on her desk were bills to be paid. Around her feet were boxes of books to be inventoried and put on the shelves. Sara looked out into the shop area to see it had filled up with patrons. A little more paper work and she would do what she did best, talk to the people, inspire them, helping them make the right selections for their needs and desires. She was so good at this and she knew it.

Having a grand old time, Carol was leafing through Betty Friedan's book, The Fountain Of Age. Maybe that would be her next area of study, women aging. It was certainly apropos of her life, that was for sure. Standing next to her, Andi pulled a book from the shelf.

"Will you listen to these titles. 'So What If Your Bladder Doesn't Listen To You, Anymore.' If that's what I have to look forward to, just kill me now!' laughed Andi.

Suddenly, Carol looked away from her book and rolled her eyes, upwards. She took a short breath, then began to fan herself with her pad. Andi took no notice of this.

"How 'bout this one, Carol? 'Women Who Love To Hate The Men They Love Too Much And The Men Who Hate To Love Them.' I love it, whatever it means." She said the title over and over out loud, trying to figure it out, but couldn't.

By the time Andi looked over to her friend, Carol was very hot and very wet.

"Car? Are you okay?" asked a now concerned Andi.

Carol could only nod, as she continued to sweat and fan herself.

Andi then took another book off the shelf. "Here's one I think you better look at and quick. 'Memories Of Menopause.' Sounds like a Barry Manilow song, doesn't it?"

"Very funny," managed Carol. "I only wish it were a memory, already."

"Will you listen to these chapters... 'Don't Let Your Depression Depress You.' Who are they kidding? Oh, and here. 'Your Drying Uterus And You.'"

"That's me, alright," said an even wetter than usual Carol.

"Yes! Here we go," continued Andi, on a roll, now. "Healing Through Hot Flashes."

"There's a way? I don't think so. It was probably written by some arrogant man who thinks he has answers for everything female," said a suddenly very hostile Carol.

Andi looked for the author's name on the front of the book. "You're right. Maurice Carothers, M.D."

All of a sudden, Carol felt very, very dizzy. She bent over and took hold of the bookshelf to steady herself.

Andi immediately put her arm around her. "Carol? Are you okay? You don't look so good."

At that moment, Sara wandered by and saw that something was wrong with one of her customers.

"Are you alright?" she asked with real concern.

A few minutes later, after Sara had sat Carol down at a large table, the top of which held all kinds of flyers for concerts, lectures and the like, she brought to Carol a large glass of water.

"Are you feeling any better? I could get you some soup or something from next door," said the still concerned bookshop owner.

After declining the sweet offer and explaining it was just Mother Nature, obviously once again punishing her for being born a woman, after they all had a light laugh about it, after Sara admitted she was still waiting to go through her change, "Well, I'm certainly not looking forward it," Sara left Carol and Andi alone.

"Let's hope she's luckier then me, huh?" Carol remarked as she drank the cool water and gained back her composure and Andi began to look over the flyers on the table. Many of them were advertisements for all kinds of self-help workshops. It made Andi wonder how people got through life before the term, "Self-Help." And did people, indeed, need all this help, self or not? One flyer especially caught her eye. As she read it she started to laugh out loud, making the feeling-better-now Carol wonder what was so funny.

"This is great! Here's what I call an interesting, fun week," said Andi, still laughing. "Going on a retreat called, 'On Becoming A Crone.' That's so funny."

"What's funny about that?" asked a slightly vexed Carol.

"Well, for one thing, do you really want to spend seven days exploring if you're a witch or not? I mean, wouldn't you know if you were one? I don't know, being able to cast evil spells on your enemies, maybe having some flying monkeys in your garage, having only large black capes and tall pointy hats in your closet. Um, let's see, mm, having a fondness for black cats... Warts on your face..."

Carol's vex turned to indignant.

"Enough, Andi! Shame on you!" A Crone isn't a witch! I just was reading something about them. A Crone, for your information, is a very wise woman. An elder! A person to be revered!" Carol could hear her voice getting louder and louder. "A Crone is a mature female whom the younger generation, like you, I might add, should listen to and learn from!"

To say this outburst was a surprise was an understatement. Andi had never seen Carol react to anything quite so emotionally.

"Okay. Okay! But what gives? You sound personally insulted."

Carol's voice rose even higher and louder, she seemingly having no control over it. "You're damn right! I am! Ya know, I'm almost one myself, damn it! And if I have to spend these years sweating, crying, drying up, being damn dizzy and bloated and feeling like crap most of the time... I, at least, want to be respected and, and... honored for it!!"

Other shop customers couldn't help but hear this outburst and casually looked over to see who was causing such a ruckus. Sara, unfortunately missed this tirade, since she was out back getting a delivery.

Then an old woman, who was eighty if she was a day, toddled up to Carol, patted her on the head and said, "Right on, Dearie, right on," then toddled away, again.

Needless to say, Carol was unbelievably embarrassed, yet strangely empowered. Not knowing quite what to do at that point, wanting more than anything to fade into the beautifully hand-crafted woodwork of the shop, to disappear from life itself if at all possible, grabbed the flyer out of Andi's hand.

"Let me see that!"

# CHAPTER SEVEN

Sara sat outside in the small patio area of her Santa Monica townhouse, drinking her morning tea. It was Monday and she pondered about what she would do, on this her only day off from the rigors of her work. Catch up on new arrivals she had brought home to read? Although an impossible job, she tried to read every word in every book she stocked in her shop. How else would she be able to sell them? But at the moment, she didn't feel like reading.

She looked around the enclosed space where she sat. It wasn't a pretty sight. A few flowerless plants and vines struggled to survive, despite her neglect at watering them, much less ever entering into a conversation with them.

When she had moved here, less than a year before, she had had such plans for this space. A place to grow her own little garden. She intended to plant night blooming jasmine, because she loved its intoxicating fragrance. A rainbow of color would liven up the five by five feet of soil next to the deck. And on that small wood-slat deck on which she now sat, would be planted in terra-cotta pots, daisies and zinnias and marigolds. But busy as she always seemed to be, she never got around to any of it. Only there now, laboring to endure, were the few wilting left-overs from the former owner.

Prior to moving here, she had remained in the large house she had bought and shared with David, half her life spent in that house. A gardener had always taken care of the foliage in the huge yard. Too big an undertaking for a brown thumb such as she.

It had been such a relief to finally rid herself of the responsibility of managing such a place, especially once Rebecca moved out, with its hints of memories always haunting her of David, later a short second marriage to an alcoholic, a talented, beautiful alcoholic, now so long ago she could hardly remember those painful years. And then her incredibly passionate 5 year live-in relationship with the long-haired blond Sean, the earth-child poet/musician.

After David, she continually seemed to find men she could and as it turned out, would have to take care of, financially and emotionally. Maybe it was because David had ruled her and one day she decided, never again. I will be in charge, she told herself. And she was, until she just didn't want to, anymore.

And then a number of years went by until Peter came back into her life. When she sold her house and moved here, the first thing she bought was a new virgin king-sized bed. No ghosts of past loves haunting her place of dreams, now. And in her much smaller bathroom, one tooth brush stood, alone, marking its territory in a ceramic rinsing cup. If you dare to leave a brush, you had better be ready to leave your heart here, forever, it seemed to say.

She had rid herself of the age-old furniture she still had that David had picked out so many, many years before, this time to decorate her own way, in country pine. Mementos from her past, her years of living, stood firm on bookcases and on built-in shelves. And recent things acquired proclaimed a new style of Sara. A cross between Native American and country. There was no longer a trace of the men she had once loved and at times hated, except for pictures and letters, neatly adhered to in now yellowing pages of scrap books, to remind her if she looked, of a life she had once lived.

She thought of Sean, who wrote her words of love on a daily basis. A beautiful man-child, young and deep, almost too lovely for words. Having a few small editions of his work published by a local company, it did not begin to bring in adequate funds to survive. And so he worked, not nearly enough, though, at a bookshop/poetry reading/coffee house type establishment, reminiscent of the ones in Greenwich Village in the fifties and sixties, where people snapped their fingers to respond to a poem well written, in lieu of clapping.

By then the eighties had arrived and beatniks had long since disappeared. So had the hippies. In came MTV, Madonna and her wannabees and then the greedies, the Young Turks, the twenty-something arrogant suits who wheeled and dealed at stocks and bonds, who definitely had no interest in esoteric mumble jumble. Poor Sean. He had been born into the wrong generation, more than half a generation after Sara. But she had found in him a sensitive soul and she had loved him deeply. It didn't matter, for a while, anyway, that he had no concept what-so-ever of the real world. He was a child of the earth, not interested in actually changing the land he inhabited, only to write about all that was wrong with it. And how he saw it had nothing to do with what it took to put food on his plate, only what was put into that food before it got onto his plate. Oh yes, he had mighty convictions about this rotten society he was born into at the wrong time in history, but was only satisfied to vent his hostility through his off-beat poems. He was an angry young man with a pen. Sadly, it turned out, not much more. And so it was no surprise that after a while their relationship got as old as she was getting. And that inevitable day arrived when she no longer felt the need or desire to take care of this physically beautiful person, anymore. And on that day, she found her love for him had vanished, too. Had she somehow mistaken love for the compulsion to take care of him? And it made her wonder just what the hell was love, anyway?

He was devastated when she said good-by. She, although sad at the loss of yet another relationship, was at least confident by the fact that he now had the ammunition for a whole 'nother book of poems of anger, more likely than not, targeted at her.

But she had to wonder why she always tended to find men who were so unavailable, men who couldn't be there for her any which way, emotionally, intellectually, realistically. Physically, well that never was the problem. If that was her script, she wanted a rewrite.

Sara took a last sip of her now cold tea. How long had she been sitting there? She picked up the flyer for the Crone Workshop that lay on her lap and read it over, again. The last few days she had contemplated not going after all. She couldn't remember the last time she had been away from her shop, her other baby, for that long a time. She could hardly stay away on her measly day off, much less for a week.

She read the flyer over for the hundredth time. It told of finding the Goddess within her. Was this about radical feminists sick of worshipping a male god, and making up one in their own image, instead? Sara hoped not, because she didn't believe in any supreme being, be it male or female.

She remembered back to when she was a little girl of ten and a sad smile curved her lips. Her mother's father, her Grampy was very ill. A born and bred atheist, she remembered looking out of her bedroom window trying to find the North Star to wish on. When she couldn't locate it, she talked out loud to the sky, in general.

"Oh, please, sky," she had said softly, lest any family member hear her. "If there is a god up there, please make my Grampy better."

He died a few days later.

When her mother traveled states away for the funeral, Sara crept, crying, to her sleeping father's bed, waking him to ask why they hadn't taught her to believe in a god, so she would know her Grandfather was in a safe place. Somewhere. Anywhere.

Half asleep and groggy, her father drowsily said to her, "Okay, Sara, you know we don't believe in that stuff."

"But why, Daddy? Tell me again," asked the pained Sara in her small and tearful voice.

Wanting to close his tired eyes, again, he rattled off to her, as quickly as possible, his truth, the truth he had taught his daughter.

"Don't you remember, Sara? I've told you a million times. We can scientifically go back to when there were lots of different gases in the air... over a very long time, billions and billions of years, the gases came together, eventually forming the sun. Then millions of years later, parts of the sun were flung off from it and after a long, long time they cooled down and one of those parts was the earth, where we live today…"

Small Sara fell asleep at the foot of her father's bed before he got to Darwin's Theory of Evolution, going back to the one-celled ameba. Too bad, because that was her favorite part of the story. But still, it was so very hard for the youngster to grow up with no connection to something greater than herself, science aside. Not because the theory didn't eventually make sense to her, but because though out her life it placed her so far apart from all her peers, leaving her to always feel different, never to really fit in, seemingly living with a one way glass in front of her, where she could see out, but no one could really see her.

And now Sara was deliberating if she chose to spend a week in the great outdoors, in reverence to the Goddess. No, she wasn't sure about this week, at all. Would she be required to dance naked at night in a field, like those Wicca women she'd read about? She didn't think she'd be up for that kind of thing.

On the other hand, the flyer also spoke so profoundly of womanhood, especially older womanhood. Crone-hood. And celebrating one's life. Well, she thought, as she picked a dead leaf off a half dead plant by her chair, she might be open to a little celebration, as long as they convinced her there was, indeed, something to celebrate in her life. At this point, she wasn't sure. She wondered what her long dead parents would think about it. She could only imagine.

Oh, what the hell, she decided. She would take the risk and go. Anyway, it was too late to get her deposit back, now.

## CHAPTER EIGHT

Carol's garden was flourishing. She tended to it the way she tended to everything in her life. Perfectly. One might say all her work and her perfection was taken for granted by her family, but it was more that it was accepted as the norm. Simply the way things were and had always been. She had set it up that way and it was only recently she had begun to resent it.

When it was pondered, could Dan really be blamed for wondering what was going on with his wife? And how could she explain to him what seeds of discontent were being sewn in her mind when she couldn't verbalize them, much less understand them, herself?

When they would fight over some insignificant happening, at least what he considered to be such and she would respond with angry tears at his insensitivity, he would later bring her flowers as some kind of archaic peace offering. And sometimes she would yell at him, inside her head, as she carefully arranged them in her favorite vase, 'Oh, so you think these will make it all better? Make up for your boorish behavior?' He made the gift of posies meaningless to her, when once so long ago they had meant a colorful symbol that she'd accept, proof positive of his undying love for her.

So now, when his offering went seemingly unappreciated, he thought, 'What do you want of me? I went out of my way and brought you your favorite flowers. What the hell do you want from me, anyway?'

Life had become a roller-coaster ride in the dark for them. Up and down. Round and round. Dan, never knowing how his wife was feeling from one moment to the next and Carol knowing her husband didn't have a clue into her psyche.

Stalemate.

But hadn't she tried to explain over and over that she no longer felt right, especially in the aging shell that housed her? Her body had become her enemy, a foe she couldn't readily identify and as the days passed by, one she had less and less control over. Hadn't she told him that these days her mind had a mind of it's own, that her body didn't seem to be her own, anymore?

So where was she in all of this, she wondered? He certainly didn't have the answer, obviously tired of hearing the question. Some part of her being wasn't going along with all the changes being thrust upon her body.

The answer, if you could call it that, from all the experts, was always the same. 'Hormones' was the operative, much used word that continued to be tossed around with such ease by the medical profession, who in truth had no other scientific findings for what ailed their aging female patients. And don't think for a moment it was only aging women this applied to. Though generation after generation it became *the* answer for all of misunderstood female society, starting back when little girls woke to find tiny buds on their chests, where before had been flatness.

"Hey! Watch out, man! She's on the rag," teenage boys laughed, describing how their girlfriends now acted depressed and testy, once a month. Once a month, ha! What about the week before and the week after, as young bodies tried to accustom themselves to nature's changes within them?

And later, when so many husbands with patronizing insensitivity patted the swelling tummies of their wives, where they secretly hoped a male heir was developing, said, "It's okay, Hon, I know what your body is going through with all those hormonal changes. I was just reading something about it. See. See what a modern, sensitive guy your husband is."

And finally, when woman's magnificent womb of evolving existence was about to retire, exhausted after years and years of toil, giving forth blood and babies, once again their feelings were belittled in the name of the substance produced in the body that stimulates an organ. Hormones. And Carol thought about all this.

Later in her learning quest, she would realize that the three most important experiences that happen in a woman's life: the beginning of fertility, fertility itself and finally the loss of that fertility had been diminished and reduced in society to a simple hormone problem. And women had bought into it and all the pills it came with, ignoring the fact that all this just might have something to do with why they had come to live their lives with so little self-worth.

Carol, experiencing yet another hot flash and a mental state that resembled a plane ride in turbulent weather, reread her Crone flyer and said out loud to herself, "And they expect me to celebrate?"

On a morning two weeks before the retreat found Carol, Dan and Jonas in their combination kitchen, breakfast room. The men had their heads buried in the newspaper, while Carol patiently waited for their toast to emerge from the toaster. When Carol brought the bronzed bread to the table, without looking up from his news, Dan said, "Aren't you eating? Not on another one of your nutty diets, are you?"

No, I'm just not very hungry. But maybe I'll have some tea." She paused a moment, to no one's interest. "I don't know. Maybe not."

Carol decided on tea, after all, poured herself a cup, then sat down at the table. She looked at each of her men, or rather at the opened papers that hid their faces. She took a deep breath, thinking this was as good a time as any to tell them.

"I've decided to go on a little... vacation," she said quickly and simply, as her heart raced.

There was no immediate response from behind the black on white pages. Then a voice from behind the print. It was Jonas.

"Whatta ya mean, Mom?"

Carol experienced immediate, perhaps un-called for annoyance. "What do you mean, what do I mean?" she said quite deliberately. "I mean what I mean. I'm going on a vacation."

Both men then peeked over their wall of news and looked at her, then looked at each other, then at her again, trying to size up this strange situation, as far as they were concerned.

Always on the defensive these days, Carol said, "What? What are you both looking at?"

"Didn't we just come back from a nice little vacation in San Diego? And what do you mean, you're going somewhere, alone?" This from Dan.

"San Diego for two days wasn't a vacation, Dan. It was a work weekend for you."

"Well, I had fun, Mom. Saw some friends. I thought it was great."

Carol bent her head down toward her tea cup and said nothing more.

And yet, again, Dan saw the unhappy wife that was his. "Are you feeling alright, Carol? You tossed all night. Why don't you go back up to bed for a while. I can handle things down here."

She quickly over-reacted with, "What's that supposed to mean? Like I can't, in the state I'm in?" Carol wanted to stop the words as they rolled off her tongue, but she was too late.

Dan was surely lost. What? What did I do now? he thought. I was just trying to be sympathetic, for crying out loud. But he didn't say anything.

Carol took another deep breath. "I'm sorry. That was my fault. What I'm going on isn't really a vacation at all. It's a retreat. It's on an island in Washington."

"A retreat? What's it for, Mom?" An innocent enough question from the son.

She tried to stay in some kind of control. But couldn't. "What's it for, Jonas? It's for growth! It's for some peace. It's for me! That's what it's for!"

"Whoa, cool," said Jonas, "like way back in the sixties, huh? Free love, hippy stuff, huh?"

Carol almost laughed. "Don't worry, dear, it's only for women."

"Only women?" said Dan, suspiciously. "So, where did all this come from, Car? Where do you come up with these... ideas?"

"What? Were you going to say *crazy* ideas, Dan?"

"Hey, I didn't say it, you did. But, well, yeah."

Now the mounting anger showing on her face told Dan to back off, which of course, he didn't heed. "Ya know, the longest time, now, I've really been trying to understand you, Carol, but I just don't have a clue where you're coming from, anymore."

"Of course you don't, Dan," she answered with more than a sarcastic edge. "How could you?"

With clear signs of impending confrontation and parental discord, Jonas did what he did best. "Whoa... I'm outta here," he said as he split from the room.

Ignoring her son's departure, that in itself a departure for the loving, good mother, Carol raged, "You don't listen to me! You're incapable of hearing me! I am unhappy! Don't you see that? By now my life should be easier! I feel empty, Dan. Empty! I've spent my whole life doing for you. Doing for Jonas. I'm still picking up after my grown son, for crying out loud! Still doing his dirty laundry!"

"So don't tell me! Tell him!" Dan said sharply, not hearing what she was really trying to tell him.

"I'm still doing yours, too!" Trying to hide her tears, she quickly got up, grabbed Jonas' dirty dishes and smashed them into the sink, breaking a plate in the process and cutting her finger. With her hand to her mouth, she sucked her blood, trying to stop its eternal flow.

Dan came up behind her, now truly concerned. "What's really going on with you, Carol? I sure don't know. Only that you've changed and like I said, I don't have a clue who you are, anymore. Whatever I say, it's the wrong thing. Do you even know what you want, 'cause I sure as hell don't."

Suddenly she burst out crying, making her husband feel even more helpless, impotent. Trying to calm her down, the only way he knew, he changed the subject. "Okay, okay, so what's this place, this retreat have to do with anything? Is it some kind of therapy or something?"

Again, trying to gain back a little of her lost composure, but not looking at him, she tired to explain. "It's a place for women like me to learn about what's happening to us. Is that alright with you? It's nothing to be threatened about."

"Threatened? I'm not threatened." He held back a little laugh. "Well, fine. It's fine if you want to go to this thing. Only I still think you make too big of a deal over every little thing, you know? We all go through shit, Carol. That's life. So your body's changing a little. If I gave into every ache and pain I woke up with, I'd never get anything done. And really, what else do you really have to complain about? I've given you a good life, haven't I?"

Whoops. Dan just lost himself at least six points.

She turned toward this person, this stranger whom she knew so well. "Go to hell, Dan!"

Now it was his anger that was on the rise. "Come on, Carol. What do you think, that only women have problems? That you hold the burden of the world on your shoulders? Well, you don't. I'm the one going out into the real world everyday, taking all kinds of crap, trying to give my family everything they could ever want.'

She spat back at him, "Well, emotionally speaking, you're damn right, we do carry the burden. After all these years, we're still struggling and with men as indifferent as you are, I guess we always will, because you'll never change! Nothing will ever change!"

"Oh, yeah? Well, for us either! Believe me, with ladies like you around, for us either!"

And with that, Dan turned on his heel and stalked angrily out of the room.

Left alone, but not in the slightest way done, Carol yelled after him. "Yeah! Well, unlike you, at least we women admit to our pain and try to do something about it!"

Carol really wasn't expecting him to reappear with an answer to her outrage, with finally some kind word. Only she hoped, somewhere inside of her, he would. She was left alone. Very much alone... with a broken plate, her still bleeding finger and with much frustration and confusion and sadness.

Part of her wanted him to come back and take her into his arms, to hold her tight, to tell her that he was there for her, with her, to tell her that he understood and that everything would be alright, that they would work all this out, together.

Another part of her wanted to run away, far, far away... from everything she knew, from him... even from herself.

## CHAPTER NINE

By the time they found themselves awkwardly sitting next to each other at the airport, Carol and Dan had made an uneasy truce. As nervous as Carol was about going, Dan seemed even more so.

"You've never done anything like this before. Gone away. Left me..."

"It's only a week, Dan. Just a week."

"I guess I still don't know why you have to go. I guess I didn't think you'd really go through with it." There wasn't anger in his voice, now, only a kind of sadness.

"You're acting like I was leaving you or something. What am I doing? I think you're making more of this than it is. I'm just trying to do something to hopefully make myself feel better. That's all."

Talking to him this way seemed to give her a kind of strength. Her own validation that what she was doing was the right thing for her to do at this time.

"You've just been doing all these weird things, that's all. What'd you think you'll find up there? Some magic potion for happiness?"

"I hope so," she sighed. "I hope so."

"There is none, Carol. Life is life. You're not going to be going through *the change* for the rest of it, ya know. Why can't you just deal with it like your friends do? Grin and bear it. None of them are running away."

In that he was right. Her friends did grin and bear it, with the help of prescribed medicines and a few belts more often than they used to. For the first time in Carol's life, though, she wasn't satisfied to do what her friends were doing. And were they really so happy to begin with? And did she even really have friends? Real friends? Good friends? Most of the women she mingled with were the wives of Dan's business associates. That is, except for Andi. And even Andi, as much as she liked her, couldn't really identify with Carol's life, or Carol hers, for that matter.

The truth was that Carol often found herself jealous of Andi's life, so seemingly carefree and lacking the responsibilities of wife and mother. But

Andi sometimes admitted her life was not all it was cracked up to be. You can't always live in the illusion of a romance novel, Andi once told her. And in a lot of ways, Carol's friend would have been willing to trade in, at least, some of her book residuals for a life closer to what she perceived Carol as living. So, the grass is not always so green on the other side and unbeknownst to the naked eye weeds hide and grow.

Dan looked at his watch.

"You can go if you want to, Dan. It should only be a few more minutes until I board." Carol never missed any of her husband's tricks.

"No," said Dan, again glancing at the time. "I'll wait."

Carol was getting more and more nervous as the hands of Dan's watch ticked closer to her departure. In a way she wouldn't have minded had Dan actually left. Then she could have indulged in her own thoughts, instead of feeling like she had to keep the conversation going with her husband until the very end, when in fact, they had said everything they had to say to each other.

The evening before, when she had carefully packed, a strange calm had come over her. She was apprehensive and excited at the same time, but also so calm. And a little sad, as if somehow she knew she was about to leave a place she would never return to, not literally, but figuratively. She felt as if she were on the cusp of embarking on a journey that would change her life. Oddly, this feeling was based only on one word printed on the Crone flyer.

Celebration.

She had thought hard about the possibility of that word, alone. She even went so far as to look it up in her dictionary.

Celebrate: To do something to show that a day or event is important. To make merry.

And from her old college thesaurus: Commemoration, triumph, jubilation, inauguration, ceremony, festival. And finally… rejoicing.

When had Carol truly rejoiced in her life? Really rejoiced? Certainly when Jonas had been born. But she hadn't even been able to share that incredible experience with her young husband. In the days when she delivered her son, having men in the delivery room was still months away, years, in some hospitals. And so, a somewhat drugged Carol, whose lower half had finally been numbed by a spinal block shared the miraculous moment of the birth of her son, a new life upon this earth, in a cold and sterile room, filled with strangers with masked covered faces.

In her doctor's office hung a framed cartoon of two doctors meeting outside their respective delivery rooms. One says to the other, "So, how was your delivery?" The other answers, "It would have been perfect, had it not been for the mother!" Back then, even Carol laughed.

And so Jonas was brought forth into this world with as little help from Carol as her doctor allowed, which was not much. Later, after kissing his wife and looking through the thick hospital glass at his newborn son, Dan celebrated, but with his buddies, smoking big smelly cigars and drinking a few bottles of beer.

Other than that, Carol couldn't remember times in her life that were real celebrations. Oh, there were birthdays and anniversaries and other milestones that parties were thrown for, but that complete and utter joy she remembered feeling in her heart the day Jonas took his first breath, the first time she held him to her breast, no, that kind of jubilation and rejoicing had never come to her, again. Perhaps, she thought, it was only something that comes with birth.

That is not to say there were not good times and fun times through the years, especially during the early times of her marriage, when it was just the two of them. When they were free to do whatever they wanted to do, whenever they wanted to do it. When love, itself, had been an adventure.

Then Dan finished his studies and became a contractor and they began to build their future. They drew the proper blueprints and ended up carefully constructing the proper marriage in their proper home. As the years passed, being so concentrated at doing the proper thing, at raising the proper son, neither of them seemed to miss that joy they used to have for simply living. They became so busy erecting the perfect life from their perfect blueprint, there seemed no time left to enjoy living it.

These days, though, Carol wasn't so sure they might have built from the wrong plans. She wasn't even sure what the right plans were, much less where to find them. Maybe, just maybe, the mistake had been to make one plan for the two of them, as opposed to merging together their two plans into one. Perhaps not, thought Carol, since at that time in her life, her only plan had been Dan.

Sitting a little ways away from Carol and Dan sat Sara and the still blushing bride, Rebecca.

"What am I going to do without you for a week, Mama?" Rebecca said, playfully, but with truth attached to it.

"Oh, now, I'm sure you'll survive, my Darling," smiled Sara.

"But I'll miss you. Didn't you miss me when I was on my honeymoon?"

"Yes. Yes, I did. Although if you were thinking of me on your honeymoon, then I'd be very, very worried!" Sara laughed and kissed her daughter's cheek.

"Oh, Mom, I always think about you. And I worry about you. I just don't understand why you're going to this place. You'll be in the middle of nowhere. And what if there are bears, or... or snakes, or... other creepy crawlers."

"Bears! Oh my!!" laughed Sara.

"C'mon, Mom, you're going to the woods. You should be going somewhere where you could meet a nice man."

"Rebecca, I know you have my best interests at heart, but I believe this retreat is in my best interest. Okay?"

"Okay," sighed the daughter. And then, "But what if something really does happen to you? You took your cell, didn't you? Will it even work up there in no man's land? And I obviously mean that literally. What if I need to get in touch with you?"

"Becca, Becca, Becca! At eighteen I let you travel all over Europe with a girlfriend. You took a ship from Israel to Greece with drunken sailors on board, you let a Frenchman you just met drive you from Cannes to Paris and you're worried about me going to an island with a bunch of women for a week?"

"Okay, okay, Mother! I get it.."

"Good. Now tell your mother to have a wonderful time and you'll miss her, but you're happy for her."

"Have a wonderful time, I'll miss you and I'm happy for you, Mom."

"That's a good daughter."

And that was their bond. Always had been. Although there was little doubt Sara was the mother, they were also such good friends. When Sara first found out she was pregnant, she hoped beyond hope it was a girl who kept her up nights, kicking her in the ribs. Already sensing her marriage to David was not meant to last a lifetime, she knew she would much rather raise a girl alone, than a boy. That thought actually crossed her mind while Rebecca was still womb-bound. It was just something about girls.

It was a time in history by the serious thinking of some, that, oh gee, women were equal, too. What a novel idea. Sara had proudly come by her belief system quite genetically. Her grandmother, fresh from Russia, a suffragette, had marched and been arrested for speaking out for women's rights almost a century before. Her mother had been an organizer for women's rights, also. Sara used to joke after her divorce that, oops, for a short while she had just forgotten everything she had ever been taught and believed in concerning her gender. David had done such a damn good job trying to make her into something she was not, had never been. Subservient. Years later, she loved to say she had failed at being a Jewish princess and was damn proud of that fact.

So Rebecca was raised knowing she could do anything she wanted to do, be anything she wanted to be, as she repeatedly listened to Marlo Thomas' record, Free To Be You And Me. Back then, Sara's great desire was to guide her daughter through childhood without ever having or wanting a Barbie doll, not to mention being a Girl Scout. But peer pressure being what it was, the child begged and then hugged her favorite Barbie at all her scout meetings. Eventually, though, the child saw the light and abandoned both of them, taking up photography, at which she now was on the road to becoming quite skilled at.

Had Sara had a son, there was no doubt he would have had dolls to play with and taught that it was alright to cry. Something had gone awry, though, Sara thought. This new generation of Rebecca's male peers seemed almost as anti-feminist as their father's and grandfather's generation. Who was raising these sons? How was it possible that from hippy parents came Alex P. Keaton?

Sara looked around the terminal for a moment and saw a man pacing back and forth. It was Dan.

"Mom?" Rebecca broke into Sara's thoughts. "Do you ever still think about Peter?"

Sara was surprised by the question. "Sometimes. Only sometimes, now." Sara was not in the mood to get into this subject. Certainly not now.

"'Cause, Mom, if I could just get back to why I think it's really so important for you to meet some nice men, ones you could really have a future with, I mean, instead of wasting a week with a bunch of women."

The kid just never gave up.

"Shame on you, Becca! That's not how I raised you! My life is fine as I'm sure my future will be. And that's whether I'm with some nice man or not!"

"I know, Mom, but I also know you don't want to be alone for the rest of your life, either. And I don't want you to be..."

Luckily for Sara, the call came over the loud speaker announcing that boarding was beginning.

"Times' up, Honey," said a relieved Sara.

Hugs were exchanged and soon Sara disappeared through the doors leading to the plane, as Rebecca didn't take her eyes off her mother until she was out of view.

Carol never saw the nice woman who had cared for her during a dizzy spell, giving her water to drink a few months before in that wonderful bookshop. And minutes later, after pecking Dan on the lips, she too walked toward the large silver bird that she hoped would take her to a better place inside her head, inside her body.

# CHAPTER TEN

After an uneventful plane ride, the two women, who still had not eyed each other, disembarked in Seattle. Carol felt like a six year old about to start first grade. Butterflies flitted inside her stomach. Suddenly she was there. Alone. She had really done it. And now she found herself in a place she had never been before, facing the unknown. This for a woman who under normal circumstances had planned every minute of every day of her life. No surprises for her. And she still wasn't sure she was ready for any.

The more sophisticated Sara was not really nervous, just rather surprised at finding herself in this new mode of self-discovery. This realization had actually come to her during the flight. Although she hated this society of the quick-fix: read a book here, join an encounter group there phenomenon, it was true that some strong force had drawn her to this week's retreat. Although she had done many things in her life, more recently she had not been a real risk-taker, but only months away from the half-century mark she had been nudged away from her now rather orderly life, a life that lately had not held too many surprises. Suddenly, Sara was ready for a surprise.

Sara and Carol, separately, searched among the throngs of humanity that filled the airport for the promised representative from the retreat. Finally, they both spotted him. How could they not! There, next to a few black-suited, neatly groomed chauffeurs holding signs with the last names of passengers written in bold print on cardboard signs, was an elderly, bearded man in a red and yellow flannel lumberjack shirt. The scrawled sign he held read, "CRONE WORKSHOP."

Some folks laughed out loud upon seeing the sign, while others with better manners simply snickered as they passed by. When Carol saw the sign she breathed a sigh of relief and made a beeline for the man.

Sara, on the other hand, wanted to melt away into invisibility, suddenly afraid she'd made a major mistake, after all. Crone Workshop! Knowing better, it still conjured up images Sara was afraid to admit to. As she walked toward the flannel-shirted man, she felt the whole airport's eyes on her, seeing not what she knew her reflection to be, but that of an old wicked-looking woman with a huge hooked nose and warts all over her face, wearing a black pointed hat with strands of gray stingy hair hanging out of it, hobbling away to her cottage to make some hideous evil brew in her huge blackened caldron. Then she thought, perhaps she had read one too many fairytales at her Saturday morning story hours.

As the three walked toward the luggage carousel, Carol saw something familiar in Sara, but couldn't put her finger on it, so said nothing. Sara just wanted to get out of the public eye and retreat to the damn retreat, already.

It wasn't until the two women sat waiting in the bearded man's old van to pick up more Crones, did Sara and Carol make the connection between them. Carol was overjoyed. She now didn't feel as if she was walking into the abyss of this great unknown, alone. Sara, at least looking secure and at ease, was damn glad, also. They became immediate friends, for no other reason than they had come from the same place and were going to the same place.

By the time the van left the airport it had gained three more inhabitants: Annie, Elaine and Beth. During the two hour long drive to wherever they were being taken, the soon-to-be bunkmates got acquainted.

In her late forties, Annie was a woman of style, even in her causal pant-suit. A career woman in the clothing industry, she had never married, although had lived with a man for twelve years. They lived together no longer.

"We were both married to our careers," she told what were to become her new friends. "I guess we were the ultimate yuppies of the Eighties. Neither of us really wanted kids, back then. Anyway, we had this great dog," Annie laughed. "Now... I don't know. I'm alone and pushing fifty. Do I wish I'd had kids? I don't know that, either."

Annie had finally gotten sick of the rat race. She had lived on the fast track with the perfect job, mate, digs and dog. She also had a pretty perfect bank account and a lifetime membership to the perfect gym. Then, when the Eighties fell from grace, as her breasts had also started doing so, her perfect mate traded her in like the stocks he owned. Yes, he had exchanged her for a newer model, just like the fast cars he loved to drive. He took their perfect dog with him. In the end, it was probably the best thing that could have happened to her, because it slowed her down enough to really start to look at her life. Then two years ago she had a cancer scare. A lump in one of her no longer perfect breasts. It turned out to be benign, but it shook her up beyond belief, starting her on a search to put some kind of real meaning into her life. Now she owned a small clothing company, designed her own fashions, didn't make as much money, but was happier. Not happy enough, but happier.

Elaine was perky, answering the age old question, does one have to lose one's perk after

80

fifty? Not if you asked the Mid-Western Elaine. A housewife, mother, grandmother and avid talk show watcher, Elaine loved experiencing what she called the little dramas of life. Mostly, of course, she was only able to live them out vicariously though watching the small screen and reading the tabloids. Lately, however, while her retired husband of over thirty years went out on his golf holidays, she walked for AIDS research, mainly so she could see real gay and lesbians holding hands and possibly kissing. If some Hollywood movie was being shot within a radius of two hundred miles from her home, she was there to see the stars, up close and personal. And she actually learned how to tame a motorcycle, so she could ride easy with the Hell's Angels when they roared though her town. She dallied with the idea of getting a tattoo, perhaps a small butterfly below her navel, but decided against it, since she was not that fond of any kind of unnecessary pain.

Elaine had read about the retreat when she saw the flyer in the office of a psychic she had been getting readings from for years. Why not, she thought? She had recently taken a course at her junior college on women's mystical and magical powers, including witchcraft. She saw this week as another interesting experience that, at the very best, would enhance her ever-growing need for excitement, first hand, in what she believed to be an otherwise not too exciting life. Hearing all this, the others were not so sure about that.

As Sara looked out the van's dirt streaked window, she noticed the city's landscape had changed dramatically. All around them now were woods. Deep thick woods. Oh my, she thought, speechless at the beauty of it. She couldn't remember the last time she had seen such natural splendor. Had she forgotten how beautiful nature could be? And this was nature at its finest. Of course, she saw the great Pacific Ocean everyday, but that sight she took for granted, now. She smiled serenely as she turned her attention back to the group, back to the women.

It was Beth's turn to introduce herself. Big Mama Beth, who in her late fifties still had a twinkle in her eye and a nose that crinkled up when she laughed. And she laughed a lot. Big Beth was a woman filled with goodness and too many sweets. She was a widow whose eyes still lit up, then misted over, when she mentioned her late husband. He had tragically died in a small plane accident a number of years before.

"Flying was his life, his passion," she told her new friends. "Yup, he went doing what he loved most of all... next to me." She laughed a sad belly laugh. "See, he was up there so high above the clouds, halfway to heaven... I guess he just decided, 'What the heck, I'll just go and check it out for myself.'"

The women all looked sympathetic, but Mama Beth would not hear of it. "Now ya'll listen, we had this wonderful life together, for a long, long time. And one of these days we're gonna see each other again, you can bet on that and we'll laugh about what a good old time we had. But, ya know, I'm still here, so I gotta do all these great things, 'cause he'll wanna know what the hell I've been up to all this time."

Carol who sat across the small aisle from Beth, gently patted Beth's knee in her usual nurturing way.

The van finally came to a stop. The red and yellow flannel lumberjack shirted, bearded man turned toward the women. "Everyone out, here."

Sara looked out the window. They were in a parking lot at the edge of a lake.

"But I thought we were going to an island," Sara questioned.

"Well, Ma'am, unless ya wanna swim, ya'll need to get yourselves on that ferry over there. This is as far as this old van goes."

Elaine was the first one out of the van. By the time the others piled out, she was turning 'round and 'round, her arms waving in the air. And she was laughing, loudly. "Is this the greatest, already? Look at this world out here!"

The others surveyed the area in awe. In front of them were the blue waters of a pristine Sound, surrounded by lush firs, maples and cedars. The beauty was breathtaking.

After the ferryman loaded their bags onto the boat, the women got on board. A few minutes later they were gliding across the smooth waters. The silence was broken only by the whistling of a light wind through the trees and a bird calling to her mate. In the teal blue sky, puffy white cumulus clouds sailed effortlessly by.

The women, quiet now, in the collective silent sanctuary of their peaceful minds, could only look out in wonder at a beauty that was beyond any words in their vocabulary. And suddenly it appeared in the distance, a small island, which would soon become *their* island, if only for a short time.

# CHAPTER ELEVEN

The sun was taking its leave of that part of the world. On its journey to give light to the other side of the earth, it seductively caressed the trees across the Sound, leaving in its trail hues of the rainbow... yellows and oranges, pinks, turning to deep violets. The message left, a peaceful night in the offing. As it relinquished the day and in its wake, a full moon rose. The perfect new oval passed by and kissed the sun as it slowly ascended into the sky. And a peace befell the land. Animals scurried to their places of sleep and dreams in nests and burrows. Flowers closed their petals, their worship of the sun temporarily suspended. It was the moon's turn now to rule the earth. And the owl came out to welcome her.

In the rustic amphitheater, around a great bonfire, twenty-six women sat on wooden benches. They were of all sizes, colors and faiths. They were all women. All women inching closer toward older age. They had come from near and far for as many reasons as one might laugh or cry in any given day's time.

As this day's warmth faded with the sun, the women bundled up in their jackets and the colorful Indian blankets they found waiting for them on the benches. And so they sat, watching the fireflies flitting over and around the great fire. Waiting.

Carol and Sara and their van friends sat amongst the others, huddled together, silently wondering what was to come next. The anticipation was palatable.

Suddenly, from out of the woods, from out of the darkness, three half-dog, half wolves came. They bounded into the theater area and instantly began to sniff the women, going from one to another, startling, frightening them, agitating this peaceful space.

A distinctive whistle pierced through the night air and the animals stopped dead in their tracks, dropping to their bellies. The women murmured between themselves. The once quiet atmosphere filled with expectancy.

And then they all saw her.

She seemed to float onto the scene, stopping gracefully in front of the great bon fire. She was probably the most beautiful woman any of them had ever seen. She, with her long, unruly silver-white hair. She, who was clothed in a flowing Indian madras dress and high-laced leather moccasins. She, who was adorned with silver and turquoise necklaces around her swan-like neck, bracelets wrapped around her wrists, feathered earrings hanging to her shoulders and silver and stone rings on her slender fingers.

She was Christina. Sixty-five year old Christina. Ageless Christina.

Whatever cold had been felt by the women, there was now warmth. She filled the void with a vibrancy of life, peace and calm all at once. Her voice, when she finally spoke was strong, yet lyrical, soothing the women like the security felt when babes pressed close to their mother's abundant breast. Such was the feeling this Christina exuded.

"Welcome, welcome, welcome, my women. I see you have met my children. There is never a need to fear them, for better friends you shall never find."

As if on cue, the three stately beasts came to her and laid at her feet. She knelt down and gave each a loving pat. And they looked up to her with unadulterated love.

"They are Demeter, La Loba and this one, this one is Sophie!"

The women watched, listened, as though in a kind of hypnotic state.

"Do you know the story of Demeter? In Greek mythology she was the Goddess of the Harvest. It was she who gave the world food a plenty, crops and vegetables and fruits, without which humanity would die. She was springtime. The earth's new abundance after the barren winter. She was sustenance, she was joy."

Christina gave the second animal another pat.

"La Loba is the Wolf Woman. The wild woman, if you will. That within each and every one of you that lets go of all inhibitions. That inherent instinct inside of us all that wants to run free. Ahh, yes. There is a La Loba in every one of us. We just must find her. Yes? And perhaps we will this week!"

The twinkle in her eye and the melody of her voice was infectious, spreading throughout the women. Even the ones so tired from their long day's journey awakened as new found energy pulsed through their bodies. What magic did this woman hold?

"And then there is this beauty... this one, of course is Sophie. No, there is no myth she is named after. Sophie was my mother's name. But she, too, was a Goddess of the Harvest, after all, she gave life to me. And a wild woman lived inside of her, to be sure."

As Sophie was being talked about, the beautiful animal rose to a sit and nuzzled her mistress. Out of a pocket in her dress, Christina bestowed on each of her brood, a treat.

"So, here we are and I welcome you all to this week of discovery. We will do many things, you and I. We will meet in large groups and small. We will hike and swim and do crafts. We shall dance and we shall sing. And sometimes, we will do nothing. We will try to not only accept the inevitable… growing older, but hopefully in this week you will learn to begin to cherish it and most of all, celebrate it. That's right! Hear me now. It is time to celebrate becoming a Crone".

The energy force in the outdoor theater was now accelerated, as the women smiled more widely and buzzed amongst themselves. They wanted to hear more of Christina's words, as they sat mesmerized by her beauty, by the sound of her voice, by the words that she was saying, for they knew instinctually that here, in front of them stood an exceptional woman, the likes of whom had never passed them by before. And they wanted everything from her. Her knowledge and her beauty and her wisdom. How, they wondered, had she gotten to be the way she was? Where had she learned all that they knew she knew?

"And this week you shall meet the Goddess, The Great Mother Earth, tapping into something deeper than your everyday existence upon this earth you have walked on for so long. Perhaps for the first time you will really feel Her beneath your feet, as She heaves and sighs, as She grows and ages. And you will feel Her pain and Her laughter, for they are your pain and your laughter. You will experience

Her anger at all the injustices brought against Her, because it is the anger you have inside of you. And most of all and finally, you will celebrate, yes celebrate being a part of Her. Where before you have fought Her gravity, now you will rejoice in the very fact that you are a woman, an aging woman. You are the Great Mother, Giver of Life. You are important and you are as precious as the stones and ore, the gold and silver inside Her vast belly. You are as delicate as Her newly grown blades of grass, as wild as Her winds and as strong as Her tides."

Christina hardly took a breath, as she continued.

"Every new line on your face, like every new ring inside the trunk of the great ancient oak will become an affirmation of your knowledge and your wisdom from living on this earth. And you will even come to celebrate this, the unheard of... the aging process. For this, my children, is the Crone. Like the earth itself, you are to be revered and respected for all the days and nights you have roamed this land. Her land. And we shall roam, my women and roam some more. Welcome, I say again. Welcome to this magical third portion of your life. Welcome the celebration, because believe me, there is much for you to celebrate."

And listening to Christina, even the most skeptical, believed this might actually be able to be true.

# CHAPTER TWELVE

After a hearty and healthy dinner in the retreat's mess hall, all the women, now full and fatigued, retired to their respective cabins for much needed sleep.

Carol and Sara, along with Annie, Beth and Elaine, walked slowly to their new home for the next week. In the woods they had yet to see in the day's full light, that they had yet to explore, all were feeling a tranquility none could remember ever feeling. Their minds were full of Christina and her inspired words and as exhausted as they all were, they lingered under a tall fir tree and looked up at the full moon.

"I feel so peaceful," said Carol. "How could that happen so fast?"

Annie shook her head. "Well, I'll admit I got swept away a little listening to Christina, tonight, but all that Goddess stuff. I hope she's not going to proselytize to us all week."

"Naw," interrupted Beth. "I don't think it's about religion, real religion, ya know? But there was something real powerful about all the similarities between us and the earth, don't ya think?"

"Yeah! Mother Earth!" piped in Elaine. "Maybe when I tell my kids and grandbabies about it, they'll appreciate me more!"

Sara, who usually had an opinion about everything said nothing, as the women again began to stroll toward Cabin Number Three. And thunder could be heard in the distance, suddenly disrupting the forest's quiet.

Inside their cabin they found two women, Penny and Victoria, their other bunkmates, who were already unpacking.

Victoria, an elegant woman, nearing sixty, was trying to neatly put her expensive clothes away into the small wood cubbyholes allotted to each of them. A tall and stately woman of society, she didn't seem to fit into this group anymore than her designer clothes didn't fit into their limited space.

Penny seemed her opposite. Not just that she was short and chunky and probably in her mid-forties, she never did say, but looked as if she belonged on a farm, from her simple clothes to her well-scrubbed Mid-western face.

After introductions were made and greetings exchanged, the eldest of the group made known her unhappiness.

"For the price of this week, you'd think the accommodations would be a lot better," complained Victoria, who was at a loss at what to do with her beautiful clothes still stacked on her bed.

"Oh, I don't mind," Sara said, in an almost dream-like voice. "I feel like all this is some kind of deja-vu. Like I'm a kid, again, back in my old camp where I spent so many fun summers." She climbed up on the top of an empty bunk bed and looked out the window. "Oh, goodie. It's started to rain. Neat." She even sounded like a kid again and hearing her own voice surprised her.

As the others picked their sleeping places and began to unpack, Penny was taking great care to make up her bed, hospital corners and all. She smoothed out her top blanket and then looked at her handiwork, proudly. Then she smiled at the framed picture she had put on her windowsill of her husband and two sons.

Elaine, who had taken the bunk above her, looked at the bed, also. "Penny! That's beautiful, but I don't think we're being graded here. This isn't the army, ya know," Elaine laughed without malice.

But Penny looked hurt. "I didn't do it for that." She was embarrassed and defensive at the same time. "I just like things right, that's all. Is that a crime? So does my husband."

A light tension filled the cabin as the women all eyed her and each other. Realizing this, Penny said, "And don't any of you say anything. It's just the way I do things. The way I like things."

Carol, who was also making her bed was taking great care *not* to do it in her own usually obsessive way. "So do I, Penny. And, personally, I think that's a wonderful quality in a person."

"Me, too, Darlin'!" This, of course from Mama Beth. "Unfortunately, I, on the other hand, am more comfortable in semi-arranged disarray!"

And thanks to this jolly woman the mild tension was broken and everyone laughed, except that is, Victoria.

"Well, this whole thing certainly isn't what I was expecting. I thought it was going to be more like a resort, to relax, to be pampered. I was so looking forward to a week of getting massages and facials. Things like that. Truthfully, I'm not sure I'm going to stay."

Beth, whom while listening to Victoria's complaints, had emptied the entire contents of her duffel-bag onto her bed and was now trying to make some sense of the mess. "Well, maybe you signed up for the wrong retreat, but if you want a great rub-down, I'd be happy to give ya one. That's what I do for a livin'. How 'bout it, Victoria?"

Victoria looked at the large woman, then, sweetly, declined the offer.

"Okay, but I think you'd have liked it."

Feeling more uncomfortable by the moment, not to mention definitely out of place and out of space for her remaining clothes, Victoria just stood there. Noticing this, Penny squeezed together in one cubby-hole some of her shirts and offered her other to Victoria.

Victoria smiled and took the younger woman up on the offer.

"I hope you stay," Penny said softly. "But I don't think you should feel bad or anything if you don't want to. Everything isn't right for everybody, you know?"

Penny's words were making Victoria feel even worse. She looked out the window, where the rain was now coming down in sheets. She knew she was stuck there for the night. She'd make the best of this uncomfortable situation and decide what to do in the morning.

The mood in the room lightened up after that, as the women readied themselves for bed. Faces were washed, moisturizers applied, teeth brushed and as the women started to put out a few of their personal items, they began to feel a little more at home.

A while later found everyone settled in, lying in the dark, listening to the rain's constant patter on the cabin roof. They were quiet now, lost in their individual thoughts as they waited for sleep to overcome them.

Sara lay in her top bunk, not yet ready to close her eyes, looking out her small window. For a moment the dark clouds parted and the moon was in her sight, high in the sky. Trees moved rhythmically, swaying back and forth in the storm's wind, lulling her, quieting her mind. And suddenly she realized how sad she was. So unexpectedly sad… for all the forgotten times in her life. For all the times life had forgotten to give her. When she thought she should feel full of all the things Christina had talked about this night, she felt empty, oddly empty, instead. Why, she wondered, as silent tears began to flow from her eyes. How strange. And she tried to analyze herself, but couldn't. She hadn't cried in so long. When had been the last time? Oh, maybe at Rebecca's wedding, but those were tears of a different kind. Happy tears. And before that, tears of sadness for Peter's loss. These were tears of cleansing, although as of yet, Sara didn't know that. All she knew was that all the beauty of this night had overwhelmed her, had opened the gate of pain inside of her she didn't even know was there. She was usually so in control of her life, her thoughts. Now, as her tears continued, she felt very much alone. It took a while, but finally, finally, she slipped off to sleep, her cheeks still wet.

During the night, the earth rested and replenished Herself. The day's activities had heated Her up and tired Her out. She needed the coolness and the quiet to survive. From Her inhabitants She had been bruised and sucked dry. The gentle night healed Her, readying the Great Mother for yet another day.

Water from the sky seeped into the earth, feeding Her dry roots. And as the hours went by She was slowly rejuvenated, the cycle of nature, never ending, repeating itself as it had done for all those millions and millions of years. And above it all, the stars watched over the Great Mother through Her hours of darkness.

And then slowly, slowly, the moon moved across the sky, heading toward the other side of the earth, its work done for now, as the sun again brushed by, beginning her ascent, peeking over the Eastern horizon, bringing forth the first rays of light again to this part of the world.

And the circle was complete. But never ending. Never ending.

# CHAPTER THIRTEEN

Victoria woke before the others, before the dawn had broken through the clouded shadows of the night sky. But outside the cabin, the day's activities had already begun. Squirrels scurried up and down the trees, looking for food to bury for afternoon treats. Baby birds screamed, their little bodies craving food, waiting for their mothers to return to the nest with their breakfast. Hopefully, a big fat worm. The forest was coming alive.

As quietly as she could, Victoria got out of bed and padded into the communal bathroom. As she looked around at the gray, dingy walls, she longed to be home in her large blue and white tiled tub filled to the brim with her favorite bubble bath and to soak in it for a long, luxurious start to her day.

She looked at her reflection in the broken mirror hanging over one of the old sinks. God, she looked awful. Her dyed, blond hair definitely in need of a root job and dark circles around her eyes made her wonder how she would get through this week, if she stayed at all, without her hairdresser and a few facials.

After washing up, she began her morning ritual of applying make-up to cover the lines and wrinkles that time had wrought. She had had some substantial work done on her face a few years before and knew it was about time to go through the worthwhile pain again.

Thinking she heard something, Victoria looked out into the bunk area. All was still quiet and she wondered how the others managed to sleep in this God-forsaken place. What should she do? She didn't belong here and she knew it. These were not her kind of people. Elaine, who couldn't talk about anything but her big, happy family. And that Penny who seemed to have attached herself to her. And oh, that big, loud-mouthed Beth. They were country bumpkins, whereas she was a lady of society. She, who lived a life they could only dream of living in her stately mansion in the Nob Hill section of San Francisco. And Christina! Who was she kidding? This woman was no more than an aging hippie who had figured out how to make a buck off problem-riddled women.

So why had she come, when she knew damn well this was no high class spa? She thought of her grown children, now scattered around the country, calling her only on the important holidays, coming into town only for weddings and funerals, but quick to cash the trust fund checks they were given, monthly. And she thought of her husband, Andrew, who no matter what lengths she went to anymore to make herself look wonderful, had lost interest in her years before. What bimbo was he fucking this week?

Oh, she and Andrew kept up a good front when they appeared in public with friends or his business associates, but in that grand house of hers there was no longer any warmth, any love. And in her lovely bedroom of carefully matching fabrics on the bed and drapes and chairs, he never touched her, anymore.

She had known for a long time now there were other women in his life, much younger women than she, but they never talked about it. That was just the way it was. And she couldn't blame him, completely. Once she had gone through her change, it was she who had lost interest, first. One day while out shopping, she had actually seen him on the street with someone who looked so close to what she had looked like thirty years before. It was then she had first rushed to a plastic surgeon. Andrew told her she looked wonderful, but still he roamed.

And yet, with all his infidelities, he still depended on her concerning business dealings, concerning his everyday life. To the world they were the town's most elegant, loving couple. To others they looked to be the most terrific twosome with a life to be envied.

It was at that moment of thought, Victoria decided she would stay. Maybe Andrew would think she had run off with some young stud for a week of passion, instead of being out here in the woods, in the middle of nowhere with none of the amenities she was so used to.

She tried on a smile and then began the long, arduous task of putting on her public face, even if it were only for a bunch of women who probably had never seen a haute couture dress up close, much less ever put one on.

Penny laid in her thin bed, not moving, but her eyes were wide open. Out of the window and through the early morning fog, she could barely make out the other cabins. She missed being home. She thought about her family and knew tears were close to welling up inside of her. She wondered how her husband, Sam and her two teen-aged boys were getting on without her, so far away in Idaho.

They had almost had to physically push her onto the bus the day she left. Too extravagant an expense she had told them when they had given her this week as a present for her forty-seventh birthday. But Sam urged her to go. He had to remind her about the fishing trip he had taken the year before. Now it was her turn to get away. Her men had heard about the retreat from a friend of a friend's wife, who had come back with glowing reports, an opportunity not to be missed by any woman. Sam was like that. Always thinking of Penny. Always doing little things to tell her how much he loved her. And in return, she lived her life for him and their sons.

Penny knew she didn't have much in common with these women she was sharing this living space with. First of all, none of them seemed very happy with their lives at all, except perhaps silly Elaine. And, of course, Victoria. Who wouldn't be happy with a life so full of all the things Penny longed to have, but knew she never would? And maybe Carol. After all, she was married, too. But the rest of them lived all alone and Penny felt badly for them, having to live a life without a man. She really felt sorry for poor Beth. Oh, the woman put on a good show with her crassness, but Penny couldn't begin to conceive going on living if Sam were to die.

And then she thought about all that Crone talk. She wasn't a Crone, yet. Yes, she had started missing her periods now and then, but a Crone? A workshop for Crones? Even with the high recommendation of this place, it was really Sam who had urged her to go, who had picked this *vacation* week for her. She never told him she would have much rather have gone to a lovely spa where she would be pampered. A place Victoria probably went to on a weekly basis. But she was here, so she would make the best of it.

As it started getting lighter outside, Penny wondered what she could even talk with the others about for a whole week. They were all so different than she. And the truth was, the night before, she had such a hard time identifying with Christina's words. They didn't apply to her. After all, her Sam already treated her like a Goddess. It was true, she didn't have many close women friends, but what did she need them for when she had her husband? He was her best friend. She was happy and fulfilled being surrounded by her little family. That was enough for her.

It was now seven and as Christina had promised, the wake-up bell sounded from the mess hall. And there wasn't a chance anyone could sleep through it, its constant ringing, so loud, so offensive, shattering whatever dreams the rest of the women were having. They silently cursed as they struggled to rise, disoriented, as they woke in this strange place, for a moment wondering where they were.

They slowly stumbled out of their beds to fully wake, unable to communicate with each other, just yet. As they dragged themselves to the bathroom, Victoria emerged, dressed and in full make-up, looking as if she was prepared for a casual, yet snazzy lunch at the club, not a ten mile hike in the forest.

# CHAPTER FOURTEEN

By the time all the retreat women breakfasted and their day got under way, the sun had made her appearance in her full and bright glory. Gone were the storm clouds of the night before, leaving the forest clean-smelling, the foliage glistening a hundred different shades of green.

The women donned active wear of one kind or another and began their trek through wooded paths. New friends made the night before, cheerfully chatted as they walked, again energized by their night's sleep and the anticipation of what this day would bring.

Leading the way were the three half-dog, half wolves, with Christina close behind. In her khaki shorts and white T shirt, wearing high-top hiking boots, her wild white hair pulled back from her beautiful face in a low ponytail and carrying a walking stick, she looked like an advertisement out of L.L. Bean's wilderness clothing catalog.

After walking for over half an hour in the shaded coolness of the lush forest, the terrain suddenly and dramatically changed. The path now became narrower and steeper, as the group, more slowly now, inched their way toward a rocky plateau.

The women started to huff and puff and complain to each other. By the time they reached the sun-drenched plateau, many of them were sure they had walked their last step on this earth.

"I thought I was in shape," said Carol, gasping for breath, who a few months before, in her effort to feel better, had taken to walking from her home to the beach and back, a distance of almost three miles.

City girl, Annie, who turned on the ignition of her car just to go to the corner to mail a letter these days, responded after trying to catch her breath, "Shape? Since I quit going to the gym, I'm lucky to walk a mile in a week."

Sara, who hadn't said much all morning, said nothing now, as she tiredly climbed the last few feet to the plateau. As the women straggled onto the large flat area, they all but collapsed. Beth rested her large body against a big rock next to Penny and Elaine.

"Hey," she said, breathing hard. "I like a challenge as much as the next guy, but I sure hope this isn't going to be one of those damn Outward Bound kind of things. Ya know, where ya do things like fall out of a tree and hope to hell someone will catch you!" And then she laughed her raucous laugh.

Penny looked worried. "You don't suppose we'll have to do that, do you?"

"Don't worry. She's kidding, Penny," laughed Elaine.

Some of the women, including Victoria, bent over in painful exhaustion. She cursed under her breath when she saw that her new, white, expensive tennis shoes were already dirty.

Christina looked over to her poor, pathetic group and smiled her radiant smile. The woman had yet to break a sweat. "The aging process sucks, doesn't it?" she said.

Although surprised by her choice of words, the women heartily agreed.

"Well, take a load off your feet, drink some of your water, relax and enjoy this glorious view. Have you even noticed it, yet?"

Christina walked to the edge of the plateau and took in a few deep breaths, her arms stretching high above her head. The women who could still move, hobbled over to her and were greatly rewarded. What they saw was so spectacular, it took what breath they had left, away.

Far in the distance was the Sound. Sail boats looked like children's toys from the height the women stood. Down below they saw small rivers and streams, winding their way through the dense woods. A huge eagle majestically soared in the cloudless, azure sky. It seemed almost motionless, its strong wings extended, as if it were floating in wind that was guiding it toward the heavens.

Christina turned to the women, again. "We're no longer young, my friends. But our soaring days are far from over. Oh, yes, our once proud breasts are hanging lower each day. Now, tell me whose mother didn't warn them in the sixties they had better keep wearing a bra? I guess we should have listened, yes?"

The women laughed and agreed, even the younger ones whose boobs hadn't yet quite started to droop.

"And what has happened to our once tiny waists? They are now slowly spreading out to our hips. Our once baby smooth skin is beginning to harden, wrinkle and sag."

Victoria automatically put her hand to her face, then quickly put it down.

A lovely black woman laughed out loud. "Hey, girl, you're depressing me! I thought we were going to celebrate getting older!"

Another woman yelled out, "Well, I intend to fight it, tooth and nail with everything I've got!"

Now it was Christina's turn to laugh. "Okay. You can all fight it, but you'll lose the battle in the end."

There were groans all around.

"To me," she continued, "fight means struggle, which I equate with an outputting of a lot of negative energy. Do you really want to spend the rest of your life neurotically watching for wrinkles to appear? Or being depressed about your cellulite, planning and saving your money for operation after operation to rid yourself of what you perceive to be ugliness?"

Victoria put her head down, positive everyone was looking at her.

"Well, not to worry," Christina went on, "because I have a much better solution."

"So do I!" It was Beth, putting in her two cents worth. "How 'bout this? We could all do what those Mid Eastern gals do. You know, how they cover their entire bodies in black veils?"

Even Christina laughed along with the other women.

"Actually, that custom was their men's idea, in fact, their rule. But, we'll talk more about that later. The fact is, we are no longer young, especially in terms of the way our society see us. After we turn, even forty, in a way we become invisible. Our worth is gone. And what a shame that is. And when we become invisible, as far as others are concerned, we somehow become invisible to ourselves. Think about what older age connotes in this country. Ugly!

Used! No longer capable! And on and on. So this is what I do to start with. Instead of thinking of being in the old age of youth... that youth which is so coveted, so desired... why not perceive yourselves as being in the youth of older age? You see, you are really only beginning this journey. Think about it. Believe me, psychologically, it makes a big difference."

The women became thoughtful. Some nodded, others talked to each other.

But Annie could not quite accept it. "Well, I'm not so sure that will work for me. Right now, this *youthful* older age body of mine feels like a damn antique!"

But Christina showed little sympathy. "You have to toughen up, women! Believe me, by the end of this week, you'll wonder how you ever lived without this kind of exercise. And it's so much healthier than riding some stationary bike in an air conditioned gym. Who thought of that dumb idea, anyway? No, no. Being close to the land... to step on Her earth and feel Her pulse of life, it will get into your bones and strengthen them. To be this close to nature can't help but inspire your soul. Look around you. This is heaven. Don't wait to die for it. It's all right here for you to be a part of each and every day."

Again the women murmured to each other, while they continued to look out at the beautiful view.

"Alright! Enough talk for now. Up and at 'em. It's only two miles to the next plateau! If you thought this was unbelievable, wait until you see the view from there!" And with that Christina bounded off up another path, with Demeter, La Loba and Sophie by her side.

The women moaned a little, but followed her lead, if not slowly.

Before she started her trek, Sara took one last look at the expansive wilderness below her, at the vastness of the land. And she could only sigh, thinking of so many things. Thinking of nothing.

Carol came up behind her. "Sara? Are you okay?"

Surprised, Sara had thought everyone had gone ahead. "Oh, yeah. Sure. It's so beautiful. I just wanted a last look."

"I've noticed how quiet you've been. I was worried about you."

"No need to worry," said Sara, her voice little more than a whisper. "Oh, I don't know. Everything feels so strange and at the same time so... right. Something's happened in my mind, or something. It's like, somewhere inside of me, I've thought or known some of the things Christina talks about, but they were, I don't know, abstract. I didn't know how to put them into words. But I feel like I've come home, in some way. You know? I know it sounds silly, saying it that way, sort of *ooh, ooh,* or something, but I don't know any other way to describe it."

"No, Sara, it doesn't sound silly at all.  I've been feeling sort of the same thing.  You can read all those books, like I have, that talk about similar things, but actually living it, looking out on the world from this vantage point, instead of it just being words on pages, that's sure something else."

"It's funny," Sara went on, "because the truth is, I don't even know why I decided to come up here. But something told me I had to.  Does that make any sense?"

""For me, I just knew I had to get away. Escape from my life."  Then Carol quickly added, "Not that I have such a bad life, or anything… I just felt I had to be with women who were going through what I am… you know, the menopause thing."

The two new friends smiled at each other and a primal feeling drew them to hug each other, these two women who had been complete strangers the day before.  They took one last, long look at the landscape below and then arm and arm began to follow those who had gone before them.

## CHAPTER FIFTEEN

By the time the group returned to their cabins after their morning island exploration, an amazing thing had happened. The women no longer were moaning and groaning. Oh yes, they were bone tired, they were sore, they were disheveled and dirty, but they were not moaning and groaning. Something rather miraculous was already changing within them. Had you asked them though, what it was, they would not have had an answer for it.

Rest was on the afternoon's agenda and some of the women napped, while others laid out in the sun and read. A few went swimming at the retreat's private cove, while still others wrote letter to loved ones back in civilization, or played cards with one another.

But no matter what they did, a kind of peace had enveloped them. It wasn't an intense feeling, a bolt of lightening kind of thing, but it was there, hovering overhead.

That evening, after dinner, the women sat circle for the first time. In the mess hall on foam mats they sat, in front of the blazing fireplace made of stone, hands clasped together.

It was then that Christina began the circle with the Self Blessing Of The Goddess:

*"Blessed be my mind, that I may always think of Her.*
*Blessed be my eyes, that they be open to all the beauty which is part of Her.*
*Blessed be my mouth, that I may always speak and sing my truth, loudly and with conviction.*
*Blessed be my heart, that it be open to all the love that's in the world, that I may trust and be vulnerable when it is safe.*
*Blessed be my breasts, formed in strength and beauty, to enfold and nurture life.*
*Blessed be my womb and yoni, for pleasure and for creating life, as She has brought forth the universe.*
*Blessed be my hands to do Her work.*
*Blessed be my legs and feet, that I may always walk and dance upon my own true path.*
*I am Goddess."*

Even those who were skeptical, even those who were atheists and the more traditionally religious, the Catholics, the Protestants, the Jews, were touched, because the words spoken in this blessing went beyond individual faith or non-faith. These words went directly to the heart of who they were, to the soul of what it was to be a woman.

Each woman then checked in, taking a few minutes to tell where they were in their lives. And they told of divorce and new marriages. They spoke of frustrations at work and at home, at having problems raising their children, of medical maladies that had begun to plague them. These twenty-six women were a microcosm of the aging woman.

And some spoke of the dreams and joys in their lives. And others, in the most pain, did not tell their complete truth, not yet secure enough in the newness of such a circle.

That night, Christina talked about the Triple Goddess… about the three stages of womanhood.

"We are first the Maiden, or if any of you still can recall it, The Virgin."

The women had to laugh at this. And through the laughter, Sara went back in time and thought of Peter and the night he had first taken her to be his, so many years before. She could still taste it, that delicious feeling of merging with another for the first time. And for a moment she was, again, shrouded in sadness.

"Then we become fertile. The bearers of life. The Mother, with the world's most beautiful power of all. Never in our lives do we have such an inner glow as when we are with child."

Annie looked around the circle. She was one of only a handful who were childless. Had she made a terrible mistake, making everything else in her life a priority, putting off having a baby until it had become too late? It was something she would certainly have to finally come to terms with.

"The last stage of the Triple Goddess is, yes, The Crone," Christina continued in her lilting voice. "Although it is this stage that leads us toward death, you are now entering, in so many ways, a most fulfilling time in your life. Yes, you are empty in your uterus, so tired now from its life work, but you are so full in every other way, as we shall soon discover. The wise elder evolves, as our ability to reproduce ends. Too bad we didn't get wiser, sooner, eh, say when our kids were teenagers!"

This brought on laughter and applause from all of those who were mothers.

Christina went on. "Now, if you look up *Crone* in the dictionary, please don't be alarmed when you see the written meaning. It will likely say withered old woman, a witch-like hag. How offensive, I say, but then we know who wrote the dictionaries, don't we? When they were written, women were not even allowed an education, for the most part. So much for definitions we are to believe and live by. But more on that, later... Of course, we should grieve each of the stages of womanhood as they pass us by, and we do, but we must also celebrate them. And again I say that magical word to all of you. Celebrate!"

"When I was going through my menopause, I felt for those years as if I didn't belong or fit in my own body, any longer. It is the same as with illness, when your body, the one thing you've always felt you had control over, that which has been such a constant in your life, now is failing you, doing things you cannot comprehend. During that time I felt so disconnected from my body, the thing I had always thought of as the whole of me. I likened it also to pregnancy, then labor. The fertile labor gives us unquestioned rewards, another life. Ahh, but this labor also gives us life. Our own!"

"Now, you might say, Well, it's a hell of a long time in coming, eh? But I truly believe we cannot honestly be free until this Crone stage of our lives. It can be the time in your life when, at last, you think of yourself first. And so I thought about it long and hard, trying to wipe away my feelings of guilt by being so self-absorbed by my body's changes, of being selfish, of being sad  And eventually, yes, eventually I stopped grieving. And when my last period was finally done and gone with, when I could have spent the rest of my days indulging in what I had first perceived to be my loss, I looked at my life, I looked at it critically, seeing it from every angle I could. And then, my friends, I took the deepest of breaths and then another and another... and it was only then that I could finally come to terms with it...ultimately able to revel in my post-menopausal zest!"

Carol thought about Christina's words, 'Post-menopausal zest,' and made a mental note of them, hoping one day soon she would feel the same way.

"You are not empty, my comrades. You are as full of life as you ever were. Fuller, in fact. Now is the time to celebrate yourselves. Celebrate your soul. Celebrate your knowledge and your strength and your courage and all that you have lived through and accomplished. It is time to celebrate your life... what you started out as and what you have become. You are all Goddesses, my women. And as you look inside yourselves, if you really look inside that which you really are, you will see it. I promise you. See how beautiful you are. Each and every one of you... Goddesses!"

It was then that Christina picked up a mirror that lay on the floor in front of her. She held it up, that glorious smile of hers reflecting back her image. And she said to it, as she said to herself out loud, "I am Goddess."

And then she passed the mirror to the woman who sat to the right of her. The woman tentatively held the mirror up to her face, her eyes darting away, then back to her reflection, then away again, then finally back, embarrassed and almost afraid to really see the image it cast back to her of herself, not yet believing the words she was supposed to say.

Softly, Christina urged her on. "It's alright, my friend. Look at yourself. No need to feel discomfort. Really look and see how beautiful you are... and say, 'I am Goddess.'

The woman, again glanced into the mirror, silently cursing how it happened that she had been what she thought to be so lucky to be sitting next to Christina that night, now having to be the first to do this, this difficult task being asked of her.

Then, in words barely audible, she somehow said it. "I... am... Goddess..."

"You are," whispered Christina.

Like a hot potato in her hands, the woman quickly passed the mirror to the next woman, feeling the burning on her cheeks.

And then a most remarkable thing occurred. As each woman looked and saw her own reflection, then handed over the mirror to the next woman, the words they said got stronger and stronger. It became a hypnotic chant. I am Goddess. I am Goddess. I am Goddess. I *am* Goddess...

And when the last woman quite nearly shouted out in glee, 'I am Goddess', every woman in the room was more than smiling, unrestrained, laughing joyfully. For at that precious moment in time, they all believed it to be so.

They *were* Goddess.

# CHAPTER SIXTEEN

The next days flew by. The women were learning so many new things about themselves. Christina told them of how life had been Twenty, Thirty, Forty Thousand years before and even before that, when it was the Goddess who had been worshipped by women and by men. She told of the artifacts that had been unearthed all over the world from that now forgotten time. They were of female deities, only female. They were forms of women with heavy, curved bodies and large hanging breasts.

And the women learned this was a peaceful time in history, when there were no wars or violence to speak of. Since no one yet knew the physiology of the human reproductive system, knowing only that women's bellies swelled, eventually bringing forth into the world a child, then another and another, there was no concept of how that happened, of the family unit, as we know of it today. Most likely the brother of the mother took on the "father" role to her children. And women were revered, because just as the Goddess, Mother Earth, burst forth with new life in springtime, so was it was also with women, for they too were the creators.

The act of sex was not connected to pregnancy then birth, but to pleasure and for joy. It was only much, much later, after man's church had been established that sex, for procreation or pleasure, for that matter, along with everything else concerning women, became controlled by men. Sex, it was ruled, was sinful for the good women of man, that is, unless it was desired by man, himself. And so women were regulated to be either Virgin, Mother or Whore.

When for thousands of years it had been instinctual and sensual and something to rejoice in, women, later, under the thumb of religious guidance, were told sex was an act only to be endured as a wife, at their husband's bidding.

The retreat women learned that during the time and worship of the Goddess, it was women who first developed agriculture, for food and for caring for the sick. It was women who first domesticated animals. They were the first users of fire, the first potters and weavers. They were, in fact, the very core of society. Men were relegated to hunt big game, for furs and meat.

And of most importance, it was the woman who was considered sacred, because it was she who gave the world new existence, continually populating the land with her species.

And so their world went on in peace and harmony centered around the most important elements of life: the women, the land and the Great Mother of them all.

This information was so new to most of the women and so exciting to learn. Why hadn't they ever been taught this before? Why had no one ever told them this, *her* story? Why had it never gotten even a bare mention in the study of human history? *His story.* Why wasn't it common knowledge, like the world wars, the Holocaust, the story of Jesus? Every invention that man created was in the history books... every expedition they led, every leader that was elected was there to learn about and analyze. But the importance of women all those eons ago... nothing.

Through the years women had been demoted to that of second class citizen, just another commodity to be used and abused in man's new society. Of course, this great change did not happen over night. Christina then told of how thousands of years before the death of Christ, before Moses had personally heard from one almighty god, himself, marauding men swept down from Northern Europe, pillaging the towns and raping the women. The

121

power of the Great Mother was on the verge of shifting away from Her. The real struggle was about to begin. Already the Goddesses of Greek and Roman mythology were becoming more evil, where before they were so strong and capable, like Diana, Goddess of the Hunt, or Athena, the Goddess of Wisdom.

As things evolved, men became more and more violent, using their brute strength to take what they wanted, looking for, needing something to worship in their own image.

"One theory," Christina explained, "was that once men finally realized it was from their own seed that pregnancy occurred in the first place, man ran with the knowledge, that which became their ultimate power. They would take their rightful place in the world, where they now felt they belonged, at the head of the table."

"Yes, and eventually a more organized religion came to pass, spoken by man, written by man. And if you think about it," Christina said, with more than a hint of anger in her voice, "the Bible became the greatest mandate against women ever conceived. Consider this. Eve was an after thought of God, made from an unneeded part of man. Kept from her were two of the most essential elements of life. Food and knowledge. In ancient mythology and in the world of the Goddess, the snake is not evil at all, but the feminine wisdom. And food, are you thinking of that apple in the Garden of Eden, is sustenance, without which we die. In the Old

Testament from the first page, women were evil, as Eve tempted Adam. Something to really think about, yes? And consider, until more recent history, woman's lack of schooling was at the sole desire of men. Jewish and Christian men, alike."

"Unfortunately, this shift in power touched every facet of women's lives. One example is whereas in those days of yore, the Goddess days, it was women who helped with the birthing of new life, in the most natural and loving way, the woman squatting, nature's gravity helping in the birthing process. But things changed dramatically once newly educated male doctors took control. Then, when it was a woman's time to bring new life into the world, as in most cases still done today, they laid her flat on her back, legs uncomfortably up in the air, against nature, Herself. And why? Because not only did these newly minted M.D.'s find it easier for *them,* but it was a way of controlling the female sex during their most important function, a function that man was unable to do, no matter how much he prayed for it in his newly built temples and churches to his newly conceived god."

"Consider how closely a woman's food intake is watched and judged, so often based by the way men like to see their women. It certainly is not in the image of those old, heavy, rounded Goddesses that were buried so long ago. How attractive would *they* have looked in a thong bikini doing a beer commercial?"

Although the women laughed at this, the point was more than well taken and one could feel the anger swelling in the retreat women's hearts and minds.

Christina went on. "Back then, women were not even allowed to enter man's new places of worship and they were tortured and killed if they were caught secretly worshipping the only thing they knew, their Goddess. This is what happened to the remaining Pagans, who, by the way, also included men. And directly over their sacred grounds, where their holy sights of worship were, Christ's churches were erected, wiping out, burying any last remains of the Great Goddess, Mother Earth."

"By Medieval times the situation became far worse. Any woman who stepped out of line was considered a witch and burned at the stake. If they inherited their dead husband's land, they were tried and murdered, again for being witches, so that the town's government, run by men, of course, could get their land."

By now the women were enraged. They listened to Christina's words, not wanting to believe what they were hearing. And they thought about their own lives, their own generation and their children's and how so little had really changed, how so many of them had been beaten down by men in one way or another, by their husbands or their male bosses. And they wondered why so much stayed the same, even with the advent of the feminist revolution, a good thirty years before. Where had the war so many of them taken part in gone wrong? And was their own sex somewhat to blame, that after all was said and done, they were still relative laborers in a man's world?

Christina suddenly softened her tone. "I know, women, this all sounds so harsh, but you must remember, men have had a long indoctrination period to their way of thinking. Men have been taught well and conditioned for thousands of years now, that they are the power, given to them by their God, the God they created in their image."

"Now I certainly know that probably most of you, like myself, in fact, have been raised with a belief in God and faith and I would never want to take that away from any of you. I simply ask that you look at what religion, at its worst, has done to propagate the sexist behavior that still exists throughout our world, today. Continue to believe the good you find in your beliefs, but also, perhaps begin to understand and reject the negative aspects of that belief. Most of all, see the possibilities of the truth of what came before these beliefs, before the male God, that which was a woman, the Goddess."

"And let me also clarify strongly… this is not some man-hating workshop. I say again, it is not. Between you and me, I have been loved and loved wonderful men in my own life, yes I have, as I'm sure many of you have, also."

At that statement, some of the women smiled and nodded, while some shook their head in the negative.

"It is simply an unfortunate fact that men have been misguided by their forefathers for years upon years. Yes, they need educating, but I would certainly not recommend you stand in the park on your soap box, spewing out this new found information. Better you should focus on yourselves, finding the beauty inside of you, gaining self-worth along the way. We must take back the power within ourselves, especially in this stage of our life. And by these actions you will regain your own power that can never be diminished by another individual. Please do not believe it is too late to change and grow. In your own ways, right the wrongs of your individual lives."

The women continued to think about all that had been said and discussed it between themselves as the days went by. And it became so clear to them how through centuries and generations, women had, indeed, become brainwashed into believing they were less than their physically stronger counterparts. That in trying to gain independence and power of their own, so many sisters ended up trying to emulate the very men who had tried to keep them down and subservient, because it seemed the only way they had to get ahead in this world.

But in truth, how could blame be put on all men, when they were just living what they had always been taught. Men were taught to be men, by men. Unfortunately, for the most part, women had been taught to be women by men, also.

"Oh, yes, my friends, we have an abundance of work to do," Christina told the women on another day, when they all sat outside in the warmth of the sun. "We are no longer the young women, with nimble bodies they still exploit in Playboy Magazines. But, fear not, or rather, fear... they haven't forgotten us, by any means. Our age makes us high paying targets for their constant greed and control, by the men and unfortunately the growing amount of women, who have played the man's game, clawing their way up that corporate ladder. They all want you to believe that with old age you lose... your face, your figure, your ability to conceive, your ability to be a force in society as a whole. And most importantly, your ability to feel good about yourselves, unless you buy their expensive cosmetic products or have their operations that supposedly will wipe away your years of living. Well, you get the idea. But what they don't know is that now we are free. Truly free. Free from the stereotypes that their society has burdened us with. Free to finally learn to love ourselves, no matter what! And if they won't listen to us, we will listen to ourselves and to each other. And from that, believe me, we will find strength and peace and joy."

"Yes, that is our weapon. We must turn all the negatives of the past millenniums into positives for ourselves. And perhaps, if we are lucky, by our own enlightenment and this new-found belief and self-love, they too will become enlightened. And hear me now! I do believe that men have been severely misguided, for the last, say… six to eight thousand years…"

The women laughed at this.

"… but it's not too late. Not for us and not for them. It's 1993, my women and I'm hoping if every one of us starts spreading the message, then by the new millennium a change will begin to happen. But it all starts with each of you, with the realization of who you really are and in the celebrating of who you have become. But until you believe it yourself, you will never be able to convince others of this truth."

There was so much for the women to think about and at that moment it was so hard not to hate men, all men… even the ones they loved. How could they take this huge picture of what they were learning and pare it down to their own individual lives? After all they were learning from Christina this week, they wanted to race home and change the world, educate the world concerning the way people thought about women, women of all ages, but especially aging women. But first they were learning that they would have to change themselves, one woman at a time.

# CHAPTER SEVENTEEN

As the week went by, Christina watched the transformation being made by her women, the natural beauty emerging from each of them. Those whom she had first seen with make-up adorning their faces had slowly ceased putting it on. Even Victoria now only dabbed on a bit of lipstick, before she rushed out to the day's activities. Hair was pulled back with ribbons or leather strings, now sans mousses or sprays. The glow in their cheeks came from the sun, not from some expensive bottled make-up. And never had they felt so healthy, so happy and so at peace with themselves.

They tried sculpting vessels, that which they were, for new life and Goddess forms and learned how to weave Dream Catchers made out of grape vines, hemp, beads and feathers. Medicines for their aches and pains ceased to be ingested, forgotten, as they did yoga and challenged each other to volley-ball tournaments. And most importantly, they continued on their quest to get closer to the earth, going out on small expeditions, walking the land that was theirs, taking with them, Demeter, La Loba or Sophie as their guides.

One afternoon, Sara, Carol and the rest of their bunkmates sunned themselves at the private cove, where the gently lapping water met the shore. They had become fast friends, by now, connecting in their common bond, no longer bothered by their differences, for here on this island, they were all the same... women of the third age.

Penny talked about the perfect wife she was and even though she loved her little family and her life, how through the years she had, in fact, resented her place, sometimes.

"Sam sometimes treats me like I was a China doll, like something breakable, you know? And I think because of this, he maybe keeps me from doing things I'd really like to try and do. Once, I remember wanting to go on a fishing trip with him, but he said the waters would get too rough and me not being the greatest swimmer, he thought it would be too dangerous for me. He wanted me to be safe at home. It's funny, because at the time, I took it as a compliment, that he loved me so much, he didn't want anything to happen to his princess."

Elaine told the group how she had come to this week as yet another fun and exciting experience, another thing to be able to tell her friends about back home that she was crazy enough to do.

"But I never expected to learn so much. I guess my life has been so small. I just always wanted it to be more like in the movies or all those, okay, stupid tabloids I'm always reading. That's why I think I'm always doing these things, to make myself feel important to others. After this, I don't think I could ever live, what's that word, vicariously, through what I read in a movie magazine. And boy, will I ever have a few things to tell my husband!"

Annie couldn't get her mind off her childless condition. The truth was, there had been a number of years when she and her live-in love had discussed her getting pregnant.

"Actually, *I* discussed it. He kept telling me it wasn't the right time for either of us. Either of us? I guess things were more important to him, like money and cars and boats. And I went along with it. I guess I was successful at believing him, that our life was full enough with all those things. And the capper is, this new woman, my replacement, this girl he left me for, well, I just found out she's pregnant and he's overjoyed about it. Hell, I want my dog back."

What Annie didn't reveal was that many years before, she had gotten pregnant and because her boyfriend was so adamant against having children, believing it would ruin their lifestyle, she believing he would leave her if he knew, when he was away on business she had an abortion without even telling him she was ever pregnant. And she grieved deeply for that unborn child, much more now, than she had at the time.

Surprising herself, Victoria confided to her new women friends about her husband's infidelities. After so many years, first of denial, then keeping the truth and the pain to herself, she now felt such a relief in the telling, like the weight of the world had been lifted from her shoulders. She could never have shared this secret with the women she lunched and played tennis with, although she wouldn't have been surprised if half of their husbands were cheating on them, also.

After hearing Victoria's story, it was harder for Sara to talk about Peter, but she eventually did. She wasn't looking for sympathy, how could she? But just perhaps a little understanding of why someone like herself could have been in such a situation. Had all along it been desperation at not wanting to be alone, that allowed herself to believe that he would, indeed, leave his wife? Had it been the dream of the fairytale that the once young lovers, first loves could find each other again and live happily ever after? She knew that it still wasn't over for her, that she still had a lot of work to do to reconcile her life and her pain. But sad as she was, this week, if anything, was giving her hope... of something.

Carol had so many thoughts churning inside of her, she didn't know which to address first. Now, at least, she had validation to all the things she had been feeling the last number of years. And that, in itself, gave her strength.

"To hell with Dan," she said angrily, "if he can't understand what I'm going through. I'm tired of trying to explain it to him."

Yes, she was angry, but determined to continue her quest for knowledge and inner peace, be it alone or not. She shared how she wished she could always be surrounded by women, like this week had provided, women who understood, because they were in the same boat, traveling the same way.

Big Mama Beth had little to say, but was there to encourage the others, to take them around the shoulder and pat them, gently, where they hurt the most. Men were no longer a question in her life. She felt she had had the best, and when he died, she knew she would continue to live a full life, but alone, with all the warm memories of her fine husband, always near-by in her heart. Out of all the women, she had come to the retreat with the most inner peace. She was not afraid of growing old, nor dying. When it finally came for her, it would be then, she believed, she would reunite with her great love. So she lived on, a busy life, believing that wherever her husband was, he was close by, watching over her.

Most importantly about these women was that no matter what story they told about their feelings or their life, they were not judged by the others. There were no disapproving looks or finding fault in each other's life stories. There was only acceptance of each other, realizing that none of them had ever walked in the other's shoes. And this was such a relief, being able to be so truthful about their lives and still being understood and loved.

They had been sitting, talking in the sun quite a while, now the bond between them even tighter, closer.

Elaine finally got up and looked longingly at the water. "Boy, it's hot. Do you think anyone can see us from here?"

"Probably not," answered Beth. "What are you thing of, going skinny dipping?"

"As a matter of fact, that's exactly what I was thinking! Why not?" laughed Elaine.

Annie laughed, too. "I sure hope *skinny* isn't the operative word, here."

The others joined in the laughter, Big Beth the loudest.

Suddenly, Elaine quickly pulled off her bathing suit and took off for the water, screaming, "To hell with it! C'mon, ladies! Last one in is a rotten egg!"

As she submerged herself in the cold wetness she screamed again, this time in sheer delight. "Oh my god... Goddess! This is absolute heaven! I haven't done this since I was a little girl. Come on in. You don't know what you're missin'.

She began to expertly swim back and forth, every now and again jumping up, hooting and hollering in pure bliss.

The others looked on from the shore, obviously tempted.

Carol was the next to go, surprising herself. Off came her suit and into the water she ran. Elaine, Annie, Sara and Beth follow suit, or as was the case, without. Now they were all screaming and laughing as they romped and swam and dived like, perhaps not young, but certainly beautiful sea nymphs.

Penny and Victoria edged closer to the water, jealous their friends had the guts to do this. Finally, if not shyly, Penny undid the straps of her conservative one piece suit, dropped it to her ankles, stepped out of it and into the water.

What freedom she experienced, as she felt the liquid touching her body. She swam over to the others, to their delight. They were all school children again, let out for recess, as they continued their water antics.

And they didn't feel one bit embarrassed or silly. They gave not one thought about their breasts, no longer firm nor high, about the dimples on their legs, or their stretch-marked, now looser stomachs. In fact, they didn't even think about their bodies, at all. For the first time in their lives that they could remember, that was not who they were, at all. They were all beautiful souls, experiencing the ultimate joy at simply being alive. And probably for the first time in their lives there was no judgment put upon them for behaving the way they felt like behaving or looking like they did. They were experiencing this pure existence in the world, a feeling of oneness with the earth, with the water.

Then, from a little distance away, they heard Victoria yelling out to them. "I did it! I did it!"

Although she had entered the wet in her bathing suit, once in, she defiantly ripped it off and was now waving it like a flag of victory for all to see.

The women all started applauding and yelling, as they got closer and closer, finally encircling her, their water dance continuing. Never before in any of their memory had they all felt so free, so open, so unencumbered, so happy, swimming in the amniotic fluid of Mother Earth.

# CHAPTER EIGHTEEN

On the second to the last day of the retreat, Carol and Sara, with Sophie in tow, threw caution to the wind and went on a canoeing trip down one of the rivers that wound its way through the island. On one hand, they were somewhat apprehensive about taking this little adventure, alone, on the other hand, some force beyond their control pushed them to do it.

Large puffy clouds sailed overhead, as they adventurously paddled past the ferns and wild flowers that lined the river bank.

For seemingly no good reason at all, Sara started laughing out loud as she moved her oars, forward and back, forward and back through the smooth water.

"Know what I feel like? Like we're in that movie 'Deliverance'".

"Jeez, I certainly hope not! Wasn't there a bunch of killing in that film?" said Carol, now also laughing, as she tried to keep her oars moving as fast as Sara's. "But I sure feel powerful. No, not 'Deliverance'. If I only had a big old shot gun and a lousy man around, I'd feel more like we could be Thelma and Louise!"

"That movie really pissed me off," said Sara. "I mean, here these women went on this journey, looking for independence and in the end, what to they do, fly off a canyon to their death! Not sure that was the feminist thing to do."

"Yeah, I guess that's true, but I sure did like when, which was it, Thelma, or was it Louise, shot that guy who almost raped her, in that parking lot," answered Carol.

"Yeah, that was fun, but acting like men, with all the violence they did, I don't know, there's gotta be a better way for women to make their point, although, on the other hand, after all the things Christina's told us this week, maybe those two gals had the right idea," Sara laughed. "Hey, I consider myself to be a feminist, always have, but half the time even I think even I'm oblivious to all the things men do to us. I mean, do we really even take in that we're still portrayed like bimbos in bikinis on TV and in the movies, in ads, everywhere. In fact, lately, I do believe it actually is getting worse. But I think the public sees it so much, they're, we're immune to the real meaning of it, that we don't really think about what it really is. Continuing exploitation of women."

"You're right. And what about us older women?" Carol added. "If they show us at all, we're senile, or out of touch, or crabby, or ugly! Or worse, what about all the aging actresses who want to try and look younger so they can still get hired to work, who've had so much plastic surgery, they don't even look human, anymore and then everyone says, "*This* is what being fifty or sixty looks like these days! I don't think so. They all look like they're fifty or sixty with a lot of plastic surgery!"

"Hey, I have an idea," said Sara, "Maybe we should start a political awareness group for better rights and more respect for the aging, but not yet really old women. Remember the Gray Berets? Well, we could be, let's see, maybe the... Beige Berets!"

Sara was feeling giddy, undeniably silly, but she was really getting a kick out of herself and Carol was glad to see her friend laughing again. This whole week, for the most part, Sara had seemed so into her own little world. So quiet.

And then suddenly, the smoothness of the river got rougher with a few mini-rapids coming out of nowhere and the two women and Sophie hung on for dear life, as the canoe pitched and surged its way through them. As the women concentrated on their paddling, trying to avoid rocks and crashing into the river banks, they cried out in both fear and a feeling of delight. Even Sophie started barking. And then, as quickly as it had come, the river once again smoothed out. The panic was over.

"Forget Deliverance! How 'bout the sinking of the Titanic! I'm soaked," laughed Carol.

A little ways down the river, they guided their canoe to the shore to feel terra firma once again and explore a little. The minute it came to rest, Sophie bolted out and disappeared into the forest. Seeing this, the women panicked and ran after her, screaming her name, wondering if this was Clarissa Pinkola Estes' true meaning of women who run with the wolves... or after them.

As the two women followed in the direction Sophie had taken, the forest grew darker and darker. Where could she be, they wondered? Was she just trying to find a private place to relieve herself, or had she decided to rendezvous with an old flame, perhaps?

They decided to try and stay calm. After all, Christina had told them her pet would never abandon them, that Sophie had been a guide for retreat women for years. But as they carefully walked through the dense woods, calling her name, there was no sign of the half-dog, half wolf.

Helping to keep their composure, was what they saw all around them, the immense beauty of this land.

"I can't believe it's almost over. Hasn't it been great?" asked Carol, not waiting for an answer. "I haven't even missed Dan and Jonas that much and now I don't even feel guilty."

"Yeah. There's something about being with women, isn't there? Especially under these circumstances. I know this will sound stupid, Carol, but I feel like if I stayed up here, I'd live forever. Like this place isn't a part of reality, you know?"

"It isn't, " Carol said thoughtfully. "But what if we get home and lose it all… forget all the things Christina has told us and most of all, lose this feeling we've had all week?" The mere thought of that happening made Carol very sad.

They looked around the forest. It was so quiet they could hear their hearts beating. Sara took a great breath, filling her lungs with the freshness and the peace. Then her eyes went up to the sky.

"Ah, oh. Look how dark the sky's gotten. Wow, I hope it doesn't rain. What'll we do then?"

Carol looked up, too, then in unison they began calling out for Sophie, again. As they picked up their pace, having no idea where they were going, not even considering they might get lost and never find the river and their canoe again, suddenly lightening streaked across the sky, followed a few seconds later by the loudest clap of thunder either of them had ever heard. The peace was gone and in that instant, the women felt scared and alone. There was no question about it. The Great Mother was having Her say.

More lightening and thunder crashed through the darkened sky. And then the rains began. Not a sprinkle, not a drizzle, but large drops, falling hard from the heavens.

The women quickly put on the rain proof jackets that had been tied around their waists that Christina insisted they take, just in case, and started running through the now eerie woods, having no earthly idea where they were going. They thought of trying to go back to the canoe, but decided it was best to try and find their four-footed guide. Anyway, they doubted how good an idea it would be to even try and paddle back to the retreat in this storm.

They were doing their damnedest to be calm, when in fact, they were frightened out of their minds, not to mention dripping wet and most probably very lost, by now. As they ran, half-blinded by the rain, Sara, who was in the lead, tripped and fell into the mud over something. On the ground, she suddenly saw what it was she had tripped over and not moving an inch, let out a shattering scream, her eyes opened wide in fear.

"What!? What's wrong, Sara? Is it Sophie? Are you alright? ... Answer me!" Carol cried, standing over her friend, shaking, but not seeing what Sara had seen. "Sara! Speak to me!"

A completely petrified Sara was mute with fear, unable to utter a single sound, now, her eyes glued on that something she had fallen over.

"Sara! You're really scaring me, now. Are you hurt? For crying out loud, say something!" In a panic, Carol started trying to drag her friend up. And that is when she saw it, too.

Laying there in the mud was an old, skinny human leg, wearing raggedy old socks and ancient, scuffed hiking boots.

Now it was Carol's turn to become hysterical. "Oh my god. Oh my god. This isn't happening."

Sara, slowly, carefully getting to her feet and full of mud from top to toe, seemed to be in shock. All she seemed capable of doing was squeaking out Sophie's name, like the beast could even hear her, and Sophie would magically appear and make an intelligent decision about what to do.

"Forget Sophie. C'mon, Sara. Let's get out of here. We gotta get out of here!" cried Carol.

But Sara, now, was taking a closer look at the leg and saw that whatever it was attached to, if anything, was covered by some large wet ferns. Feeling scared out of her wits and somewhat brave at the same time, Sara slowly, slowly started pulling back the large drenched leaves, quite afraid to see what was underneath them.

"What are you doing?" hissed Carol. "Don't do that."

And then both women looked down at their now uncovered discovery and screamed so loud, it probably scared the Goddess Herself.

They hugged each other in terror, for what they saw was that connected to that skinny, wet limb, was the body of a very, very, very old woman.

Then, frightening the women even more, Sophie suddenly appeared. She completely ignored Sara and Carol and went directly over to the body. This set the women screaming, again. But Sophie heeded not and began to lick the face of the little, old, old, wet woman.

"Sophie! Stop it! Stop it! No, Sophie! Will you stop it!" Sara pleaded with the animal, in a loud frantic whisper.

Sophie didn't.

Then the scariest thing of all happened. The old woman's body jerked! This set the women off on another screaming jag, although it didn't seem to have any effect on the half-dog, half-wolf in the slightest. She just continued her licking.

"Sophie, damn it! Stop it! I mean it!"

And then a very, very queer sound emoted from the body.

"Bluiicckkk... Uckkkkiiee..."

That was it! The two women completely lost it, running away from the body, running back to it, running away, running back. Sophie looked at them as if they were nuts, then calmly continued her licking.

"Go 'way. Go 'way, you silly," the body said, pushing Sophie away gently with her spindly arm.

Sophie immediately backed away and sat next to the two open-mouthed women.

The old woman lifted her head, blinked her eyes open, then closed, then open again.

"She's alive! She's alive!" Carol cried out.

The women quickly bent down to the now talking old, old body, trying to help her up, as they uncontrollably laughed out loud out of relieved tension, panic and fear."

"What's so funny? And who are you? And speak up, will ya? I'm a little deaf, ya know?!"

This set Sara and Carol off again, as they got a good look at their find. It was then they realized that behind all her wrinkles and beyond her ancient body, bent with age, that once upon a time, this obviously very alive, mud-covered old Crone, had been so very beautiful.

As they carefully helped her get her footing, Sara said, her laughter now somewhat quelled, "We thought you were… well, that you had…"

"What? That I was dead? Kicked the bucket?" The old woman had spunk, that was for sure. "Don't be silly, sillies. I was just taking my afternoon nap."

Feeling the rain for the first time, she looked up at the sky.

"Damn! It's raining and I left all my windows open."

Carol and Sara convulsed into laughter, once again.

"C'mon, girls, whoever you are. Control yourselves," she said as she started hobbling down the path in the rain. "How does some nice hot tea and freshly baked cookies sound to you?"

The two women, with Sophie by their side, followed behind the little old woman, wondering if this was all a dream. Or better still, a bad fairytale.

# CHAPTER NINETEEN

A while later found Sara and Carol sitting on a handmade braided rug in front of a stone fireplace, now cleaned up, warming themselves in the glowing heat. They were wrapped in Indian blankets given to them by the old woman, as their clothes dried, nearby.

The old woman's name was Jane. The younger women thought she should have had a more exotic moniker, perhaps something from the Indian tribe she told them she was one quarter from, but alas, she was simply Jane.

The cabin where she lived was small, but filled with artifacts of the land, rocks and shells, ragged wood sticks she used to help steady herself when she went out walking. As rustic as the cabin was, she did have electricity, but that was pretty much all. No television, no radio, no microwave, just a big, black stove and refrigerator that looked to be as old as she.

As Jane fixed her guests their snack, the women studied some large and small baskets, filled to the brim with dried flowers, that sat on the floor near to the fireplace.

"These baskets are so beautiful," Carol said, examining them, closely.

"Well, thank you. I made 'em myself, ya know." Jane said, as she bustled around her tiny kitchen area. Her nap in the woods had done her good, for now she moved quickly, a frenzy of energy.

"You're kidding?" Sara exclaimed, as she picked an empty one up, running her hand over the meticulous handiwork.

"No. Learned from the Indians when I was a mere babe. I could teach you, gals. It isn't that hard. You just need patience and strong hands. Do you have that?"

"I think so," Carol answered. "But we're leaving the island day after tomorrow."

"Too bad. Well, maybe next time. Now come on over to the table. Tea's ready."

They sat down at the old dented wood table and had the herb tea and cookies Jane had put out for them. Neither woman realized how hungry they were, as they gobbled up the goodies.

"This is such a wonderful place you have here, Jane," said Sara, as the heat of the tea warmed her insides, the way the fire had warmed her outsides. "But you don't live up here all by yourself, do you?"

"Of course I do! I'm not an invalid, ya know!"

Sara, quick to clarify her possibly misconstrued words said, "Of course you're not. But you're so isolated here. Don't you have any family? Someone to help you out?"

"Help me out with what?" was Jane's response. "I grow my own vegetables out back, in my garden. And I can still chop my own wood for the fire. And I have a few friends on the island who bring me my other supplies when I need 'em. Anyway, my sons wouldn't be caught dead up here. They like things modern. They couldn't survive out here for a minute, or would they want to, for that matter."

Carol glanced around the cabin. "I'm not sure I could, either."

"Oh, sure you could. Just have to get used to it. And want to. Ya know, all my children were born here. Right in the other room, but no, it's not good enough for them, now. My two sons live in some snazzy retirement home in the city. Well, you know how kids are these days, don't ya? I, personally, think they're way too young to retire, they're only sixty-eight and seventy-two, for God's sake, but you think they listen to their mother?

Now, my daughter, she is something else. She's a country doctor up north. Still makes house calls, she does."

Sara and Carol could hardly contain their delight in this woman. They smiled at her as she gave Sophie a cookie. The animal ate it quickly, then begged for another. Jane complied.

"But don't you get lonely up here? Carol asked.

"Oh, I did for a while, I can tell you that, especially after my last husband passed over. But that was some twenty-five years ago. Eventually, there are just some things a person has to accept. I buried him not far from here and everyday I go out and have a nice chat with him. He's not a very good conversationalist anymore, so I just talk and talk and tell him what I've been up to."

The women smiled sadly, for a moment thinking of Mama Beth communing with her lost love. Then they tried to picture what it would really be like to be Jane, to be so old and alone, yet so amazingly self-sufficient and seemingly happy.

Jane was in the mood to talk and that she did.

"I'm not giving up, though, but the truth is, it's a little tougher to find true love at my age. But then, you two youngin's probably don't have problems like that."

Sara laughed. "Oh, you'd be surprised."

"Well, I'll be darned if I'm gonna settle for less, just to have some companionship around this place. I'd rather live the rest of my life alone." And Jane slapped the table with her old, arthritic hand.

"I hope I feel that way when I'm your age, if I end up by myself," said Carol, momentarily thinking of Dan and then wondering just how old Jane really was. Ninety? Closer to a hundred?

"I hope I feel that way next week," laughed Sara.

Jane looked at her young visitors and reached out her wrinkled hands, patting Sara's and Carol's.

"This is real nice. Real nice. Ya know, I have grandkids about your age. Some of them make the trek up here twice a year or so just to visit me." Jane smiled her half toothless grin as she thought of them.

"One just finally got her law degree and the other one just opened up a dance studio, something she'd always dreamed of doing. Nice kids. Nice kids. Now, see the difference between girls and boys? All my granddaughters have new careers, since their own kiddies grew up, but my grandsons are all ready to retire. Can you imagine that? Just in their fifties? God only knows what they're gonna do with the rest of their lives"

Jane scowled at the thought of it, then continued. "Probably go and live with their daddies in that Home. Play golf! Boys! Got no sense, at all!"

As the three women talked a while longer, Sara and Carol relished every minute spent with this remarkable woman. And they silently thanked

Sophie for running off like that, giving them the opportunity to meet her and be so welcomed in her home.

Jane was delighted to hear about Sara's bookshop, being an avid reader, herself. "I don't go in for those modern books they put out these days telling you how to do this, how to do that, how to be happy, or those silly romantic stories that never come true in real life. What crap! I like the old classics, like Jane Eyre and Louisa May Alcott. And that Anais Nin. Now that gal was something else, wasn't she, though? What a hoot!"

The women were getting such a kick out of Jane, they could have stayed with her for hours more. But they noticed the sun had reappeared again, the storm over for now and decided they had better get on their way, before Christina sent out a search party for them.

After getting dressed in their now dry and warmed clothes, they stepped outside the cabin into the brilliant sunlight. They couldn't help but notice the sight of the most glorious rainbow arching across the sky.

"Oh, look, Carol. It must be some sort of a sign, don't you think?" said Sara, always breathless at the sight of another one of nature's miracles of which she had seen so many of this week.

"I think it means there is hope for us. That our life will be better when we get back home," added Carol, as she too stared at the magnificent sight.

The old and wise Jane couldn't help but laugh at these two youngin's.

"Oh, phooey!, she said. "It's just a rainbow, girls. You two are much too serious. Just get out there and have some fun while you're still young! Ya know, there's not some deep meaning to everything. Things are! Accept 'em and go on. Then you'll end up living as long as me. Everything in the world doesn't need to be analyzed, ya know? You think Freud was a happy man? No! The guy was crazy! Just go and live. A rainbow is just a rainbow. And I'll tell you a secret. There's no pot of gold at the end of it. You gotta make your own pot and fill it with your own goodies of gold"

This certainly gave the women pause.

Then, before they took their leave of the old Crone Jane, they thanked her profusely for her wonderful hospitality, hugged and kissed her good-bye.

"Now, if you can, you come back and see me someday and I'll teach you how to weave a basket." And with that, she waved the women off in the right direction so they would find their way home.

As Sara and Carol followed Sophie down the wooded path toward their canoe, to the flowing river which would take them back to the retreat, they turned around to get one last look at Jane. But she had disappeared.

# CHAPTER TWENTY

That night, in front of the great bonfire at the amphitheater, all the women listened to Christina for the last time.

"It's hard to believe this week has gone by so quickly. I can only hope that all of you have had as wonderful a time as I have. And I hope that you will always keep what you have experienced this week inside of you. Study the Goddess and learn more about Her and how She relates to your lives. And She does, believe me. Take all you have learned and be Crones, Crones supreme, when the time comes, if it hasn't already. And to your skeptical friends and families, especially to other women, show them what you're really made of, so they won't be afraid or depressed to enter this stage of their lives. You are all so vibrant. You are all alive with endless possibilities. And you are all fantastic. Celebrate, my women. Celebrate! And may the Goddess be with all of you."

And with that, Christina raised her arms into the night air and applauded her women.

Everyone then went wild, exuberantly cheering their fierce leader back. It was much like the end of a graduation ceremony.

"And so, to end this week and to begin your life anew, this journey of your rebirth with your new-found spirit, born from self-discovery, let us dance in celebration."

Christina then turned on a portable tape machine and music thundered into the night air, wild music of African origin. With no prodding whatsoever, the women leaped to their feet and around the fire and beneath the stars and the now less full moon, they danced in untamed abandon, their souls taking flight. They felt primal, as they moved to the rhythmic beat of the drums. And they came together in a circle, individuals always, but most certainly in oneness, in oneness with each other and in oneness with the Great Mother. And they danced until they could dance no more.

Later that night in their cabin, the bunkmates were finally quiet, immersed in their own thoughts as they packed up their belongings for the journey they would take the next morning, back to their real lives.

Penny stood by the cabin door, looking out into the blackness of the night, tears streaming down her cheeks.

Sensing her sadness, Beth came up behind her, putting her strong, yet gentle arms around Penny's shoulders. "Ahh... what's the matter, baby?"

"I don't know. I feel so good up here. I don't think I want to leave. I don't want it to be over."

In her always motherly tone, Beth said quietly, "I know, Darlin', I know. I think that's how we all feel."

Then Penny start to cry in earnest. "What's wrong with me? I love my life at home. I love Sam and my boys."

"Of course you do," said Beth soothingly. "This has nothing to do with that. It's just been a very special week for us gals. I don't think any of us thought what kind of impact this week would have on any of us."

Annie joined the two women.

"Let's make a pact to stay in touch with each other, okay? Let's not just say it, let's really do it."

Now it was Victoria who stopped her packing to join the others.

"I own this cabin in Northern California. We don't go there very often, anymore. Maybe we could meet up there a few times a year or something. It's in the middle of nowhere and we could hike and sort of rough it, just like this week. The way I'm feeling, now, maybe I'll just go and live up there by myself."

"And to think, Victoria, you were ready to leave us after the first night." This from Elaine.

"But I didn't. Maybe I'll leave *him*, instead." Then she smiled widely, her make-up free, now tanned face crinkling in delight. "I would have loved to see what my husband would have thought had he heard I swam naked in a cold lake!"

"He'd probably be jealous he hadn't been with you." Said Sara.

"Oh, I don't think so. He'd have probably told me what a fool I was making of myself," Victoria said, suddenly wondering if she really cared anymore about anything he said to her or thought about her. And she wondered, too, what he would do if she actually kicked him out, to let him live with one of his twenty-something screws, who she knew were only after his money.

"Well, I'm not sure I'm even going to mention it to Dan," Carol confided. "He would never understand and then most likely try and make me feel how stupid the whole thing was to do, trying to pretend I was a teenager again, doing silly things. No, I don't think he'll understand much of anything I'll tell him about this week."

The women now all stood near to the open cabin door, slowly joining hands, then lifting up their arms, putting them around each other's shoulders, then slowly swaying back and forth in unison.

They had come together as strangers seven days before, so diverse in their life's experiences and now this incredible retreat had bonded them together, forever, even if it happened they were never to see each other again in this life. Here, now, they knew they were among sisters.

The next morning dawned cloudy, nature once again on the verge of watering Her land, as the retreat women bid their final farewells to Christina and her half-dog, half-wolves, Demeter, La Loba and the dear, dear Sophie, with hugs and pats and kisses. And as used to all these tearful adieus Christina was, summer after summer, even her eyes filled up some.

After all, she once again was sending women back into their own worlds with new-found knowledge and strength, as they took those tentative, uneasy steps toward becoming Crones. And she so hoped they would all fare well on their journey.

"But do not tread lightly upon this earth," she finally told them. "Walk with your heads held high, with conviction and energy and power and dignity. And remember always... you are Goddess. You *are* Goddess, so celebrate it! Celebrate... Celebrate..."

Christina's last words rang in the ears of the women, as the ferry that a mere week before had brought them to this wooded paradise, was now taking them back to their own homes, to their individual realities.

Bundled up in the cold morning air, the women looked ahead, as the ferry pulled away from the island's shore. And then when they turned back a few moments later to take one last look at the place they now knew and loved so well, the place they acknowledged they were not quite ready to take leave of, a thick mist had engulfed the island, now which had all but vanished from their sight.

## CHAPTER TWENTY-ONE

Carol and Sara sat next to each other as their plane headed back toward Los Angeles and home. While Carol gazed out the small air-tight window, Sara looked over the long book list of suggested reading Christina had given all the women the last night of the retreat. Could it be that she, the consummate reader, not to mention bookseller, had never heard of most of these titles? Of course, the study of the Goddess had never before been her priority, much less in her realm of thought.

She made the decision, right then and there to enlarge the women's section of her shop. Perhaps she would even start a women's circle one evening a week. She could picture it in her mind's eye, women entering Cronehood sitting around the old stove on large, cushy pillows. A Goddess altar, lit with candles would be in the center, as women shared their fears and joys, their disappointments and frustrations with each other. And talk, of course, about what they were all going through, the aging process. Suddenly, she couldn't wait to get home and start her reading, a new education before her, picking up where Christina had thirstily whet her appetite. Sara felt absolutely inspired.

Carol, on the other hand, felt absolutely perspired. Moments before she had felt peaceful, her mind full of the last week, of Christina, her bunkmates and of wonderful old Jane. Of dancing in the moonlight and hiking on the Goddess's land. She had felt so liberated. Then she thought of home and Dan and Jonas and she worried how she would keep in her mind and in her body all the serenity she had newly experienced. She felt desperate that it would all be fleeting, passing her by, that she would be unable to hold on to it no matter how hard she tried. And it was then she felt that old familiar heat begin to rise up from her chest.

"Oh, no," she said, unaware she was verbalizing out loud. She began to wave her hand in front of her already wet neck and face.

Sara stopped her reading and looked over to her friend. What she saw shocked her. Carol's face was flushed pink, the wetness literally dripping from her temples, down her neck.

"Oh, my goodness, Carol! Are you alright?"

"No!" Carol responded, looking quite panicky. "My damn hot flashes have come back, with obvious vengeance."

Sara studied her friend's physical condition. "This might sound stupid, but I've never really seen one up close, one so severe. Jeez, I wonder what it will be like for me."

"Hopefully, not this bad. Well, feast your eyes, kiddo!" Carol said as she grabbed the book list out of Sara's hands and started wildly fanning herself with it.

Finally the episode passed and as Carol wiped the remaining wetness from her brow, she said, "Know what's so strange? All this week I never had one, well, maybe a few little itty-bitty ones the first day or two, but not like this. These are the kind I was getting two dozen times a day back home. That never occurred to me until now, since we were so busy and active all week."

Sara thought this mighty interesting. "Well, I'm no expert, Car, but is it possible they're partially stressed induced. I mean, of course, it's physical, but I wonder if stress can exaggerate it?"

Sara always liked to figure out the psychological reasoning behind everything, something that drove her daughter nuts. When Sara pulled this kind of thing on Rebecca, the child would reply, 'Mom! Maybe things just happen for no damn good reason at all!' Even though old Jane had echoed this same sentiment, it still seemed an impossible thought to the mother. Everything had, just had to have a good reason behind it.

Through all her doctor's visits and all her reading up on menopause, Carol had never thought of this as even a possibility. Hot flashes to her were simply another depressing reminder of the lack of control she had over her aging body. But she certainly gave it some thought now.

"Stressed induced," Carol repeated. "I don't know. What I do know is how great I was feeling all week. And now that I think about it, I really haven't had any of my other symptoms, either. No dizziness or aches. They all went away. I guess I just thought that maybe I was starting another phase of it. But now…"

"Well, you were probably eating healthier and doing all that exercise. Maybe that had something to do with it," Sara said, still trying for some rational explanation.

Carol turned back to the window and stared out at the blue, cloudless sky that was brightened by the sun, which she was now closer to by thirty thousand feet or so. Could it be Sara was right, though? Could it be she was really dreading going home, that the mere thought of continuing not to be understood by her family had kicked off this attack? It was true that since boarding the plane, her stomach had knotted. And there was no doubting she felt torn between wanting more hours, more days in the safe womb of the island, the guilty feelings she had had leaving Dan and Jonas in the first place and in some small secret place, not wanting to go home at all, just like Penny. She had been opened up to so many new possibilities in her life, but she continued to wonder where they would fit into the days and nights and years in her life that would follow.

"What's it like?" Sara's voice invaded Carol's thoughts.

"What're they like?" Carol took a deep breath. "Well, they're like this very, very wet expanding sensation. See, it starts on your chest, then rises slowly up your neck, then to your face, from bottom to top, until it reaches the end of your hair follicles. And you feel yourself getting redder and redder and redder, inside and out. Remember what a contraction felt like? It's sort of like that, but without the pain and on the top half of your body, instead of the bottom half!"

As Carol gave Sara this graphic explanation, her voice raised, higher and louder, her arms moving up her body, waving madly, finally ending above her head.

At that moment, a man who was walking innocently down the aisle, probably heading for the plane's tiny toilet to take a piss, couldn't help but notice what looked to him to be a possibly unstable passenger.

Sara noticed his reaction and couldn't help but look embarrassed for her friend.

"Okay... I get the picture," Sara said in a low voice.

Never noticing the man, herself, Carol moaned, "No, Sara. You couldn't unless you've lived through them. And luckily you haven't, yet."

The sullen Carol returned her gaze to the sky. Sara went back to her now damp reading list.

A few moments later Carol groaned loudly, as she began to experience yet another flash. Seeing this, a powerless Sara had an idea.

"Carol? Maybe you could actually learn to control them. If they're like contractions, like you said, maybe doing breathing exercises while you're having them would help. You know, like in natural childbirth."

Although, in all honesty, Sara didn't think deep breathing would have any effect, whatsoever on Carol's continual plight, she felt the need to say something of a positive possibility, not being able to stand seeing her friend so miserable.

"Hey, I'll try anything," answered Carol. The heated woman immediately started exaggerated breath intakes that quickly turned into short, loud pants.

As she sweated profusely, panting hard and loud, the same man, happily relieved, made his way back to his seat. He again couldn't help but notice Carol's bizarre, but now, exaggerated behavior. As far as he was concerned, this plane couldn't land soon enough for him.

Forty-five minutes outside of LAX, the seat belt sign came on early, followed by the pilot's voice over the loud-speaker. In an overly calm tone that pilots must have to take lessons to learn, in case of emergencies, he explained how they would soon be experiencing some turbulence, due to unexpected thunderstorms in the area.

He hardly had a chance to finish when the big bird suddenly began to pitch, shake and dive. Never really mentally prepared for anything but a smooth flight, passengers screamed out in fright.

Carol and Sara looked at each other, words not forthcoming out of fear, as they gripped their arm-rests for dear life. Then Carol dared to peek out her window, thinking she might see the cause of the plane's erratic behavior. All looked calm enough, as they swiftly bumped along through the still sunshine. She saw in the distance white billowy clouds. But underneath were darker, more ominous ones. It seemed so unrelated to all the shaking going on inside the plane's cabin, as hearts sunk to the pits of passenger's guts.

The flying machine stabilized a few minutes later, giving everyone a false sense of security, only to begin again its violent air dance.

Again the pilot's voice could be heard, asking for forgiveness, vocal cords trembling, because of his plane's uncontrollable movements. "Please stay calm," he said. "We are not in any danger. All planes in the area are experiencing what we are and we should be out of this in ten to fifteen minutes."

Well! That sure as hell made everyone feel better, as passengers thought of loved ones on the ground, praying to God they would see them again this day.

Trying her damnedest to remain calm in the storm, Sara did not see her life pass before her eyes, as the shaking, dipping and diving got worse. With not so steady a voice, she said to Carol, "I guess the Great Mother is pissed about something, huh?"

Carol closed her eyes, afraid she might be on the verge of getting sick from the plane's turbulent motion. "I was thinking this was, maybe, another sign, you know, like the rainbow we saw in the woods. But I know if Jane was here, she'd pooh-pooh it as just some bad weather." Carol was hoping if she kept talking she wouldn't puke her guts out.

Through their fear, both women then laughed, stiffly, in truth, terrified, but just thinking of the wonderful, ancient Jane made them feel a little better, a little safer.

After another few minutes of their nauseating ride, it all stopped as quickly as it had begun. The plane continued, now smoothly, on its downward path back to earth.

Carol, once again dared to look outside her temporary home in the sky, waiting for another inevitable lurch in the wild ride, when she saw a wonderful, delicious sight. Land! Below her, through the now wispy clouds, was the city of angels and devils. She saw the freeways, packed with ant-sized cars making their way to and fro. She saw all the playschool-sized houses with their blue swimming pools, a sure sign they were about to land in the city of glitz and glamour. Above her, dark clouds still loomed, but they were now safely flying below the fray.

When the plane finally did touch down, the passengers, a hundred and some strangers, now forever bonded by their terrifying experience, broke out in grateful applause. Carol broke out in another terrifying sweat.

# CHAPTER TWENTY-TWO

Rebecca had been the dutiful daughter in Sara's week long absence. She had watered house plants, filled the fridge, brought in the mail and sorted it, throwing out those pesky advertisements, took all messages off her mother's answering machine, among which were numerous hang-ups, checked in on Book, Nook and Crannies, warmed up Sara's car once or twice and even brought fresh flowers for her mother's bedroom.

After eyeing all this organization and neatness, Sara decided that she really must go away more often. She had taught her daughter well, making her a neurotic, obsessive, just like herself, she laughed to herself.

"You're such a good daughter, Becca."

"Thank you, Mama. I try."

That night as Sara snuggled up in her own bed, after a wonderfully long and hot bath, she realized that she was glad to be home, after all, in her own space, in her own bed, once again.

She already felt far removed from the forest she had so quickly come to love. Had it all been a dream? Had she really canoed down a river with a wolf as her guide? Had she really swam naked in the Sound, jumping, happily around like a child with other naked women? Was she really a Goddess?

As tired as she was, Sara got out of the sweet comfort of her comfy bed and went to the glass door, sliding it open. Barefoot, she stepped onto her patio, out into the balmy night, in search of the moon.

There it was, her now beloved Luna, in all her glory, high in the sky. Not far from it, she saw a twinkling star.

Bring me peace, thought Sara. Bring me happiness and peace, she wished upon it, silently. Bring me love.

Upon returning to the coziness of her thick, down comforter, she lit the candle on her bed stand. It glowed and flickered in the dark, as Sara lay there, still. As drowsiness began to over-take her, she blew out the flame and quickly fell into a deep slumber.

That same night, Carol was just getting around to unpacking. She had not had the luxury of puttering around a clean house, while soft music echoed from the stereo, as Sara had.

Carol came home to chaos, a week's worth of things that had gone wrong, that had been left, undone, for her to deal with. She came home to hear Jonas' complaints, his missing her filling, tasty cooking, his dirty laundry piled high on his bedroom floor.

And Dan wasn't much better. He had neglected to bring in her car to be serviced, as he had promised. Overdue rented videos sat atop their big screen TV. The dogs hadn't been groomed and the plants hadn't been watered.

Hot flash after hot flash attacked Carol that night. But was she really surprised by the state of her house and family? The answer was, not at all. In fact, in a not very healthy way, it made her feel needed and wanted. Her men obviously couldn't survive very well without her motherly and wifely touch, even for a week.

She knew she should be angry and part of her was. But another part of her, that part which had had a lifetime of indoctrination, as Christina had talked about, took it all in stride. This is what was expected of her as a woman and she filled that expectation, fully and completely.

The mild anger she showed her husband and son that night was all part of the dance of a relationship that had been around for thousands of years. No. Tonight she was too exhausted to be the gatherer to her men's hunter. Tonight she again assumed the role of the perfect mother, not the Great Mother.

Even though it seemed to be the case, Carol had not already forgotten the past week. Rather, she savored it, silently. She would grow stronger on her own and use her newly acquired knowledge when the time was right for her, and then she would slowly try and educate her men.

Temporarily alone in her bedroom, she neatly piled her soiled retreat clothes in her wicker laundry basket, then put her still clean things and sundries away. Among the items was the Dream Catcher she had made during the week. She held it up and smiled, remembering the day the women had sat outside at long picnic tables, making them. She had been proud of her handiwork, making hers slowly, trying for perfection, as she picked the beads and the feathers, so carefully, as she wove the web, leaving a perfect hole for which good dreams could pass through.

Carol looked around her bedroom, then hung it on the bedpost on her side of the bed. She happily stared at it a few seconds, then went back to her unpacking.

She felt from behind her Dan's arms go around her waist.

"Ya know, I missed you, Car," he said.

Carol smiled. "So... your heart is fonder, now, huh?"

"Yeah, I guess so."

"See, maybe my going away wasn't such a bad thing, after all."

"Well, just don't make a habit of it. It was a damn long week. I'm sorry the place is such a mess, but I've had a bitch of a week."

Carol noticed the female reference, reacted inside, but said nothing.

Then Dan saw the Dream Catcher on the bedpost. "What's that thing hanging on the bed?"

Carol was looking forward to explaining it to him. "It's a Dream Catcher. The Indians made them for their baby's cradles. See the web? Well, during the night the baby's bad dreams get caught in it, saving them from having nightmares. And see the hole in the middle? The myth goes that the good dreams find their way through it, then float down that hanging feather into the child's subconscious. Isn't that lovely?"

It was quickly obvious that Dan was not as enchanted with the story as was Carol.

"You're not going to keep it there, are you?" he said, as he went over to take a closer look at the primitive craft. "It really doesn't go with the room, you know."

Carol tried to ignore him, hurt in her heart in a place he could not see.

"See the colored beads?" she went on. "The red one inside the web signifies the beating heart. And the ones right above the feather are for the different races of people... white, black, brown and yellow."

"So... I guess this means you want to keep it up, huh?"

Carol now gave Dan a dirty look.

"Okay, okay, if you really have to."

Thank you so very much for your kind indulgence, thought Carol with hostility.

"So, what else did you do up there? Hopefully, not make a lot of other crafty things," Dan lightly laughed, then had a vision of his beautiful house suddenly filled with unprofessional looking arts and crafts made by his wife.

"What's the point of telling you anything, Dan. You'll just have some negative comment to make about it, anyway. I knew you wouldn't understand anything of what I've just experienced. You'll just have some negative comment to make about it."

"No, I won't. I really want to know," he said in the most interest-filled voice he could muster.

But Carol wasn't buying it.

"It was women's stuff, Dan. Any which way I explain it to you, it will come out sounding dumb and trite. I guess you just had to be there. But if you want to know the truth, it was the best week I can ever remember having."

And with that, Carol turned on her bare-footed heel and went back to her unpacking, not seeing the hurt and being left out look on her husband's face.

# CHAPTER TWENTY-THREE

After being home for a week, Sara's glow was still intact. Wanting to share her new-found appreciation for all nature had to offer, she invited her friend, Bonnie, to join her for an afternoon in the city's wild. Although balking at first, wondering why they couldn't spend the day, instead, shopping in Beverly Hills, Bonnie finally relented and joined Sara for what she thought would be a nice little walk in the park.

Bonnie, dressed in a trendy aerobics outfit, her face heavily and perfectly made up, was none too thrilled when she found herself on a dusty fire road in the Santa Monica Mountains, trying to keep up with her newly energetic friend.

Wearing hiking shorts and boots, a fanny-pack holding a bottle of water, slung around her waist, Sara happily made her way up the steep path. Bonnie huffed and puffed behind her.

Brave souls on dirt bikes whizzed by, kicking up the dust, while other hikers voiced greetings as they passed.

Finally, Bonnie slowed to a crawl, then stopped, leaning over in exhaustion and pain, much like the retreat women had done on their first hike up to the plateau.

"Sara, hold on. I gotta rest a minute." Bonnie somehow got out.

Sara shook her head and went back to her friend.

"What's wrong?" asked Sara, not too concerned.

"You said we were going to take a little walk, not climb Mount Everest!"

"Toughen up, kid! We've only been out here ten minutes."

Sara laughed to herself, knowing she sounded just like Christina, egging her retreat women on.

"Ten minutes? That's all?" panted Bonnie. "It seems more like ten hours."

Bonnie then looked at her tanned and healthy looking girlfriend. "You know, I think you've gone off your rocker. What're you going to do next? Bungee jumping?"

Sara took Bonnie's hand and led her over to a partially shaded area on the road and sat her down on a rock.

"Here, have a little water," Sara said in mocked sympathy, as she pulled the bottle out of her pack.

As Bonnie drank the cool liquid, she now really studied Sara's face. Then it hit her.

"Wait a minute!" she exclaimed. Then in a sing-song voice added, "I know your secret. I know your secret."

"What the hell are you talking about?" was Sara's response.

Bonnie smiled widely. "You just told me you went to that stupid place, that retreat thing. You really had your eyes done, didn't you. And nice job the tanning booth did for you. C'mon, Sara. It's me. You can fess up the truth to me."

An amused Sara couldn't believe what she was hearing, as Bonnie continued to peer closely at her face.

"Mm, and maybe around your lips, too, hmmm? You sneaky girl, you."

Sara burst out laughing.

"You don't have to be embarrassed, Sara. I think it's wonderful that you finally took my advice. Now, wasn't it worth every last dime? You look great!"

Then Bonnie reached out and touched Sara under the eyes with her finger. "Mm, whoever did it, did a terrific job. What's his name? I maybe would have gotten it a little tighter, but overall, good job. But how did it heal so fast? Was it that new laser surgery I've been hearing about? Yeah, but even with that, you should still be red or something. Why aren't you still red and blotchy?"

Bonnie continued to study Sara's face, amazed.

"Bonnie, Bonnie, Bonnie! I didn't have plastic surgery!"

"Of course you did. Why can't you just admit it? How else could you look so good?"

Sara laughed out loud. "Because, you ninny, I *feel* good!"

Sara started stretching her tanned legs, ready to move again, while Bonnie was having a hard time comprehending any of it.

"So, what, you had a peel, then, right?"

"Nope!"

"Well," said Bonnie, not wanting to give this up, "You had to have had something done to look like this."

Laughing again, Sara said, "A couple of hours a week of hiking and you too can kiss your surgeon good-bye. Now, let's go, woman."

And with that, Sara took off up the road, leaving Bonnie sitting dumfounded. Then, suddenly, she heard something rustling through the near-by bushes. She jumped up and started running, trying, frantically, to catch up with her friend.

"Sara! Wait! I think I heard something! I think it was a snake! Sara! Wait for me!"

Sara turned around, saw Bonnie was in no imminent danger, laughed and continued on her way.

"Sara! This isn't funny! Wait for me!!"

As the days went by, Sara continued working on feeling mellow, which unfortunately turned out to be much more of a struggle to attain than she had first thought, now that she was back to the daily grind of her real life.

She was well enough versed in the language of words and their meanings to know that *mellow* and *struggle* should not, by all logic, belong in the same sentence. To even think of struggling toward mellowness, she thought to be a kind of oxymoron. Not a true figure of speech, but contradictory, none the less.

As she finally began to take a crack at gardening her small plot of patio soil, as she walked on the beach during her lunch breaks, wanting to experience the great outdoors as much as possible and as she buried her head into book after book, delving into the myths of the Goddess, still there were too many in-your-face reminders of the patriarchal society in which she had to dwell.

And Sara was starting to get incredibly annoyed. Everywhere she looked were the cruel signs of how men ruled this, The Great Mother Earth. Of course, there were the obvious, political and religious power, but almost more disturbing to her were the less obvious, words, mere words that made up sentences that all of humanity completely took for granted and worst of all, lived by.

Fore-*FATHERS*, *MAN*-kind, *MAN*-made, *MAN*-power, *MAN*ned. Were machines never *WOMAN*ened?

*MAN*-hours, *MAN*hunt, *FATHER* figure, *FATHER* time, He's your *MAN*, *MAN* on the street, *MAN* of the house, to be one's own *MAN*. And of course... *AMEN*!

A woman, according to the dictionary, was an 'adult fe-*male* person,' and not much more. A man, on the other hand, was a 'human being, distinguished from other animals by superior mental development.'

These were all more than just words to Sara. This was defining what people were and ultimately what they could do. But the definition that pissed Sara off the most was 'Woman's Rights.' 'the right of women to have a position of legal and social equality with men.' Which meant, women were not born equal to begin with.

What were the real ramifications of this statement, wondered Sara, that equality, like women, themselves, were a much later after-thought of man's, just like women were God's afterthought after making man? That being born from day one, much less being equal was not a woman's right of birth? This must have been the case, since the words, 'Man's Rights' were nowhere mentioned in the most authoritative dictionary of American usage. They obviously didn't have to be, since these inalienable rights had already been given to man by their very own god.

Sara knew one might argue that the term, 'man' was at least in some cases used generically, meant to encompass all human beings, but semantics aside, this did not come close to satisfying her.

How, in fact, would modern man feel if for every use of the word 'man,' the word 'woman' was interjected, instead? She could only imagine the gender war that would most probably ensue, most probably would have ensued centuries before.

A good ten years ago, Sara remembered, the always sexiest Hollywood had a wonderful idea. How terrific it would be to acknowledge their female counter-parts in the industry. And so that year's Academy Awards heralded it The Year Of The Woman. And some women at the time actually cheered, 'Hey, now we're finally getting somewhere in this town!'

Tokenism. Sheer tokenism, thought Sara, as she had watched along with the millions of others, of course, wondering what Cher would have the guts to wear that year. Would next they honor the likes of Lassie and Rin Tin Tin in the Year Of The Dog? The fact was, Sara thought, if one has to make a big deal, give an award to a certain group of people (or animals) it is because they are not considered the norm, say, like... MEN!!!

How offensive, pondered Sara, as she sat crossed-legged in front of her newly set-up Goddess altar. Oh, yes, peace and mellowness were going to be hard to come by living on the Great Mother who in the last thousands of years had been so completely man-remade.

Later, while glancing over an article in what was considered to be a 'new' woman's magazine, a female anthropologist had the audacity to explain women's evolution regarding finding love. It said in essence, that millions of years ago, needing man's protection ( of course) and hunting abilities for life-sustaining food, women naturally responded to those who seemed both strong and important in the tribe, that because of evolutionary forces, males, driven by desire to reproduce, picked sweet young, good-looking females that seemed most likely to produce viable heirs for them.

Get your facts straight, female anthropologist! Millions of years ago, men didn't even know it was from them that got a woman pregnant in the first place! Sara was feeling indignant! Rubbish! So angry was she, she shot off a seven page, didactic epic to the editor explaining the true story of the ancient world and how the magazine should really check their writer's facts before printing them! Needless to say, her letter-to-the-editor never saw the light of page. Sara immediately canceled her subscription.

Then she came to a momentous decision. Seething with enraged infuriation at the day in and day out injustices of the world pertaining to women, as she saw them, was certainly not doing her any good. She would now force herself to concentrate all her energies on the positive. On herself. On the

Goddess. She couldn't fight all of mankind alone and she knew it. Instead she would continue her search, trying to recall all of what Christina had said. And she would make it work for her. She would find peace and happiness and serenity within, if it was the last damn thing she did! And then, she would somehow figure out how she could make a difference in, at least other women's lives. Sara was on a mission in her mind.

## CHAPTER TWENTY-FOUR

On a morning after Dan had gone off to his work and Jonas had split for places unknown to her, Carol took a tour of her lovely house. Walking from one beautifully decorated room to the next, she was struck by the fact that her men had a special place for themselves and she did not.

When they had first moved in, Dan had taken one of the upstairs bedrooms and made it into a home office where he occasionally worked out of. Jonas had his bedroom, plus a small adjoining room where he puttered in his art of cartooning. As Carol looked at her son's talent, hung all over the walls with scotch tape, a look of worry crossed her face. There was no question he had a flair for it, albeit a strange flair. Carol had to wonder what he would do with this talent. His bizarre little people and animals certainly did not fit into the mold of Disney or Hanna Barbera and even with his art degree, she was very concerned what her less than ambitious son was going to do for the rest of his life. Thus far, in his early twenties, he still showed no signs of either finding a job or wanting to move out on his own. He dreamed of his work and sardonically drawn wit gracing the pages of the New Yorker Magazine or the like and did not want to settle for less. Carol, even more than Dan, had always encouraged his creativity to the point of his never wanting to compromise himself in his art. The result was that now he couldn't even think of taking a job that did not fulfill himself and his talents, completely. This had been accepted and respected during his college years, when his parents saw his idealism as something to be proud of, but the truth was, there was no sense of reality to it, now. But Jonas was steadfast, holding on to his dream, a dream his parents helped to cultivate, while comfortably being solely supported by them.

Downstairs again, Carol found herself in what was the maid's room, although they had never used it as such. Since Carol held that title, along with that of mother and wife, the small room behind the kitchen and laundry room had always been used as a large closet, a place to dump everything that everyone didn't know where else to put.

"What'd you need it for?" asked Dan, when Carol broached the subject with him of making it her own. "You have the living room and the family room, the kitchen, all the rooms are yours, aren't they?"

"It's not the same, Dan," she said, somewhat irritated. "Both you and Jonas have your own private places in this house. I want one, too." Carol heard her voice sounding like a four year old, pleading for her own toy, not wanting to share it with anyone else.

"Fine," conceded Dan, as if doing her some big favor. "But what are you going to do in there, anyway?"

This, Carol hadn't figured out as of yet. "I don't quite know. But I want it."

And so for the next number of weeks, Carol worked on her new little project of carving out a special place for herself. Perhaps, she thought, if she accomplished this in the physical sense, the mental would follow.

It took her days just to go through the junk that had accumulated in the room. She threw out unwanted, unneeded things and moved rarely used things into the garage.

When the room was finally empty, she painted her new private place, herself, and was proud of her accomplishment. She had not physically worked so hard in years and was sore from head to toe. But the result was well worth it. Although her men never offered their help, she would have turned them down, anyway. This was something she was creating for herself and it was so important that she did it alone. She believed that as she created the outside that would surround her, perhaps she could then recreate the inside of herself.

Carol then bought a large Indian throw-rug to cover the stained carpet. She found a desk, some bookcases and a low table that would ultimately become her Goddess altar. She also added to the room a comfortable reading chair and end table. She loved the process, as the room, her new sanctuary began to take shape.

Then the real fun began. She went around her house taking down a few special mementos and photos, to be the first items to grace her new room. All this excited Carol no end, as she continued to create something out of nothing. Newly bought books on the Goddess were put on the shelves and long forgotten paintings she found in the garage, she loved, but ones Dan didn't think fit his house, were hung on the new white walls. In the back of one of her closets she found a box filled with stones and shells she had collected from long-ago seaside vacations and these too were put around the room in small baskets. And she was reminded of old Jane's cabin deep in the woods of the island.

On a day's outing with Sara, Carol found candles and incense and crystals and, of course more books to add to her growing collection. She couldn't wait to finish her room and then to sit, curled up in her new chair and read all of them. At that time,

Sara was still waiting for her shipments of Goddess books to arrive at her shop, but even still, Carol felt bad about buying them elsewhere.

Carol filled her desk with pens and clips and rubber bands. She had an extension phone installed, despite her husband balking at the expense and need for all these things.

And finally she was done. She sat in her new room and looked around for the longest time. Outside the window she could see her flower-filled backyard garden, as Renaissance music played on her new CD player. As she sat, she felt warm and content and fulfilled, although still not quite sure herself what exactly she was going to do in this newly created magical space she had made for herself, knowing only it was something she had had to do and have.

Dan and Jonas didn't take much interest in Carol's indulgence and were only vaguely aware of the fact that she seemed happier than she had. During the room's remake they had hardly stopped by and then only to ask of her something concerning their own needs, truthfully glad she hadn't wanted their help with the renovation. Most importantly to them was that whatever she was doing for herself didn't adversely affect their lives and their needs. And so they continued to indulge her in her new fancy.

Carol made very sure that on the outside of that room everything seemed the same. She did for her husband and son as she always had. Yet, when she heard the front door close, when she was sure she was alone in the house, she hurried to her now special place of quiet and new discoveries.

And it was there, as she held in her hand a newly bought clay figure of what was a primitive Goddess she had found in a new age store, she tinkered with the idea of going back to nursing, or of doing something in her life that would make a difference, that would fulfill her need to nurture, to help people with their own pain. No, she thought, not any people, but women.

Carol continued to sit in front of her newly built shrine, daily, breathing in the fragrance of the sandalwood incense and candles, meditating, lost in thoughts of herself, her life and her Goddess and then one morning a male voice disrupted her quiet.

"Mom?"

Pulled back into reality so abruptly, her space now invaded, intruded upon, Carol turned quickly to see her son standing there in the once closed, now half-open doorway. The uninvited son took a step into the room to get a closer look at his mother and her altar. And he laughed.

"What's all this stuff, Mom?"

A now fully blushed Carol quickly got up, embarrassed, speechless and finally angry. Very, very angry.

"What're you doing back in the house? I thought you'd left," she said in an accusatory tone, really meaning, 'How dare you return to this house without a warning!'

"I did, but I forgot my wallet. I was calling for you all over the house to help me find it. So? What're you doing?"

"This is *my* room, Jonas! The door was closed and you didn't even knock! You just barged in, with no regard for me or my privacy!"

"Well, I didn't think…"

"No! That's the problem with you. You don't think! How would you like it if I came into your room day or night, unannounced?"

Carol was near tears as she quickly blew out the candles, trying to now hide what her son at already seen.

"I'm a human being, too, Jonas and I'd like a little respect around here!"

"I respect you, Mom."

"No, you obviously don't even know what that word means."

The grown boy was confused and at a complete loss at his once stable mother's reaction, or over-reaction. Although really, how stable had she been acting, recently? The truth was, Jonas hadn't a clue what it meant that his mother was in the throes of menopause, only that she had been prone to yell at him a lot more, in the recent past, for what he considered no good reason.

And so, oblivious to any needs other than his own, he continued to question her. "So… what is all this?" he pressed, as he pointed to the altar.

Carol was so upset, her sacred space now somehow soiled. She would explain nothing to him. What could she say, anyway? That she had taken to praying to a female deity? How foolish would that sound, especially since when she had come back from the retreat, she hadn't discussed her week with him at any great length and he hadn't inquired, other than to ask if she'd had fun. The little she had told both him and his father had been met with skepticism, so why try, she decided. If anything, both men had decided to simply ignore what they considered to be some harmless phase she was going through, finding it rather humorous and having nothing to do with reality, at least theirs.

Carol was trying hard to regain her composure. "Now, if you don't mind, please get out of my room."

Carol, the oh-so-good mother could hardly believe her own words, casting her son out with nary a word of a real explanation. Jonas now looked like a little boy, again, hurt and not understanding.

"Okay... fine."

"And close the door behind you... please."

After Jonas left, Carol crumbled in front of her Goddess statue and started to cry. Feeling alone and mean and stupid and most of all guilty for treating her own flesh and blood with such harshness, she again lit her candles and continued to cry.

# CHAPTER TWENTY-FIVE

It was closing time in the Malibu plaza. Shop owners locked their doors as they waved good-bye to each other and headed for their cars and home after the long work day. Within minutes the plaza was deserted and quiet.

Sara, after straightening up the last of the out of place books, looked over her once again neat and tidy shop. How she loved this place she had created over fifteen years before. She prided herself on being one of the very few independent booksellers in the city that still survived.

Since her new found interest in all things feminine, she had also found a renewed energy for her work. Her women's section was by now filling up with collection after collection of books on women's studies, both the psychological and the mythical. And they were selling. Whenever she had the chance, she discussed these books with customers who showed even the slightest interest. Some were skeptical of the theory of the Goddess, while others embraced the ideas and the books.

Within the perimeters of her little shop, she began to see an awaking to the possibilities, an opening up to the ancient, but newly emerging ideology in some circles of that long forgotten matriarchal society that had once existed. Word of mouth was slowly spreading that Book, Nook and Crannies was the place to come for female spiritual enlightenment.

Sara was encouraged that perhaps a new wave of thinking might be coming, that the future of women might well lie in their past. Most of all, she was excited that she was a part of it, however small.

Looking around one last time, she finally turned off the inside shop lights, leaving on the ones that lit up her window displays, walked outside and double-locked her doors.

"Hello, Sara," came a familiar voice from behind her.

Sara whipped around to face Peter.

She was visibly shaken by the sight of him, speechless for more than a long moment. And in that short space of time she was instantly filled with remembrances and love and hate and anger.

"What are you doing here, Peter?" she heard come out of her mouth.

"Can I talk to you, Sara? I really need to talk to you."

She tried to compose herself, to quiet her heart that now beat so hard and fast and loud inside of her. You need, she thought? When I needed to talk to you, you hung up on me.

He stood before her, this man whom she had loved so much, this man who had done irrevocable damage to her heart. This man who now stood before her looking like a sad and lost puppy.

She had seen that look on his face, before, most often when he had been incapable of making the final decision to leave his wife, as he had promised he would, over and over again, when they had lain next to each other after making love. He only wanted to be with her, he told her, then, but was so concerned over hurting his wife in the process. And Sara remembered how she had tried to soothe away his fear with her always wise words, telling him how this lie he was living would ultimately hurt his wife even more in the long run.

"I've left her," Peter then said.

Sara heard the words, but said nothing. Was she now supposed to run into his arms? Was she to forget all the pain he had caused her close to two years before?

He looked at her pleadingly.

"Please, Sara... let me explain everything to you. Please..."

Why she followed his car in her own, why she allowed him even this small opening back into her life, she had no idea, as they drove to their favorite place, a private cove by the ocean's edge.

As she parked her car next to his, the coastal sky was turning vibrant shades of pink and orange, as the sun readied to make its decent behind the mountains. Seagulls flew across the water, then landed on the beach in search of scraps of left-over food by the day's beach dwellers. They were all unaware that in Sara's life had come this sudden upheaval.

She stood a few feet from Peter, her eyes focused on the waves as they crashed onto the shore, again and again. But at this moment, the beauty and infinity of it passed her by, as she listened to his voice, now so close to her. How long had she waited to be with him, again? How long had she dreamed of a moment like this? How long had it taken her to forget and to begin to finally heal all the wounds he had inflicted on her?

"I couldn't leave her, then, Sara. I just couldn't. Everything was so screwed up, you know? She found your phone number, hidden in my wallet. She accused me of having an affair with you. I guess I had once told her about us, when we were talking about old girl and boyfriends and she must have remembered your name, or something."

Sara listened, but still said nothing.

"I know you have every right to hate me... Do you still hate me?"

His voice begged for a response from her, but she gave him none. Sara wanted to scream out, 'Hate you? Hate you? That hardly begins to express what I feel for you.' But she continued to remain quiet, surprising even herself.

"Please talk to me, Sara. I know what I did seemed awful, but I didn't know what else to do. She never gave me a chance to even talk to you, again."

Sara's mind raced, the way it had that rainy morning when she had received his fateful last call. Had his wife actually kept him locked away all this time? Had in all these months that had turned into years, his wife never let him out of her sight? And what of him? Had his wife really such control over him? Was he such a pune, such a wretch of a man that he went along with his wife's demands?

Sara's heart and mind had swelled to capacity with a sadness and an anger she had not felt in so long a time. She did not like this feeling of remembering that period in her life of such incredible misery and pain.

"You son of a bitch!" she finally heard herself spew out to him. "You don't get it, do you? You decided to stay with her, well fine. Somehow I could have dealt with that. It would have hurt, but if that's what you wanted, then what could I do? But how could you have ended it with me the way you did? A god-damn five minute phone call? After a year of supposedly loving me... of all the promises you made to me? You're a coward, Peter!"

And the flood gates opened up inside of her, of everything she had had to keep inside of her for all that time, all those many months of bleakness and pain. Not able to even look at him as she spoke, she did not notice his head bent down, his staring blankly at the ground in front of his feet.

"Is that all I was to you after a year? Coming over to my house at six in the morning before work, then all those long lunches and again for hours in the evening, day after day after day, for a year!? How dare you treat me worse than some... cheap one night stand, you bastard!"

Tears were so close to emerging from her eyes, but she was not half done.

"What about all the plans we made? Our marriage? You had the gall to get down on one knee and ask me. And our honeymoon, driving up the eastern seaboard, staying at bed and breakfasts? We planned the whole thing! Remember? And what about the house we were going to build up the coast? We planned a life together, Peter! Did you just forget all that? Or was our whole relationship just a fucking lie, like your marriage was? Was I so damned blind, so in love with you that I truly believed everything you told me?"

Everything, every word she screamed at him had festered inside of her, until now, unable to ever let him know the depth of her anger and her pain. As she yelled and yelled at him, it all came back to her, every moment they had spent together that year. All the love and the tenderness, all the hours of intimacy they had shared, all the dreams and laughter. And as all these memories washed over her, as her tears now could not help but spill out, as she seemed once again swallowed up by the enormity of her now raw again despair, she cried out to him.

"We were going to grow old together! And you took that away, Peter. You were my future, my life. And you took that away from me in one five minute phone call."

Her mind continued to tumble back and forth between sadness and outrage. She wanted to say every damn word to him she had never been given the opportunity to say. She would not be so cheated again.

"What the hell were you doing with me, anyway? Were you telling me all those lies just so I would sleep with you, because your wife wouldn't? Because I would gladly do all those things you loved, that your wife couldn't stand to do?"

And Sara remembered their love-making, their exhausted, enchanted love-making. So long before, he had been her first and he had taught her well. And a lifetime later, they were still so beautifully, impeccably divine for each other, with the merging of their flesh and their minds and their souls.

So when it was over, finished without a real ending, for her, at least, Sara had to wonder if he had simply used her as his whore. But that had been too terribly painful for her to even conceive of. It was too excruciating an idea to even begin to bear the thought of. No. It was clearly better to believe anything but that, that instead, she had evidently misjudged him. That, in fact, he was a spineless, coward of a man, who would rather give up this great love, than admit to his wife he no longer loved her, as he had finally admitted to Sara about his marriage. And that was his great sorrow... that he had married for a second time for the wrong reasons and hating divorce, failure, he knew not how to end this, his greatest lie.

When they had started their illicit affair, Sara had her own theories of his marriage. Hadn't she told him she believed that deep down she felt, if given the choice, he would rather have this wondrous relationship with wife, instead of her, considering all the years invested in that marriage? But he denied it. It was she he loved, he told her again and again. It was she he had always loved, since they were barely out of high school.

But Sara was not that stupid in the ways of love. She knew for him and his wife to have lasted all those many years, both must be getting something from the union. So eventually Sara bought into the fact that one reason Peter stayed was because of his wife's supposed helplessness. He often mentioned that if he left, what would the poor woman do without him? As time went by, though, Sara had to wonder what Peter would do with an independent woman like herself, one who did not so obviously need him. And she knew she had hit upon something. He did, after all, have this desperate need to be needed. Was that the real reason he decided to stay with his wife?

For months after his last phone call, Sara thought and thought about all of this. She remembered word for word things he had said, things she had said. She had tried so hard to figure out what had actually happened and how he could have done to her what he did. She would not let it go in her mind, a mind at times she was fearful she was on the verge of losing. But eventually, what did it matter? He was gone from her life. What was the point of any longer wasting time trying to analyze the bastard?

Somehow she knew her only salvation would be to simply close that chapter of her life as a tragedy she had no control over. So that is what she had tried so damn hard to do. She never called his house. She never drove by it, hoping for one more glance at him, like heartbroken teenagers do. She never contacted his office, where she knew his secretary and partner were well aware of his involvement with her.

She could only live with her pain until it lessened, which eventually, after too long a time, if finally did. It was never completely gone, though. The dull ache reappeared, usually late at night when she felt alone and desolate, wondering how she would get through the rest of her life without anyone to share it with. Without him.

There was something Peter had once told her she never forgot, when he was wrestling over the thought of ending his marriage. "You know, I sometimes wish I could just disappear... from everything. Not die. Just maybe walk into the ocean and disappear from my life as it is now."

"And then lead another life?" she had asked him.

"Yes. With you," he had sadly said.

And Sara remembered telling him how that was impossible, that he must take responsibility for his actions, no matter how painful. Considering his actions with her, he obviously had not heard her words, or simply chose to ignore them.

Now Sara turned her teary eyes away from the wave's constant ebbing and flowing and looked at him for a long time.

"You loved me, Peter. How could you have treated me this way? Was I wrong? I really thought you loved me." But she couldn't keep her gaze on him and sobbing, ran from him, down the little path that led to the sand and the ocean's edge.

He ran after her, calling her name, finally catching up with her as she neared the water. The beach was empty now, as the sky darkened, ushering in the night.

"I did love you, Sara. I do love you. You've got to believe me. I'm so sorry, Sara. I'm so very sorry."

She turned to him quickly, her anger rising up again. "You're sorry? You're a lying ass-hole!

That's what you are. You have no moral feelings for anyone or anything! You lied to me and to your wife and to everyone!"

She again turned from him and started running down the beach.

Following her, again, now beyond desperation to be understood, he grabbed her, trying to stop her movement. But she would have none of it.

"Oh, God, Sara. I never lied to you. I didn't. You've got to believe me. All I ever wanted my whole damn life, all I've ever dreamed about, starting back when we were still kids, when we first went together, was to be with you. I never wanted it to end in the first place. You were the one who first broke up with me. Remember?"

"Oh, so now you're going to blame me for this? What, were you getting back at me for something that happened thirty years ago? I went off to college. We were too young. It was you who couldn't be alone and ended up marrying someone you admitted to me later you didn't really love. It's obvious what you do, again and again."

"Okay, okay, you're right. But I never stopped loving you. Not for all these years. Never."

"Then why did you cut me out of your life as if I never existed? We had a chance this time. Did you even give me another thought? What the hell was going on in your brain, anyway?"

Peter was sobbing now. "Please, Sara. Please. I know. I was crazy. She kept threatening me. She said if I didn't stop seeing you she'd do something terrible, something we'd both regret. I didn't know what to do... what she was capable of. I was scared. I thought maybe she'd do harm to herself. I know I made a horrible mistake. This, especially the last 2 years without you, has been such a terrible time in my life. I don't know what else to say, except I love you. I have always loved you."

And he continued on and on, telling her how, yes, it was he who kept calling her and hanging up, just to hear her voice. How he couldn't work, couldn't do anything except think of her and what he'd lost. And how finally it had all become too much for him and no longer caring about the consequences, no matter what his wife might threaten to do, he had finally left her. And she did nothing. Surprise.

"Please let me make it up to you, Sara," he cried as he tried again and again to take her in his arms. "Please, please just say you'll forgive me."

"You brought me too much pain," she sobbed to him. "Too much pain. I don't think I'll ever be able to forgive you. I don't know if I could ever believe anything you say to me, again."

But this time when he tried to draw her near to him, suddenly feeling his never forgotten strength around her body, again, holding her so close... when she felt him, his same touch, his same smell, all so familiar, so long missed, she gave in to him.

"I love you so much, Darling," he said to her as he tried to kiss away her tears. Please don't make me live without you. I don't want to live my life without you, anymore"

Now so emotionally wrought, so close to total collapse, so very much confused, she allowed him to continue to hold her. And while she found herself kissing him once again, as if magically in her mind, all the time and pain hadn't passed since last she'd kissed him, part of her wondered if this was really happening, or if it was yet another one of her dreams. And then for one split second, she let slip through her mind if this really was the way she wanted her dream to end.

# CHAPTER TWENTY-SIX

"I can't believe you, Mom! How could you even talk to him, again? Tell me you haven't slept with him! You haven't, have you?" Rebecca was angrily pacing around the small living room of her still newlywed apartment.

Sitting on the overly-stuffed couch, Sara matched her daughter in wrath. "I'm sorry I even told you, Becca. And it's none of your business if I slept with him or not! Stop treating me as if I were a child!"

The first fact was that, no, Sara had not slept with Peter. The second was, yes, she felt like a child right then. She had visited her daughter for some kind of guidance, guidance she knew she really didn't want to hear, knowing exactly what her daughter would say and how violently she would react. But perhaps that's exactly what Sara needed to hear… even if she didn't really want to hear it.

Rebecca hated Peter for the way he had treated her mother and she would never forgive him, the way her mother obviously had.

Sara hated how their roles continued to get reversed, blurred on occasion, how righteous Rebecca had become in her growing opinions on life and how it should be lived. And most of all how some of the time her child was right. Boy, that was the kicker.

After that fateful encounter of the evening before, Sara had torn herself free from Peter, running, driving as far away from him as she could possibly get. How tortured she had been that night, alone in her bedroom, as she sat in the dark, tears streaming down her face. Why had he reappeared in her life? Why now, when she was beginning to feel so good, so focused on her own life, again? Why now, when she hardly ever dreamed of him, anymore, when his image had become so much dimmer, almost non-existent? Was this is test, she wondered? Was this is cruel joke, his walking back into her life, if she dared let him? And was it too late?

Her phone rang incessantly that night, but she had the courage to let it ring and ring, no machine turned on to take a message. She knew it was him and she knew she wasn't strong enough to hear his voice, his words, his pleas.

"He's going to hurt you again, Mother."

God... dess, how Sara hated when Rebecca called her "Mother."

"You know he will. How can you just forget what he put you through?"

Why did Sara's daughter sound exactly like she had years earlier, when Rebecca had been dating that asshole kid in high school who had so abused her? Sara had been right about that boy, but that hadn't stopped her daughter from loving him, going back to him time and time again, getting so hurt from all the grief he gave her.

"Believe me, Becca, I haven't forgotten anything. And nobody said I'm seeing him again. I saw him once and not by my doing, believe me."

Oh, how Sara hoped this child of hers would not ask if she would see him again, because she not yet knew the answer to that yet, unasked question.

"C'mon, Mom. I'm not stupid. And I know you. Even with all he did to you, you always hoped he'd leave his wife and come back. You can't deny it."

"So what?" Her voice was now raised. "Why shouldn't I have? I loved him. I loved him with all my heart. I know you hated me for seeing him, Rebecca, how wrong you thought it was because he was married, and it was wrong, but that's what happened. There are sometimes circumstances...

and it happened." Tears were so close to coming for Sara.

Rebecca saw this and drew back a little.

"Oh, Mom, so fine, you did it. Even I thought he'd leave her at one point. He conned me, too, back then. I remember when he came to me and swore he'd leave her and told me how much he loved you. And even I believed him. But now you know what kind of person he is. We both do. He's a creep, Mom. You've got to know you're better off alone than with him."

Sara's mind flashed back to all the holidays and birthdays and New Year's Eve's she'd spent alone. All the times of joy she'd shared with no one, even at Rebecca's wedding. No, her daughter had no idea what loneliness was really like. It wasn't like a rare Saturday night when a kid finds themselves with nothing to do. It was night after night and day after day alone, by oneself, on one's own. It was an emptiness and a desolation that envelopes one's whole being until sometimes you think, one more minute and I will go crazy. Completely mad.

And it was fear.

Sara put her head down, now wanting to hide from the person closet in the world to her, as her tears began to fall in earnest.

"I don't want to grow old all alone, Becca. I don't want to do that."

Rebecca hated this. She could not bear to see her mother, her strong mother, acting like this. Who was she to now be in the position to have to comfort the great comforter of them all? No, it was way too painful to see her own mother so vulnerable. She had seen Sara angry, but close as they were, it was so rare to see her like this, so much more than sad. So heavy of heart. So filled with sorrow.

The child knelt at her mother's feet, not knowing how to console her elder.

"Oh, Mama, you're not alone. You have me. And Thomas. And all your friends and your shop. And you'll find love again. I know you will. You're so terrific. You'll meet another man, a good man, I know you will. You just have to go out and..."

Sara cut her off. "... Don't, Becca. Maybe I don't want another man. Don't you see? He was my future. My everything. It was supposed to be for the rest of my life."

Sara continued to be so lost in her own misery. Seeing this, Rebecca felt so helpless. She kept thinking that this wasn't the way it was supposed to be. She didn't know how to do this, to console her inconsolable parent.

Even in her pain, Sara was still aware of the position her daughter was being put in. She was still the mother, ever explaining, ever trying to take the rough edges off of life's sufferings.

"I'm not some rock, Honey," Sara managed, "even though you'd like to believe I am. Even I feel hurt. Even I get tired of always doing everything myself. Even I get lonely. I know you don't want to hear this, but it's true."

"I know you do, Mom. But please, please don't be with Peter. He doesn't deserve you. He doesn't deserve your forgiveness. And how could you even trust him again? Maybe he's just lying about having left his wife, just to be with you, again."

Anger once again surfaced in Sara, for a moment quelling her sadness. Sadness. Anger. Anger. Sadness.

"Alright! Enough! I didn't say I forgave him. I didn't say I was even going to see him, again. I just said I saw him. I listened to him, that's all. And if it will make you happier, I screamed and yelled at him and told him everything I never got a chance to tell him, before! Everything!" Then Sara actually smiled. "The truth is, you'd have been very proud of me."

"Well, good," laughed Rebecca, the tension between them now somewhat broken. "'Cause he deserved it. I'd like to tell him a thing or two, myself!"

Soon after that, Sara fled from her daughter, too. She drove around for hours, aimlessly, in the hills above the city, just like she used to in her '57 Chevy convertible, when she was a teenager. Up and down the winding roads of Mulhouland drive, she drove, thinking of Peter and David and Sean and all the relationships she'd had in her life. And she wondered why none of them had worked out. Was there something wrong with her? Did she have such high expectations for happiness? Until this, until

210

this last time with Peter, it had always been she who had called it quits, ending the marriage or the affairs. Was she never to find lasting love in her life? Was it really because she would never settle for less? And what was more? Who would or could fill her expectations of love? And were those expectations much to high for any man to fulfill to begin with?

As she stood near her parked car on the top of the world, in Hollywood standards, looking out over the city's vastness, she wondered if somewhere down there was someone for her, someone to ride off together with into the sunset of their years. And couldn't she still be a feminist, a fighter for rights due her, a hater of all injustices of life, a new lover of the Goddess and still be with a man, find happiness with a man?

That night when Sara opened her door and allowed Peter in, she wasn't thinking of anything. She wasn't thinking of her womanhood. She wasn't thinking of what he had done to her, not of her pain, not of her past, not of her future. But even in the haze she found herself in, Sara, for a short moment wondered how that could be so. It was so unlike her. But it was.

And later, when they lay together, her haze continued. In those minutes that turned to hours, she again opened to him the door of her heart. And he gladly entered.

It was fragile making of love, tender and gentle. And through it all, Sara found she was outside of herself, inside of herself, treading somewhere in the past. Transported back to another time, she was eighteen again, in Peter's old room in his parents house. Inside of her, he was once again the dark-haired, muscled young man he once had been, the boy who had loved her so deeply, so innocently, who lived to please her.

She was encircled by him and by her memories, wrapped in the warmth of that long ago and far away past of all her hopes and dreams. And later, when they were so spent, in such sweet exhaustion, he silently stroked the strands of damp hair off her forehead. And then they slept. And then they slept, never uttering so much as a word to each other, because that was the way she wanted it to be.

## CHAPTER TWENTY-SEVEN

"You have learned to dance and to sing this week. And so as you go back to the lives you left seven days ago, remember to do just that. Please, please remember to sing and dance. Remember to look up at the moon. Remember to honor the sun. Remember your ancestors. And most importantly, remember to touch the earth every chance you can."

These were Christina's words that Carol now remembered, as she sat on a bluff, over-looking the long, winding coastline from past Venice Beach to the south, all the way to Malibu up to the north.

And she thought about her life, something she seemed to be doing so much of late. The problem was, though, she was thinking about it more than she seemed to be living it. Was she to spend all her days just reading about women and studying the history of the Goddess? How could she explain how she felt... that she was constantly teetering on some cusp, a cusp she still didn't know how to describe? And the truth was, it was getting a little boring to her. She longed for less thought. She longed for some action in her life. She longed to dance and sing.

Carol knew what was lacking in her life. A concrete dream for herself. Something for her, alone, to conquer. A hill to be charged, a mountain to be climbed. A battle to be won.

When she had been a little girl, she, like her frilly Southern peers had dreamed of being a wife, fantasizing of the day they would receive their *MRS.* degrees. Then, as she grew older and worshipping her doctor father, she dreamed of following in his footsteps. But they were too large and too deep, at least that was what she had been told. And so she became, instead, a nurse.

And when she married Dan, even those dreams were eventually left behind, because her husband didn't want a wife of his working. The very thought had been an assault to his manhood.

So she lived her life without dreams, instead with milestones. Other's milestones. A husband's promotion, a son's birthday, a husband's new business, a son's graduation.

What, she wondered, would be written on her epithet? Good wife? Good mother. Good volunteer? Today that didn't seem half good enough for Carol. But what then? What was she going to do with her life, in her life?

She wanted to scream out in frustration. Instead, she finally turned away from her beloved ocean. Once in her car, she decided she had better stop at the market on her way home. She had to laugh, be it quietly, at the irony of her thoughts, for she knew, once there, she would be buying her men's favorite eats for their dinner that night.

Dan had come home early from work to find his house empty. In the kitchen he found a plate of newly baked brownies and helped himself to one. Then he looked around the room for the usual note from his wife, telling him of her where-a-bouts. Yet again, there was none.

He realized she was doing that more and more of late, leaving the house without a word. It made him uncomfortable. Not that he really thought there was anything to worry about, that she was doing something she shouldn't be doing, only that he liked to know where she was during the day, who she saw and what she did.

It wasn't that Carol was secretive about her activities, just more quiet about them these days. Things had changed since she had gone on the retreat. She wasn't her old self, he thought. It was true she seemed in a little better mood these days, but he attributed that to the easing up of her hot flashes and other symptoms of her change. And she had finally gotten some kind of lubricant from her doctor, making intercourse less painful for her and more enjoyable for him, again.

A moment later he found himself wandering through the always closed door and into Carol's special room. He paused and looked back into the kitchen. The house was still. As he looked around the room, he wondered why he felt like he was doing something wrong. How silly, since after all, it was his house and this room was part of it.

And so he stepped further into Carol's private place. It wasn't as if he had never set foot inside, but always only when she had been in attendance, either at her desk or sitting in her chair, reading. Then, he had asked his question of her and quickly left, always feeling like an intruder, a strange feeling for him, especially in his own domain.

It had never crossed his mind to really inspect the place, to question his wife about the contents the room held, that in all honesty he had hardly noticed. Then Jonas told him about finding his wife in front of this candle-lit altar thing and it was true, he had become curious. Of course, he had seen it, but thought it only to be a little table filled with odds and ends he certainly wouldn't have wanted sitting in any other part of his house. That Dream Catcher thing hanging on his bedpost was enough for him.

So what the hell was his wife getting herself into? But as curious as he was, he never wanted her to know he was.

Dan picked up off the floor near the altar, a gourd rattle. He shook it, smiled and shrugged. As he looked around he had to wonder what all this stuff was for, the stones, the clay figure that looked somewhat like a fat woman's form, the awful smelling incense whose musty fragrance still lingered in the room.

He knew all this had something to do with that retreat and that damn Goddess Carol had so lovingly spoken of. After she came home he had decided to indulge his wife in this new interest of hers. Fine, he thought, if some women wanted to pray to a thousands of years old woman, good for them. Carol had never been the outwardly praying kind, but if all this stuff made her feel better, be in a better mood, then who was he to complain? What harm could it do since, as usual, he didn't see it having anything to do with his life.

His eyes wandered over to the bookcase and he started to scan the titles. Wow, he thought, there were certainly a lot of books written on the topic and he was surprised by this. One title caught his eye, 'When God Was A Woman,' Dan laughed out loud. He had never been very religious, but even the mere thought of God being anything but a man was preposterous. It was an undisputed fact, God was a man. The Bible said so. Hadn't Christ died for our sins? Hadn't he been created in His image? It was right there in black and white for all to see.

Dan opened the book and read the first few sentences of the preface. It didn't take him long to figure out what he had already supposed was true. This was a man-bashing book. Why couldn't women be happy without blaming men for everything, he thought? It wasn't fair.

He replaced the book carefully and looked at some other titles. Crone, The Great Cosmic Mother, The Myth Of The Goddess. That was what all this was, nothing but myths. Stories women thought up to get ammunition against men so that they could get further in the world. Why couldn't women be happy with all they had, all that had been given to them? They had it easy, thought Dan, never having the stress and strife men had to go through to get ahead in this world. And what did women really have to complain about, especially Carol? Hadn't he made a good life for her? Hadn't he given her anything she wanted? For crying out loud, hadn't he paid for all the stuff she had bought to fill this room?

"Dan? What're you doing in here?"

He was caught. How long had she been standing there, watching him? Why did he suddenly feel so guilty, there in his own house?

"Oh, hi. I was... looking for that Stephen King book I was reading last night. Have you seen it?"

"It's on your bed stand, where you left it." Her space had again been violated and she was not amused. "So, what're you doing?"

"Aren't I allowed in here?" Dan took a breath and puffed out his chest, showing his manliness, claiming his territory, not unlike that of the male ape.

"I didn't say that," said Carol. "You've just never really bothered before, at least not when I was in here."

Dan changed the subject. "So… these are your things, huh?"

"Yes," she answered, not unaware of what strangers they seemed to be at that moment.

"So, whatta you do with all this stuff, anyway?" he said as he again picked up the gourd rattle and shook it. "Ward off evil spirits?" he laughed.

She ignored his comment, not wanting to admit he was close to the truth. She wasn't about to tell him that she shook it over her head from time to time to cleanse the air above her, so her visions, her thoughts would be clearer.

"I think in here, Dan   I sort of meditate. It makes me feel good. I read."

"Yeah?   Well, I was looking over some of your books and did you know they're full of man-hating crap?"

Carol shook her head, not wanting to get into this discussion right then, but entering into it anyway. "Well, Dan, if you had been subjected to what women have for thousands of years, you might be hostile, too. But it goes much deeper than that, if you're interested…"

"Please, Carol. I'm not in the mood for a sermon. So, is that what you're going to do the rest of your life? Blame us for everything that's wrong in the world?"

"If the shoe fits..." her voice dropped off after that, leaving a silence between them that had become so much a part of their existence together.

Then Dan said something Carol found interesting.

"You know, you can't always blame someone else. Instead of always whining, why don't women take responsibility for their own lives and their own problems?"

Carol looked at him and genuinely smiled. "Well, Dear, that's exactly what I'm learning to do."

Why did his wife's words suddenly sound so ominous, so threatening to him? He put the gourd back down in its place, careful to position it the way he's found it. He felt awkward now, like he really didn't belong in this room.

"Well, I'm going to look for my book, now. Will dinner be ready, soon?"

"Sure, in a little while." She answered.

They locked eyes for a moment, then he gave her a quick kiss on the cheek before leaving.

Staring after him, Carol felt rather empowered, although she wasn't quite sure why. But she liked the feeling.

# CHAPTER TWENTY-EIGHT

Sara's life had become a blur. It had been less than a week since she had started seeing Peter again and so quickly her once orderly, if not lonely life had become a dizzying joy ride, fun while you were on, but once off a feeling of not quite knowing where your center was. Wanting to go again, yet having that feeling of being slightly nauseous.

She craved him much like an addict craves their drug of choice, knowing it was bad for their health, yet still wanting more and ashamed of their desire. And so, not unlike the alcoholic, she kept it hidden.

Overnight, her life had become one of yearning, then emptiness, then desperation for another drop of that sweet, quite possibly poisoness nectar that was Peter. The roller-coaster of highs and lows, of lies, deceit and addiction.

And so she did what anyone in her position would do. She rationalized. Didn't she deserve some happiness, some relief from her pain? After all, she wasn't really doing anything wrong, this time, she told herself. He was free now, almost free, a soon-to-be free man. And yet, now it was she who felt caged, closed in, confused and not at all as happy as she thought she would be by his unexpected reappearance into her life. Rebecca had been right. She had longed for this day, but now that it had come, she wasn't at all sure what her longings had been about.

What was wrong? Was it because she couldn't completely believe all his words? Was it because nothing could really be as perfect as it was in dreams? Was it because she was not sure what perfect was to begin with?

She could not yet bring herself to admit to her daughter she was once again involved with Peter. The simple answer was that she didn't want to hear Rebecca's scorn and anger and disappointment in her. But it was more than that. She was not yet ready to admit to herself that she was really involved with him, again.

It all seemed to be happening so fast, too fast, the words said, the flowers constantly bought, the plans he wanted made for them. Stop the world, she wanted to scream! Just stop for a moment and let me catch my breath!

Suddenly, where there had been nothing, there was now too much. And she was overwhelmed, blown along like tumbleweeds in the wind, out of control, unable to chart her own direction.

Peter wanted to pick up where they had left off almost two years before, as if not one painful moment had past since they had last been together. But how could she do that? He also wanted to forget the fourteen years he had spent with his wife, as if they had never existed, to simply delete them from his memory. But how could he do that? Where then would be the closure, the grieving, the adjustment? And all this troubled Sara, more than a little.

Staying temporarily with a friend, he walked out of his marriage with no physical baggage except his clothes. His wife could keep everything, he told Sara, expecting a positive reaction from her. Nice guy he was. But again, Sara had to question this. Why did he have such a great need for others to think good of him?

Sara remembered during their year long affair how he had once told her that he thought he had been put on this earth to make others happy. But then he certainly had not done that in her case, had he?

She remembered telling him that it was an illusion, that one can't make another happy, especially if that one is not happy within themselves.

And he had kissed her and said, "I'm happy. Being with you makes me as happy as I ever want to be." But still, he had stayed with his wife, out of what, guilt, afraid of hurting her because she needed him? He used to tell Sara how strong she was, not like his wife, who acted like a veritable cripple, unable to function alone.

And now Sara thought about all that. She relived every conversation she'd ever had with Peter, trying to find the answer to this uneasy feeling she had. Something was not quite right and much as she wanted to put her finger on it, she also could not seem to help herself from putting her fingers all over him.

When they were in bed, she was swept away, drawn back to a place that time, past, present and future was irrelevant. And had she never had to get out from under her blankets with him... well, unfortunately, or fortunately, she did.

But while there, in the dark, her sexuality reemerged with a thunderous power she had quite forgotten she possessed. It did not matter to her, or to him, either, the extra inch or two on her body parts. She was the wild woman and the Goddess in one, as they did their dance of love in wild abandon. And her feminist thinking aside, her belief that she didn't need a man to be whole, oh my, it was good to be with one, again. To be loved again. Yes, it was oh so very good.

What thin line there was between need and want, Sara thought. It was hard for her to admit how nice it was to have someone do the driving, instead of her, to run out for milk, to fix the leaky shower head, to do a multitude of things, instead of having to always do them herself, something she, in fact, was quite capable of doing. But having a man, having Peter do these things, did that take away her strength as an independent woman? Was it enough for a woman to know she can, just not have to, always? But did it somehow shift the power from one gender to the other?

And Sara realized how quickly, how in just these few days her role, that much hated word, had changed. Was this what happened with only the mere appearance of a male in a female's life, as the two sexes did their lover's jig? And if there was fault to be laid for this, whose feet should it be laid at? Where was the line between what and whom women really were, to that of what and whom they were to and for men? Could a woman even be defined by themselves, alone, or had this patriarchal society even allowed women that possibility?

Even after the last hundred years of women's struggles for any kind of equality, their strengths and their weaknesses were still based on the bottom line of man's definition of what they were or were not. Even the word equality, itself, was defined by women trying to climb their way up to where men already were from the start. Everything was first seen through men's eyes, even the struggle, itself, always and still interpreted from a male perspective.

A few thousand years before it was not women who had decided to be good and pious. It was the men who decided for them. And if they did not comply it was the fiery stake for them. Women have dressed for men, done for men and worst of all, women have judged themselves by the standards set up by men. They have changed themselves and their bodies for men. They have had to sacrifice their dreams because of men. And Sara thought about all of this.

And then she thought about the almost indistinguishable line between how men wanted their women and how women really wanted to be. And she had to wonder if a woman could really be herself after so many centuries of this male domination, if they even knew what self was without man's definition of them. Was that even possible?

So few women in history had broken away. Free spirits they were called. But free from what? From the male mandate of what women should, must be like? How interesting to think that of these free spirits, the Amelia Earharts', the Georgia O'Keefes', the Eleanor Roosevelts', the Billie Jean Kings', the Hillary Clintons'... how they all had what male society considered to be masculine characteristics, from their looks to their actions.

And Sara knew the words to describe these women and others like them: strong, tough, aggressive, power-hungry, ambitious, assertive, persistent, headstrong. These were all positive words when used to describe men, but the inference of these words when used to describe women was notably negative. Why was it alright in the city Sara dwelled, for men to produce, direct, write and star in movies, but 'oy' if you did the same thing and your name happened to be Barbra Streisand...? Now, only years away from a new millennium women liked to think things had radically changed for their sex, but in truth, they really hadn't.

How had Sara gotten off on this tangent of thought? Perhaps it was all connected. And this brought her back to thoughts of Peter and her and their relationship. And she sat, as Carol did, in front of her altar, shaking her gourd rattle over her head, beating her drum, tightly holding onto her rose quartz crystal of healing. And she asked the Goddess for guidance. She knew the answer to her questions were somewhere within her, yet still just beyond her grasp.

# CHAPTER TWENTY-NINE

Carol wasn't having a much better time at figuring out her own life. She was so confused, especially about her marriage. When had it crossed that line from all right to tolerable to intolerable? When had qualities, habits of Dan's that used to be funny or cute become so stupid, obnoxious, even crude? Had he changed? Or had she?

Hadn't he used to be more sympathetic to her needs, or had her needs accelerated to such outrageous proportions it was now asking too much of him to treat them with understanding and tenderness?

She could remember a time when they would talk about everything. Now, in the last number of years, they seemed to disagree about everything. Had she become so cynical about life, or had he? What had really changed? Did it have something to do with knowing more and expecting more of this life? It was true that Carol had been happier in her marriage when she had simply accepted the status quo of what a wife should be. But then what status quo had she accepted to begin with? Her mother's, who so long ago had lectured her about marriage and what she must do to make her husband happy? Or was it from her husband, who let it be known from day one how their life should and would be? Or did it also come from all the articles in all the magazines like Good Housekeeping, that all the good little wives read as the Gospel? Good Housekeeping! She certainly did that with honors. A Stepford wife was she.

But Carol was also coming to the conclusion that life was not only tough for women, but for men, also. She believed that even her macho Dan, hidden somewhere deep inside, wanted to more often show a softer side, a side of him he was afraid to display to a world that was still wary, threatened by a tender man. And why not? If you were such a man who cared, then you were tagged a sensitive male, this another oxymoron, giving the impression that normal men could not be born that way, that it must be some kind of mysterious genetic defect that happened in their mother's womb.

And so most men spent their years proving their masculinity by making lewd remarks about women's tits, guzzling beer, then belching loudly, strutting the avenues with guts sucked in and chests puffed out and in the worst scenarios raping and battering, all to show, who indeed wore the pants in the family.

Carol felt badly for her husband, who so resisted even the thought that he might have that other side to him. And so she wavered between wanting to murder him and wanting to help him see the light.

Carol knew her existence on this earth was so short as she inched her way closer to the Crone. Should she spend these precious days trying to change the men in her life, or continue to focus on herself? And by doing so, this activity that went against every grain she had been taught, would she be able to bear the guilt?

She so wanted a loving relationship, one of deep communication, of sharing the beauty of a starlit night. Dan, unfortunately, seemed incapable of doing any of this. Had she never realized this lacking in her husband, or could she also be to blame at the place she now found herself and her marriage in?

The saddest part for Carol was knowing that Dan thought nothing was wrong with their union. And at the rare times she voiced her displeasure, he blamed it on her being too emotional, most probably due to her change of life. But life always changes.

"No," she had told him more than once. "It's not my menopause. It's just how I feel."

"You never felt this way before as far as I knew," he had said.

And in this he was right. She never had. She had gone along for years, excepting the life he had given her, the life they led on his terms.

But in his own way he tried to figure out what was wrong with her. What else could it be but depression about getting older... knowing she was not what she used to be?

"No!" she had said in anger. "I'm better now than ever!"

What then could he do but to blame her frustrations and unhappiness on that damn retreat she had gone on. It had given her all these crazy new ideas that had nothing to do with real life, that had nothing to do with their life.

"You've changed, Carol," he said. "I liked you better, before."

"I like me better, now," she had answered him back.

But if that were true, why didn't she feel better? Why wasn't her marriage better? She not only wanted to feel good when she was reading her new books, or spending time alone in her room, or doing things with Sara, she wanted to feel good with her husband and her son. But she didn't and hadn't in a long time. In fact, since the retreat, things had gone progressively down hill at an even faster pace. Maybe Dan had a point, after all.

Was new knowledge the culprit? Was ignorance really bliss? Sadly, maybe.

The dramatic thought of leaving Dan had crossed her mind. It was a drastic possibility, she knew, but how long could she remain in this house where she was so taken for granted, so misunderstood, when any semblance of passion had diminished to the low point of a fizzle? She wanted so much from her marriage and she was getting so little.

But had she tried hard enough to get through to him? So much of what she now thought had to do with women's worth in society and how they had been wronged for so many years. But to this kind of talk, Dan turned a deaf ear. He didn't want to hear about the Goddess or Mother Earth or a time when women were held sacred. And so she stopped talking about it, but had not stopped thinking about it. In fact, she obsessed about it.

She wanted to share her life with someone whose thoughts and desires and paths intertwined with her own. Instead, these days she and Dan were chugging along on parallel tracks, hardly ever meeting in word, notion or body.

Sometimes, late at night, as Dan's light snoring broke the night's silence, she fantasized about living on her own, in an apartment like Sara's, where all her own things could be spread about the house, where her music would blare out from the stereo, where the fridge held only the kinds of foods she liked. It would be a place that looked the same when she came home as when she left. There would be washing of only her clothes and picking up only of her things.

She dreamed of being surrounded by people who understood her, who did not want to change her, who did not chide her if she did not add up to their expectations. She wanted to be herself and to be loved for simply that.

Carol no longer wanted to have to leave notes of where she was and when she would be back, while also wanting someone to care enough about her, not always themselves and their needs, to really want to know... about her. She wished that person was Dan, because despite all that he was and was not, she did love him. He had been part of her life well over half her years on this earth. How does one give that up? But she was now suffocating from his neglect of seeing who she was, who she was becoming, suffocating in the empty expanse of her life in her beautiful home with him.

Then her dream, her fantasy turned quickly into a nightmare. Could she even survive on her own, for the first time in her life? And what could the future be for a nearing fifty year old woman who hadn't been out in the work force in close to twenty-five years?

And what would happen to Jonas if she left Dan? In the deepest recesses of her heart, she knew her son would side with his father. And she wasn't sure if she could handle that kind of pain of making him choose, of already knowing the outcome of that choice.

During his early years, Jonas had been her little darling, hanging onto only her for dear life, guzzling at the sustenance only a mother can provide. But as he grew, his influence shifted toward his father. 'My son,' Dan would always say, as he taught Jonas to be a man, not a cry baby, at the many innocent altercations that happened in the smaller than average young boy's life. 'Ya gotta fight like a man,' Dan taught him.

And when Jonas first became interested in art, Dan immediately took the boy outside to throw around a brand new football.

The stage was set, although Jonas rewrote one act, as art remained his one great love. Dan wasn't happy about this, although when fine art eventually evolved into cartooning, it didn't seem quite so sissy to the father. The weirder and more bizarre Jonas' art became, the better Dan like it.

Carol remembered Christina's words, "Men are taught to be men by men..."

So as the years passed, Carol had less and less influence over the boy. The truth was, she had not been all that aware of its consequences until recently, when her own awareness had been heightened.

Now it was lonely living in a household that belittled women's worth, bringing it down to the level of housekeeper at best, complainer at worst. She wanted to make it better and flee at the same time, not knowing how to do either.

Soaking in a hot bath, she took this long, hard look at her life. And it was there amidst the lemon scented bubbles, she made a decision. She would go back to school. She would take whatever courses necessary to get back into nursing. She knew it would be hard to become a student again, a mature woman walking the halls with pretty little girls who had energy she wasn't sure she still had, but she was determined to do something again in her life, worthwhile, something she could make a living at that would afford her a future, if one day she did decide to leave and go off on her own.

As her skin softened and wrinkled from her extended time in the water, she felt so very excited and so very scared.

# CHAPTER THIRTY

Although Sara had been hesitant to share her renewed affair with Peter, even with Carol, she finally did. Unlike her own daughter, Carol was nonjudgmental, although she too worried about this man's true intentions, considering all that Sara told her about his past behavior.

Sara was glad to be with Carol, out on one of their day-long excursions with this woman who had become her closest of friends. And Carol felt the same. New friends were much harder to come by this late in life. Old friends seemed harder to keep. But perhaps that was because as the years went by, at least for Sara, she felt more removed from most of them than ever, seemingly having less in common with them. And now that she was so entrenched in the Goddess and Her history, the chasm grew even wider.

And even though she had become more solitary as she aged, she savored her friendship with Carol, this woman who had explored what she had, whose eyes and ears and mind had run with those wolves, who had experienced that wild woman inside of themselves.

On this beautiful of days, they drove up the coast, past Ventura, then onto the winding two land highway that led to the little town of Ojai. They planned to lunch there, then would meander down the main street filled with little shops and art galleries.

They talked non-stop on their road trip. Somehow, no matter how many hours they spent together, they never ran out of things to talk about, things to share with each other. This day Sara wanted to talk about Peter. In verbalizing her feelings she seemed better able to sort things out in her own mind and Carol was the only one she felt she could do this with.

She had finally told Rebecca she was seeing him again, much to her daughter's dismay. Well, she was and Rebecca had better get used to it. Sara couldn't live her life the exact way her daughter wanted her to, anymore than the other way around.

"Fine! But just don't ask me to see him, Mom," her daughter had told her, "because I won't!

He's going to hurt you again and I don't want to be a part of it."

When Sara told Carol this, she sympathized with her friend, knowing how many times she had decided not to do something because of how she knew Jonas would feel about it.

"You have to do what you think is right for you," Carol now said.

"I know," said Sara, "only part of me knows that my kid is probably right."

Then Carol asked how the relationship was going, a tad jealous that her friend was in the throes of such passion with another.

"You think I know?  Sometimes I think I love him so much, then I wonder how I could, after everything that happened.  But then I look at him and, oh, I don't know.  He's been so sweet and attentive.  In fact, sometimes I actually feel smothered by all his attention."

Sara laughed, never thinking she would ever feel something like that, after having been so lonely so long a time.  But it was true.

"He calls me so many times a day.  He stops by the shop, then acts neglected if I'm busy and can't sit around and talk with him.  He even wanted to come with us today!  Can you believe that?"

She laughed again, but wondered if she could be with someone like that for the rest of her life, someone who seemed to be so insecure when, unbelievably, not invited in when she went to the bathroom.  This, she told Carol, had actually happened a few days before. Just saying all this out loud made Sara think even harder.

And Carol could only ponder on how wonderful it would be to get that kind of attentiveness from Dan.

"Maybe he's just trying to make up for the way he treated you, before. It seems obvious he loves you," Carol said.

Sara smiled, continuing to think about Peter. "Yeah, I think he really does. And I admit it is wonderful being with him, again. Only... I don't know. I'm scared. I don't trust it, you know?"

"Come on, Sara. You deserve it, for crying out loud. You do. Why don't you just take each day and see how it goes? And I really think after a while Rebecca will start to trust him again, too. She loves you too much not to."

"Thanks, Car, I hope so. But I have to tell you, it's hard to take each day for what it is when all he talks about is the future. When are we going to get married? When can he move in with me? He wants to travel. He really would like to move out of LA. Well, I can't just move. My business is here. And Becca. My whole life it here. I like it here! I don't want to move, anywhere."

Carol had stopped listening after the mention of travel. "Boy, I should have such problems. Dan hates to go anywhere. I'm this old and hardly been anywhere. Mexico and Canada, but that's about it. I'd give my eye-teeth to just take off for a few months and see the world."

And so they talked and commiserated with each other about their different lives, as it were, almost opposite lives. And as always, wherever they were together, the discussion went the way of the Goddess and Christina and the days they'd spent at the retreat. Although they had both struggled so hard against it, they had lost that feeling. That loving feeling. All their reading had given them some solace, but neither of them knew how to really adopt all they had learned into their daily lives. And they wondered if the others, Elaine and Annie, Beth, Penny and Victoria were having the same problems as they were. They had all exchanged brief notes of greetings and missing each other, but so far that was all.

"I feel lost, Sara. I sort of thought I'd been found, but now I'm lost, again," confided a sad looking Carol.

"I know what you mean," was all Sara could say.

"Yeah, but you have your work and now Peter. I feel like I have nothing. My son thinks I'm crazy and my husband has taken to spying on me. I caught him sneaking around my room one day when he thought I wasn't home."

"Maybe he just wanted to take a look at one of your books."

"Yeah, only to make fun of their titles. No, I think both he and Jonas think I'm into some kind of devil worship or something."

Sara laughed, while Carol did not.

Then Carol told Sara her idea of going back to school.

"That's a great idea, Carol. I think you should go for it."

What Carol didn't tell her friend was just how bad her marriage was, how she thought she wanted out of it. But she couldn't bring herself to actually mouth those words out loud.

"Actually, at first I thought of maybe going back to nursing, but I'm not sure I still have it in me, to see that kind of physical pain. Then I thought maybe I'd go for my masters in psychology."

"Yes, yes! Oh, Carol, I think you'd be a terrific therapist. You're so bright and such a good listener and you have such wonderful instincts."

"You think?"

"Yes, I absolutely think!"

"Know what I feel," admitted Carol. "I feel like my life is in this big transition. But then I always feel like it's on the verge of something and then that something never happens."

"Amen!" laughed Sara. "Or should I saw A-woman?"

"No, forget everything I just said," went on Carol. "I think what I really want is to just be alone. Just to sit in an old rocking chair, somewhere real pretty... and rock. And maybe take up knitting. And be a god damn Crone, already."

Now Sara had to disagree. "No! I'm certainly not wise enough, yet. Lately I feel more like a stupid old child than a wise old woman." And

241

then Sara thought a moment before going on. "It's so crazy. Do we have to wait 'til we're near dead to finally get the answer to life? Everything seemed so beautiful and so much simpler up on the island. How did it get so complicated, again?"

"Maybe we should just go and move in with old Jane," Carol said, remembering their brief time spent with that Crone of all Crones. "What a character she was."

Sara suddenly got very sad and wasn't quite sure why. "I love that old woman. She is who I want to be someday… now."

"I want to go back there, Sara. I want to feel that way, again. I can't stand feeling this way, any longer. Now I know it's possible. I had it and I lost it and I want it back. Only I don't think I can get it here." Carol was on the verge of crying.

"I know," agreed Sara. "I walk on the earth here and it isn't the same, you know? Everything was so relevant up there and nothing seems to be down here. And yet, I know it's all in my head."

On the way back home, the two women decided to stop at the beach, north of Zuma. They locked the car above a rocky cove and headed down a little switch-back trail to the sand. And they walked, knowing it was getting late, but not caring.

Suddenly Sara took off, running down the beach. And Carol followed her. They ran hard until their bodies gave out. Then bent out of breath, but exhilarated, they rested a moment.

"That felt so good." Sara was the first to catch her breath. "I feel better now," she said through huffs and puffs.

"You're nuts," laughed Carol, as she flopped down on the sand.

"Come on, don't you feel better, too?" said Sara, joining her friend.

Carol looked out at the water, out toward the horizon. "I do, now that you mention it."

Carol continued to gaze at the water, at a lone small boat sailing by, pulling a water-skier. He looked so free of any care in the world as he glided over the waves.

"Oh, Sara, what're we going do?"

"Damned if I know," was Sara's reply.

# CHAPTER THIRTY-ONE

Carol was very late coming home. She had had such a wonderful day with Sara, they both had lost track of time until they were well on their way back to Santa Monica. Now she worried that her family would think something terrible had happened to her. She worried about what she would make for dinner at this late hour. Dan hated coming home after a long day on the site of one of his new houses to find his sanctuary not in order, his food not on the table. Not that that was hardly ever the case, until this day.

Nervousness pulsed through Carol as she said good-bye to her friend and then timidly walked through her front door. She immediately smelled the aroma of food cooking, as she headed for the kitchen. Ready with a storehouse of apologies and excuses for her tardiness, she first saw the table set, lit with candles. Then she saw her husband, his back to her, hovering over the stove, stirring whatever it was that smelled so delicious.

"Dan?" she said, more than surprised at the sight in front of her. "I'm home."

He didn't turn around, engrossed in his cooking, but said, "Hi, I was getting worried about you. Dinner's almost ready."

Well, you could have pushed her over with a feather. Was she in the Twilight Zone? Was this her husband or had he mysteriously been replaced by a wonderful pod person?

"I'm so sorry I'm so late. I guess time got away from us and then there was all this traffic…"

"Yeah, I figured it was something like that, but I wish you'd remember to take your cell. That's why I bought it for you. Did you have a nice time with your friend?"

Carol was completely bewildered. "Yeah, yeah. We had a really nice time. And sorry about the phone."

She edged closer to see what was cooking, staring at her husband to again make sure it was really him.

"What're you doing, Dan?"

Dan turned off the stove, then looked over his culinary accomplishments before turning to his wife for the first time.

"Well, I got home early and since you weren't here, I decided to whip us up something to eat."

Whip us up something? thought Carol, as she half-smiled. She couldn't remember the last time he had used a kitchen utensil, barring his own knife and fork to dig into the elaborate dinners she made for him. That is not to say he couldn't cook. He just never did. When they were first married it had been a different story. He had done all the cooking. Unlike Carol, he had lived on his own for a while and it was either cook or starve. A great lover of food, he chose the former.

But something strange was going on here and she wanted an explanation. Cooking was one thing, but the table set with flowers and candles? The first thing that flew across her mind was that he was having an affair. Wasn't something like this an obvious sign of a husband straying? Things hadn't been very wonderful between them, but would Dan, so morally correct, do something like that... to her? In all their years together, it was one fear she had never had, for some reason. Should she have it now?

"It's really been fun cooking, again. I forgot how much I enjoy it," he said, cool as a cucumber.

No, she thought, he seemed too poised, too in control, too casual, like he really meant it. But, was that the first sign?

Dan went on, "Jonas went out with a friend. I think he was afraid my cooking would poison him, Dan laughed.

Who was this man, Carol had to wonder, as she eyed him closely?

They sat down and began dinner. At first Dan popped up and down to get the warmed bread, the wine, the grated cheese for the pasta. Carol was amazed, but it was only the beginning.

"We really have to do something about Jonas," Dan said, surprising his wife for the umpteenth time in a few minutes. "He has no direction, whatsoever. When I was his age, I had already fought in a war, was home, going to school and was working, part-time. Remember?"

"I remember," Carol said as she wondered why he had suddenly taken notice of the non-activities of their son.

"I think we should give him some kind of ultimatum, you know, either get a job or, I don't know, get out! My father never indulged me this way."

"Dan, I've been telling him that, to get a job, for ages. It's you who's never put your foot down. We've made it much too easy for him not to do anything, I think. So… what gave you this sudden change of heart?"

"I don't know. I guess it just hit me. I came home today and he was in his room, sleeping. At four in the afternoon! And his room was a pigsty. It really pissed me off. Is that the way it is everyday?"

This from a man who wasn't too adept at picking up after himself, either, taking for granted Carol was always around to do it. She was about to mention that, but decided against it, as she took another luscious bite of the dinner she hadn't cooked. So she only remarked, "Welcome to the club."

"Well, it's going to stop! I'm not going to have my son hanging around the house like a bum! If the only job he can find is at some burger joint, then that's what he'll do! Has he even been trying to get something happening with his cartooning, lately?"

But Dan didn't give her a chance to answer. "I think we have to give him a time limit. He's almost twenty-three, for crying out loud! Why does he even want to live at home at his age?"

Suddenly it was Carol who felt just a small pang of sympathy for her son for the first time in a long while. "Well, we can't just kick him out. It's our fault, granted, but we've given him the message it's okay. Maybe we should all sit down and have a serious talk about it with him."

Later, while Carol did the dishes, she went over the entire evening in her mind. It had been such a lovely dinner. They had actually talked, communicated with each other, although there was never a mention, from her, about her husband's sudden change of... being.

Had she been so into her own little world of late that she had not seen that her husband had a few good qualities? That he had a sense of humor, she seemed to have forgotten about? They had laughed a few times while they ate and he had commented how nice it was to see her laughing, again. Had she made him out to be more of a monster than he really was?

And how strange that just when she felt she couldn't take it anymore, when she was actually having thoughts of leaving him, he would make her dinner, out of nowhere. Something very weird was going on and Carol didn't quite know what to make of it. But she had to admit, it had been a much welcomed surprise.

After a few more days of discussion, the couple sat their son down for a real heart to heart. When they voiced their concern about his life and his future, Jonas went on the defensive.

"So, you're kicking me out? It's not my fault it's so hard to break into my field."

"Are you even knocking at its door?" Dan asked. "And maybe you should really think about another related field you might also be interested in, one there are real job possibilities of actually getting work."

"I can't believe you'd say that, Dad! Maybe Mom, but not you. I thought you liked my work. You always tell me how talented you think I am."

Although she had always encouraged her son, Carol sat quiet, enjoying the fact that Dan was running with this ball.

"Unfortunately, my liking your work is irrelevant, Jonas. And truthfully, talent sometimes has nothing to do with it. Grow up, boy! You're living in some dream world and dreams don't pay the rent!"

Carol saw that her son looked like he was about to cry and she had that mother's urge to take him in her arms, the way she had when he was small and fell off his bike and skinned his knee. Nothing, but nothing is worse for a mother than to see their child in pain, be it physical or emotional. But her little boy, wasn't little anymore, now standing a foot taller than she, and coddling him would only make things worse. Wasn't that why things were the way they were with him, to begin with? Carol the coddler?

"Jonas, your father and I love you very much, but it's time you take some responsibility for your own life."

Jonas lashed back at her. "What about you, Mom? What do you do all day? You live off Dad just the way you say I do!"

Suddenly wanting to smack the little brat across his face, Carol was beyond shocked and hurt by his words, to the point of speechlessness.

Dan was not. "That's enough, Jonas! Don't you dare talk to your mother like that! She does everything around her, including picking up your god damn mess and from what I've seen lately, that's a full time job!"

Is that what her own son thought of her? Hurt seeped through Carol. But at the same time, she couldn't believe how Dan had stepped up to the plate for her. Maybe, even though he never voiced it, he did appreciate her and saw her worth, even though that worth seemed to be that of a maid. But for her husband to acknowledge her in any positive, yet convoluted way, was a beginning. And a surge of affection for Dan went through her. Cooking her dinner and now this.

Eventually, a few things were settled, or mandated, as the case was. Jonas would look for work, any work. If he didn't clean his room and do his own laundry, Carol would not. For the always sacrificing, doing mother, this was the epitome of tough love.

Three weeks later, it was Carol who was in the kitchen, preparing for Dan his favorite meal of rib roast. Having finally gotten the message that his parents were serious, Jonas was out job hunting.

Recent behavior aside, it could not be said that Dan had magically changed, never to return to his former macho-self, but it was clearer to Carol that he seemed to making a concerted effort toward her. She still had yet to figure out, though, what had triggered this change in him.

Carol was nervous as she sat down to eat with him. Her newly, more seemingly sensitive husband sensed something was going on with her.

"You don't look so good, Carol. Have your hot flashes started up, again? God, I hope not."

"No, I'm fine," she said, trying to muster up the guts to tell him what she had gone and done. It wasn't until well into the meal that she finally did. She told him she had decided to go back to school

In fact, she had already registered for the coming fall semester.

A forkful of tender roast stuck in Dan's throat. It took him a minute to swallow before he could respond. "You're what?"

"I'm going back to school! I'm going to study to become a therapist. First a marriage and family counselor and then maybe I'll even continue for a Ph. D." Carol even surprised herself by how adamant her own voice sounded.

"But why? What'd you want to do that for?" He sounded more mad than anything. "And a therapist?" She knew how he hated all that psycho-babble crap.

"Because I want to do something with my life, Dan. I want to help people, again. Especially women. And I think I'd be good at it."

"Well, how 'bout me? Helping me?" Did Dan sound almost frantic?

"What are you so upset about? I'll still be able to do everything I do, now. I'm only going to take two courses at a time, so don't worry. It won't cut into anything I do around here for you, okay?"

"It just seems stupid, going back to school at your age, especially when you don't have to."

"I'm not doing it because I have to, I'm doing it because I *want* to!"

"That's my point. Why would you want to? We don't need the money."

Dan wasn't making any sense and even he knew it.

But Carol wasn't thinking about Dan's sense. It had been too good to be true. His little dinner for her had been a fluke, as was obviously his temporary sensitivity. He wanted her home, under his thumb, devoting her whole life to only him.

But she was confused. Hadn't the last few weeks been better? Hadn't she been happier. He had even been more affectionate, more loving, even at times he knew he wasn't going to be getting any. Maybe she shouldn't rock the boat, after all.

But why were things better? Because her husband was treating her with more respect about the scrub work she did around the house? Could it be that he was really threatened by the mere idea of her having a life of her own, outside these walls? Hadn't he acted in a similar fashion when she went off for her retreat week?

"Listen, I have a better idea than you trying to slave away at some school, staying up all night doing homework, like a kid. Let's go somewhere. Just the two of us. I'll take some good time off after I finish this job and we'll go to Europe for a month or so. How 'bout that! Didn't you always want to go to France and Italy and Spain?" There seemed to be this great desperation in his voice.

Carol had no idea what to think.

"Why now, Dan? I've asked you if we could travel for years and years and you never wanted to. Why did you think of this now, just when I've decided to do something for myself?"

"No, you're wrong. I've thought about it for a while. I swear, I have. I just didn't tell you. I was just waiting for a lull in my work."

Carol looked at her husband and knew that wasn't the truth, just as he did. As tempting as the idea was, it was the wrong time for her and she suspected for the wrong reason, although she had no idea why. No! She was going to do this. She was going back to school, just as she planned, with or without his blessing.

Her dessert of home-made apple pie, made especially for him, was eaten by both of them in silence.

# CHAPTER THIRTY-TWO

After Sara had been to Ojai with Carol, she had spent three, close to idyllic, weeks with Peter. The reason was simple. She had decided to stop thinking about anything concerning her past or her future. She was being here now, living every moment as it happened, having sex every chance she could. And it was good. It was very, very good.

Sara had always been a romantic in the truest sense of the word. Whenever she gave herself to a man, there always had to, at least, be some semblance of love. And she had garnered quite a lot of semblance in her life.

Sex was strange, thought Sara. It was possible to live without it, until you got it, again.

Then you wondered how you ever could have lived without it to begin with. Sara like life with it, better.

And what of love? For those few weeks she was in love. Quite passionately, in fact. It seemed to her that she had loved Peter for a very long time, although more of that time than not, she hadn't even been with him, because he had been with his wife. At the time, she hated herself for being able to love such a cad, but she had. Minds seemed to learn their lessons so much faster than hearts.

And now Peter was back with a vengeance.

But after these weeks of incessant love-making, constantly dripping with flaming passion, Sara started her downward spiral from rapture to fervor to delight to earthbound reality.

For those weeks he had respected her request not to pressure her about anything. She just wanted to take life with him day by day. She wanted to get to know him again. She wanted to fuck him with no strings attached. She wanted voluptuous, seductive, lewd and lascivious physical contact with him and that was all.

And she got it.

In bed with Peter, she was not less than two months from being half a century old. She was ageless. She was Goddess. And she loved the feeling and the power.

She floated through the days, hardly able to wait to lock her shop door, than race to meet him. At dinners out they left before coffee, so eager to run back to her house, so hot for each other they could have melted ice. They didn't even attempt going to the movies, knowing they would never last through the first plot twist. When he forgot his promise and tried to talk about the two of them, she hushed him with her lips on his.

But after these three physically exhausting weeks, she wanted rest. And he wanted a plan. He wanted commitment from her, now.

But something was wrong. The more Peter spoke of their life together, his moving in, being a family with her and even Rebecca, the more wrong everything seemed to her.

It was more than wrong and she was aghast at the truth. She had been using him, using his manliness! Could that honestly be true?

Sara spent the next week trying to figure out her actions. Had she subconsciously blocked out who he really was and what he had done to her and how easy it might be for him to do it again? Was this her way of getting back at him, using his body parts for nothing but her own gratification? No, that couldn't be it. She was too decent a human being, too honest a person to do something like that. And why would she do that which would also give him such pleasure, if it were true a part of her still hated him on some level? Had she spent these weeks of bliss in search of some redeeming qualities, to find them only inside his pants?

And what had really drawn her back to him, again and again? The romantic notion of first love ending up to being last love? The truth was he never showed that much interest in what she did and what she thought and what her passions were, like her bookshop, reading books in general, for that matter, her inspiration from the Goddess, her political beliefs of radical thinking, of feminist outrage.

After much thought, she was no closer to knowing what she was feeling. Why couldn't she accept what was today, that Peter was back in her life, lavishing on her all of this love? But how could she distinguish between his motives and her own? And what were those motives? Why couldn't she just be happy, ecstatic they were together, again, forget some of the other things because her future was now secure, simply that she would not have to grow old, alone, as she had so feared? Isn't that what she had wanted?

What was it then, that seemed to be impairing that vision she had so long dreamed of? Maybe that was the key... what she had dreamed of, not to spend her remaining years alone. Peter had been her last and she had invested so much of herself in him. Then she had been so hurt by him. Had she just continued to insert him into her dreams, because she had no other?

Was that why so many women made wrong decisions when it came to love? Oh, their dreams were substantial enough, but then in the desperation of trying to fulfill them, had they tried to fit the unable to fit man into them?

To add to her confusion, she talked with her daughter.

"I think I've been too hard on you, Mama," said Rebecca, as they sat, eating lunch together one day.

"Too hard?"

"You know, about Peter," Rebecca said. "You were right. Who am I to judge your life? You've seemed so happy, lately. I don't want to ruin that for you. I love you, Mom. I just want to see you happy."

"Does that mean you've forgiven him?" Sara asked.

"No, not really. He still has some proving to do as far as I'm concerned, but I'm not you. Anyway, you're too smart. I know you'll make the right decision for your own life."

Sara laughed. "Don't give me so much credit, Dear. I've certainly made my share of mistakes."

"So, who hasn't? Listen, Mom, if Peter has changed, if everything he told you was true and if you really love him, I say, go for it. Even though he acted despicably before, maybe he did feel it was the only thing he could have done at the time. I don't know. I just hope the two of you have a more truthful relationship than he had with his wife."

Sara smiled warmly at Rebecca. Her daughter had grown up and at times seemed wiser and more perceptive than herself. Sara wasn't sure she liked that in a kid, her kid.

It was a mild summer evening, but a fire blazed in Sara's hearth, as she and Peter sat drinking tea. Peter was looking at a picture that sat on the coffee table of a younger Sara, holding her baby daughter.

"I wish we could have a child. If we'd have gotten married when we first went together, he'd be close to thirty, by now."

"He?" said the ever gender conscious Sara.

"He, she. It would have been great, wouldn't it have? We've wasted our lives, Sara, not being together."

Sara said nothing, continuing sipping her tea.

"Why do you always get quiet when I say things like that? When I talk about when we were young?"

"I guess because I don't think I've wasted my life. And it's sad to know you think you have. I've had a pretty good life, in fact. It could've been better, it could've been worse. But it's certainly been an interesting life, not a wasted one."

"Okay, maybe not wasted, but we could have been together all these years."

There it was again, that sad voice of his, his 'the world has done me wrong' voice.

"But we weren't, Peter. We were kids, then. And who knows if we'd have even stayed together all this time."

"We would have. I know we would have. But the important thing is now we'll be together, forever."

Again Sara was quiet.

"Sara? What's wrong? Did I say something wrong?"

Sara got up and went over to the warmth of the fire, because suddenly she felt chilled at the truth that was inside of her.

Then she turned and looked at him, this man who for some cosmic reason, a thread had connected one to the other for so much of their lives. Her, never to be forgotten first love, his, marrying others while still loving her, always... meeting again, leaving, and finally this.

"I've been thinking, Peter..."

He didn't let her finish, "... about me? About us?"

"Some of it, yes."

Peter's eyes lit up. "About us living together? Getting married?"

Sara turned her eyes away from his.

"What, Sara?" he implored. "It's Rebecca, isn't it? Don't worry, Honey, she'll come around. She can't stay mad at me, forever, especially when I'm her step-father. Remember how much she used to love me?"

"Peter, it's not about Rebecca." was all Sara said.

Why was this so hard for her to do, to tell him the truth? Maybe it was because his beautiful, still beautiful face ached so much for her love. Maybe it was because she was not yet sure of her own decision.

"Then what is it?" his voice pleaded.

She turned away from him and looked into the fire for answers, as she felt her tears close by.

"I can't do this." Had she said it out loud? She wasn't sure.

"What? What'd you mean? Can't do what?" Now alarm was in his voice.

She turned back to him and simply said. "It, this isn't working, Peter. I'm sorry."

He jumped up off the couch and went to her. "It *is* working, Sara. It's wonderful and you know it. I love you. I've always loved you. What else can I do to show you?"

"It's not you. It's me," she said softly.

"But we were meant to be together. We *have* to be together after everything we've been through."

How she hated the desperation in his voice.

"You just need more time, that's all," he went on. "I'm sorry I started pressuring you, again. I'll stop, I promise."

He sounded like a little boy, apologizing to his mother for the broken vase.

"That's not it, Peter. Listen to me. It's not about you. It's about me, just me. Don't you see?"

"No! I don't see!" Now he was angry. "What were these last weeks about, then? You told me you loved me. You do love me!"

This was so eerie, thought Sara. The last time these same words had been spoken, the two saying them were reversed. Hadn't she said almost those very words to him that day he stood in the phone booth, in the rain? Had all the pain finally come full circle?

262

"Don't ruin this, Sara. Please don't do this to me." He said this with such an over-abundance of grief and anger.

Sara moved away from him, but told him, "I loved you so much, Peter, and then you broke my heart. Maybe it is too hard for me to forget. Maybe that's it. Something's just not right for me."

"But I'm here, now, Sara. We can be together, just like we planned, for the rest of our lives."

"Yes, and we had planned that before, hadn't we?"

"I know, but…"

"You know, I told Rebecca a while ago, of all the things I feared that I didn't want to happen to me, was to have to grow old, alone."

"And you won't have to now, Baby. I'll be with you forever."

She was trying so damn hard to stay focused, not to be emotionally moved by his words. If she just kept talking…

"Then it hit me. I want to, I have to make decisions about my life, now, what's right for me *today*, not about what I hope it will be thirty years from now."

"But we are right! You and me. And we will be right a hundred years from now," he pleaded with all the passion he had inside of him.

Although Sara suddenly wanted to end this, now, wanted him to just leave her alone, she didn't know how. She didn't know what more she could say, so all she repeated was, "I'm sorry. I'm sorry."

It was then that Peter's eyes squinted and turned very close to mean.

"But what about me, Sara? What about me, damn it? You're doing exactly what *she* did! You're not listening to me!"

Sara tried to make sense of his words. And then, looking into his once soft eyes that were no longer, it suddenly hit her.

"*You* didn't leave her, did you?"

Peter transformed in front of her and now looked like a trapped animal.

Quickly, all her sadness for hurting him turned back into her forgotten anger.

"She kicked you out didn't she? Then you came crawling back to me, lying and pretending about this whole damn thing, right? And I can't believe I fell for it. I can't believe I ever believed one word you have ever said! Oh, you're good, Peter. You're really good. My instinct about you was right, all along. I just couldn't put my finger on what was not right. But now I know. All you've ever cared about was yourself! You were a bastard then and you're a bastard now! Get out, Peter. I can't stand to even look at you another moment! Get out of here, I said!"

Finally alone in the quiet and emptiness of her home, she sat in front of the fire, now only left, red embers and burnt wood. And she cried.

264

How close she had come to again giving her life and her love to him. And she cried not for what could not be, but for what obviously and painfully never was.

How could she not have seen the truth of him, before? He had taken her to hell and back, twice. At that moment, she wasn't even sure if she hated him for all his lies, or hated herself more for her blind stupidity, born out of her own need for love, her own desperation. It did not matter that she had decided to end it with him, anyway. She could now only think how close she had come to choosing to spend her life with him. And that, she would not forget for a long, long time.

# CHAPTER THIRTY-THREE

The Great Mother Earth was angry. How much more injustice could She take? They had drilled into Her tender soil, extracting from Her precious body all they could find. They cut down Her forests, leaving Her creatures homeless, many soon to die, others to die out, completely. Slowly but surely they were destroying Her eco-system that sustained all of life. Her ozone layer was getting depleted. Her waters were now so polluted, killing its inhabitants from all the poison waste they had dumped into Her. Test war missiles exploded inside of Her and above Her into Her atmosphere. They desecrated Her, day by day and She was angry!

Leave me alone, She yelled, as She sent tidal waves onto the shores. Leave me alone, She cried out in a frenzy, as she whipped up tornadoes and hurricanes through the land.

Yes, there had always been these forces of Her nature, as She stretched and rolled and yawned, forces that had made Her mountains and Her valleys over the millions and millions of years, but this was different. Now Her very survival was at stake.

But in man's greed and ignorance they realized not, that in the doing, in destroying the Great Mother, they were also destroying themselves. Did they not find sacred even their own lives, even the lives of their children and their children's children, She wondered, as She felt another sharp pain of their bulldozers and their drills as the oil, once Her life's blood, now spilled back into Her oceans, killing Her fish and seals and dolphins, whales and birds?

How could they treat one who was once so hallowed as She with such hateful negligence? How could they take Her so for granted? Did they think, after being treated this way, She would just continue to give them food and water and all the tools to build from... that She could continue to love them, unconditionally?

She would not! Her children would have to be taught a lesson for their misbehavior before it was too late. And if they did not learn their lesson soon, She knew She would die, taking them all with Her.

Then what would be the worth of all the black oil they pumped from Her veins? What would be the worth of all the gold and silver they cut out of Her belly? And as the rains came down, flooding the land, wreaking havoc on human and animal life, The Great Mother wept for the stupidity of man for neglecting to see all the beauty She had created, that was She, all the beauty they seemed to be trying so hard to make ugly.

It wasn't always that way. Once, so long ago even She could hardly remember, She was worshipped and prayed to for all She gave Her children. Back then they only took from Her what they needed to survive. And it was given back to Her tenfold. All those eons ago, Her children had sung and danced in Her honor of all She bestowed on them and in return they treated her with dignity and gentleness and love. But no longer.

And so it was that one day, before the sun rose, The Great Mother was so angry, She began to shake and shake some more. She didn't want to hurt Her good people, the ones who had never done harm to Her fragile blades of grass, who still took delight in Her clear, stone-filled streams, the ones who roamed Her land in awe of the great power She possessed. But sometimes the good ones must be sacrificed to wake up the others and to make them see that She, the Great Mother of them all was not expendable.

And so She screamed in anguish for Her own survival.

Sara thought her brain was outside of her head, as it violently shook back and forth. That was the only way she could describe it. Why was her peaceful dream suddenly turning into such a nightmare?

It took her long seconds to wake and realize this was not a dream or nightmare, at all. This was really happening. The shaking, the excruciating noise of the safe sanctuary of her home, lifting off its foundation. The indistinguishably horrid sounds of things breaking and falling and moving all around her. The piercing screams of car alarms going off, a cacophony so loud she thought she had descended into a hell she didn't believe in. And the shaking, the never-ending wild and powerful intensity of it. How long is forty-five seconds, when the Great Mother's wrath is exposed? It is endless, endless terror. A feeling of such great magnitude, of such deep dread and fear and beyond terror it cannot be explained in words.

And then it was over, just like that. The Great Mother had had her say, for now. The car alarms continued to wail, but all else was quiet, the eerie quiet that comes after the earth's shaking subsides.

Sara opened her tightly shut eyes, in the dark. Had she stayed lying down the whole terror-filled time, hidden under her pillows and blankets? When had she sat up? The fan near her bed she used to lull herself to sleep was miraculously still on, yet fallen over on its side. Then it suddenly went silent, terrifying her even more. She sat there alone in the dark, not knowing what to do. A minute later the fan again went on, signaling she again had power.

Hesitantly, afraid of what she would see, she turned on her bedside light, which, incredibly, had remained upright. If she thought she had been frightened by the force of what had just occurred, it was nothing compared to seeing what that power had done.

Books had been thrown off their shelves, her dresser had moved feet away from the wall, drawers were all open, clothes strewn all over the floor. Everything that had been neatly placed in her bathroom cabinets, now lay broken on the tile. By some miracle, the large framed picture over her bed still hung, although crooked, on the wall. Had it fallen, she would have been severely injured, at best.

In total shock and disbelief, she gingerly got out of bed, her legs so weak they barely held her up. In a fog, she found a pair of jeans, a sweatshirt and her tennis shoes and put them on.

So disoriented, having no idea what to do, she carefully made her bed, feeling compelled to put some kind of order back into what had become such a quickly disrupted life.

The lights went out and again terror pulsed through her. And she thought she felt the floor underneath her sway. She quickly sat down on her bed. Then she thought of Rebecca. Was her child alright? The lights went on again and she dashed for the phone, feeling hysteria filling her very being. The line was dead. Sara wanted to cry, scream out at how terrified she was, for herself and for her daughter, but she did not. She sat there a few more moments in a petrified numbness.

Trying desperately hard to compose herself and her thoughts, she finally got up and timidly ventured out of her bedroom. And it was then that she began to fully realize the enormity of the disaster. Shaking, she walked into her office down the hall from her bedroom on the second floor. The room looked like a bomb had hit it. Everything she owned had fallen, books, pictures, her computer, precious odds and ends, things she collected through the years, things she held sacred. Her heavy, floor big screen TV had moved away from the wall by a foot or two. And again, she had that frightening thought of what kind of force could do all this?

Downstairs there came an even bigger shock. Couches and chairs were feet away from where they had been, when the night before she had plumped their pillows before turning out the lights and going upstairs for a pleasant night's sleep. Now she could hardly see the wood floor, for it was covered with every possession she owned. All her standing bookcases had fallen over.

She heard herself gasping out loud, "Oh my god, oh my god, oh my god…"

She turned on the downstairs TV. She heard a newscaster reporting about a large earthquake, but there was no picture, signaling to her that the cable must be out. She listened for a few minutes, desperate for any information, but there was little to tell at this time.

Then she went outside, hoping for possible comfort from her neighbors. Even though she lived in 'earthquake country' and had heard tips of safety in the event of one, it never crossed her befuddled mind that her building might no longer be safe to inhabit, that water might be undrinkable, that there might be a gas leak that could lead to an explosion, even that electricity might go out, again, this time for good, leaving her to live for days in darkness. Oh yes, like most other Angelenos, she had a little extra bottled water, two flashlights and a small first aid kit, but had the very worst happened to her home, none of this would have been much help.

Sara had been through numerous earthquakes in her life, but nothing compared to what she had just experienced. She had become almost used to the rocking and rolling of a four or five pointer, but this, well, this scared the bejeezes out of her. But she and luckily her building were still standing. She was on her own, all alone, but she had survived it.

Finally her neighbor, Mary, came outside and they hugged each other, tightly and that was when Sara started to cry, then quickly pulled herself together. Mary's husband was kind enough to right the fallen bookcases for Sara. Only a half hour had gone by since her world, and so many others, had fallen apart and for so many, far worse than hers. Sara's daze continued, her daughter still was unreachable, her TV cable still not restored. Not knowing what else to do and learning from neighbors their small apartment complex was safe from leaks, Sara started the long, arduous task of trying to put her house back in order, again. The sun had still yet to rise.

An hour later, as daylight finally began to lighten the city and the real damage was able to be seen, Sara's phone line was restored. She quickly called Rebecca and got through. Her child was alright, shaken also, but alive. As hard as the quake had hit in Santa Monica, miles east where Rebecca and Thomas lived, only a plant or two had fallen in their apartment. As soon as things settled down and more safety information was at hand, she and Thomas would come over and help Sara with her clean up.

Hours later, the extent of the damage was becoming all too clear. Mother Nature's wrath had made its mark on the inhabitants of the City of Angels. Freeways had collapsed. Houses were destroyed. People were injured and a few even killed. No one wanted to think what would have happened had it occurred during the day, when people were at work and children were at school.

Of course, labeled the Northridge Earthquake, it was days before the news realized that Santa Monica had been struck about as hard, as one fault line that extended from the West Valley through the Santa Monica mountains had touched off another fault line going directly south into the usually quiet beach community. Eventually more than half the houses and apartments in Sara's neighborhood were Red Tagged, uninhabitable.

Rebecca and Thomas stayed with Sara that night. Glued to the constant images on the now cable restored TV, of the city's destruction, they tried to cope with wave after wave of aftershocks. Hearts took giant dives each time the earth moved. And cope they would all have to learn to do, when they learned there could be thousands more of these shakers to come in the ensuing weeks and months.

Sara had been a lucky one. She had lost many items that had broken with this force of nature and her walls were full of cracks, but that was all. In a day's time, unless one looked closely, no one would have believed any devastation had even occurred in her home, her books quickly back in bookshelves, alphabetized as they had been before, pictures hung again on the walls and odds and ends neatly back in their rightful places.

Except, this shift of the earth had deeply affected Sara. Damage aside, she hated the fact that she had been alone when it happened. Feeling desperate, she had come so close to calling Peter back into her life, so she would never again have to go through such a terrifying experience alone, again. But she did not and was proud of herself for that.

But amidst all the city's rubble, something became so clear to her about life and how fragile it really is and how she wanted to live that life fully, from that day forth.

And as the city, once again, settled down and people became a little more secure about the earth beneath their feet, although now so wary of it, Sara felt a strange kind of freedom and peace. Suddenly things that had always seemed so important, were no longer so. And other things, so taken for granted, suddenly were. She would not soon forget how precious life was and how insignificant everything else really was.

And that was the beginning. That was what the Great Mother, the Great Creator and the Great Destroyer was hoping for. If only all of Her children would realize it. As the Great Goddess continued to sigh and turn, more gently now, She had a feeling She would have to continue to remind Her children, over and over again, until they really understood what was at stake.

But Sara had to wonder if the price that had to be paid for this enlightenment, this rude awakening, would have to be to live the rest of her life in fear of that something that was so immensely greater than herself.

# CHAPTER THIRTY-FOUR

A week before the horrific experience that would change so many lives, forever, Jonas told his parents some good news. Up until that time, he had been job hunting, but without much vigor. He had sent out his skimpy resume to Spielberg and Lucas and Disney and when they didn't respond, he felt downcast and dejected. When Dan continued to put pressure on him to take any kind of job to begin with, he had balked. Then he got doubly depressed when he realize that without any background in management, he could hardly even get a job better than slinging hash at some fast food restaurant.

"Welcome to the real world," his father had told him, followed by a lecture about wasting his college years doing artsy-fartsy things instead of preparing himself for the realities of life.

"If you don't find work in the next two weeks, you're coming to work for me," continued Dan. "You'll start at the bottom and work your way up. You're lucky to have this opportunity I'm giving you."

But Jonas didn't feel lucky. In fact, he couldn't think of anything worse than doing construction work in the hot sun, everyday. He was an artist, after all. This was not how he had pictured his life to be. He tried to gain sympathy from his mother. It all but killed Carol to see her boy so frustrated and unhappy, but this time she backed her husband, knowing he was right.

"I wish I could snap my fingers and make the job of your dreams appear, Honey," she had told him, "but I can't. And even though you might hate us now, later you'll thank us. It's not good, not healthy for someone your age to just hang out and do nothing all day. Any work now will be better than none."

And with that too long speech for Jonas' liking, Carol hoped she had softened the fact that she, too was standing firm.

And then a few days before Jonas would have had to turn in his pens and inks for a hard hat, a friend of his called with the news.

"I'm going to San Diego for an interview at this small animation company!" an excited Jonas told his parents.

While Dan showed immediate enthusiasm, knowing Jonas would not have lasted a week nailing and hammering, Carol had mixed emotions. Of course she wanted Jonas to get a job that would satisfy his creativity, but all the way down in San Diego?

As much as she was tired of cleaning up after him and frustrated at seeing him languishing aimlessly around the house, it had never crossed her mind that he would ever leave the city, in effect, leave her.

She had vividly pictured helping him set up his first apartment, near to her, later stopping by, loaded with his favorite home-made food, even occasionally doing him the favor  of washing his laundry. How, she wondered, would he manage if he lived two hundred miles from her? How would she manage?

It was true that recently there was a tension between mother and son, but he was, had always been the love of her life, her only child, her son. And she had to wonder if the tension was caused more by her recent change of direction than anything he had done. With all the new things she was learning and her recent defiance against women's roles, in this still Patriarchal society, not to mention her own body's defiance against her, had she abandoned her own flesh and blood? And she wondered if in gaining all this insight, would she have to lose those nearest and dearest to her?

Carol had always wanted a large family, a household of multiple bare feet running to and fro, little one's laughter echoing through the halls, daughters and sons. But it was never to be. And so Carol put all the love she had inside of her, all her attention and energy into Jonas. And the little boy reciprocated by being good and smart and mostly well-behaved.

In the early years she used a sitter as little as possible, always wanting and needing to be the one to feed and bathe and teach him. She couldn't bear the thought of being out of the house and, god forbid, missing when he did some new and wonderful thing, putting the square into the square hole, uttering some new word never uttered before, lifting his cup of milk to his mouth and drinking from it for the first time, without spilling it.

She remembered his first day of school and how she had wept after he disappeared around the corner and into his classroom. What would he do without her all day? As it turned out, he survived the separation with much greater success than she did.

She had wanted him to be strong and independent and yet, in the name of love and deep concern for his well-being, she helped to enable him to stay home all these years, to attend a local college instead of going to an out of town school, to depend on her for everything.

And perhaps, just perhaps, it was the case that Dan, afraid of his son becoming a 'mommy's boy,' forever, countered Carol's gentleness and loving manner with his own brand of macho influence. And this had left Jonas torn. He loved and needed his mother, yet as he grew older he felt superior to women, in general. After all, he was a man and Dan made damn sure he knew it.

Is this how it happens, thought Carol, that men could rationalize treating women poorly, while putting their mothers on pedestals, willing to kill if anything dared harm them? Didn't they realize the women they abused, one way or another, would also one day become someone's mother?

And so now it was Carol's turn to feel torn. She knew this could be the chance of a lifetime for Jonas, but the realization that the day might be very near that he would leave her, greatly depressed her. A premature sensation of emptiness spread throughout her body. Her rational side knew that this day would come, perhaps should have already come. But knowing the time was at last on hand, upset her. Somewhere inside she knew he would get this job, he would pack up his belongings and he would leave her.

As Carol waved Jonas off on his trip and interview, down to the south, she told him to drive safely, something she had said each and every time he left the house, something she had said to him a thousand times before. "Drive safe," she repeated, tears filling her eyes as she watched his car go down the street, then turn the corner, disappearing from her sight.

Dan came home from work to find his wife sitting outside on the patio near her colorful, well-tended garden.

"What're you doing?" he asked.

"Nothing. Just thinking."

"Jonas get off, okay?

"Mm, mm."

Seeing that his wife didn't look very happy, he thought it a perfect time to tell her of his surprise. "Pack a bag, Honey. I'm taking you away for the week-end, up to Santa Barbara. I already made reservations at that little Bed and Breakfast you love so much."

To say Carol was surprised was an understatement. She couldn't remember the last time Dan surprised her with anything, barring his home-made dinner, much less a spur of the moment get-a-way. Unfortunately, he had picked a very bad time, as far as she was concerned.

"I can't go, Dan. Not now."

"What'd ya mean, not now? Jonas isn't here and what else do you have on your agenda?"

Carol took his words to be a real snipe at her temporarily, more than usually, empty life.

"As a matter of fact, I just got a bunch of books I have to read for my up-coming classes."

"But you still have months before school begins," he said, reasonably.

The truth was Dan had planned this little vacation to try and talk his wife out of going back to school to begin with. The funny thing was, though, he wasn't quite sure why. He only knew it wasn't something he wanted her to be doing.

"Come on, Carol. It'll be so much fun. And all your books will be here when you get home. It's only a few days and it's too late to cancel the reservation."

Finally Carol conceded. She was in no mood to read, anyway. All her thoughts were now filled with Jonas and the possibility of his moving away.

And so it was that as Dan and Carol slept peacefully after two surprisingly nice days up the coast, where Dan had yet to mention his wife's scholarly intentions, miles away, underneath their home, the earth began to pitch and shift and shake.

That morning at breakfast, overlooking the calm blue Pacific, they learned of the disaster. They quickly packed their things and after a very nervous, two hour drive, returned to find their dream house thankfully intact. Like Sara's home, theirs had no structural damage, only a multitude of cracks. And oddly, even though Carol lived only blocks from her good friend, she lost virtually nothing of value. They came home to only a slight mess, some broken glasses and a dish or two, but luckily, that was all. Their furniture had hardly moved and pictures hung askew on the walls. But such was the nature of an earthquake. One side of a street could be totally destroyed, the other not.

It was a very bizarre feeling for Carol to know that something like this had happened to her home and her things, yet because of some kind of fate, a mere last minute idea of her husband's, it had not also happened to her.

On the one hand she felt violated, like one would feel if their house had been vandalized. On the other, she felt strange guilt. Her friends and neighbors had experienced this hell she should have, by all rights, experienced, also. Yet somehow she had escaped the terror. Somewhat like survivors of a plane crash when others lost their lives, simply because of where they were sitting.

How could she complain about the much less severe aftershocks, when everyone else she knew had felt, 'the big one,' a feeling of which she had absolutely no conception. And hard as she tried to imagine it, she couldn't. Where others lived in fear, she could not. And this alone made her feel removed from all the talk and all the fright. She had not heard that awful creaking and cracking and banging and breaking, as if the world, itself, was being torn apart. In a very strange way, she almost wished that she had. Then, she thought, she could better understand how all this damage just blocks away, could have happened.

Dan didn't concern himself with all the psychological drama and the usual 24/7 media blitz that accompanied such a tragedy. He was more concerned about his precious house and any damage it might have incurred, not to mention all the homes he had built and were building.

Seven years before, on this land, sat a fifty year old cottage. He had bulldozed it down and built his magnificent shrine. He had worked daily with the architect, making sure every piece of wood fit perfectly, every piece of granite and tile was just right. It had been his beloved vision, his baby and his alone. So impressed with him was his architect, that he mentioned to Dan that he, himself should really become an architect. At the time, Dan just laughed, knowing he didn't have the patience for all that schooling that would be required. He did what he did through sheer instinct.

Carol would have been happy in a smaller, cozier place, a house with more of a country feel to it. But instead of fighting her husband, she acquiesced to Dan's more elegant taste. Once it was finally finished and they moved in, she certainly saw the beauty of it, but it wasn't until she had recently fixed up her little room that she finally felt she had a niche to really feel comfortable in, to really feel like she was home.

Dan walked around his trophy house checking every crack, the water heater, the pipes under the house and was happy and satisfied. He had built a strong fortress with his own hands and where others had fallen, his labor of love continued to stand erect. And he considered this to be a testament to his skill as a builder.

After cleaning up the litter of broken glass in her kitchen, Carol walked into her private refuge, dreading what she would find there.

When she peeked in, it wasn't as bad as she had expected. Some of her books were on the floor, but thanks to Dan's foresight, the bookshelves stood, still secured to the wall. Things had fallen off her desk and her chairs had moved from the quake's force, but all else remained pretty much in place.

Then she looked at her treasured altar and burst into tears. There, on the floor, lay the clay figure of the first Goddess she had ever gotten. It was broken beyond repair. She gingerly picked it up and tried to piece it back together in her hands. But she could not. Too many little parts had broken off and now lay on the rug, some hardly more than dust.

It had only been a piece of clay that had cost less than twenty dollars, but to Carol it had always represented the beginning of her love affair with the Great Mother. Of all the knickknacks in her room, why had this been the only one to break, she wondered? Had the Great Goddess abandoned her and if so, why? Would she now have to work harder to find Her, again? Carol sat down in front of her altar and carefully laid the broken Goddess down. Then she slowly moved all of her stones and shells and other Goddess figures she's acquired, back into their rightful places, the way they were before the earth had used all Her power and all Her force to disrupt life. And feeling so disconnected to the catastrophe, yet seeing the brute strength it had wrought, she continued to cry.

# CHAPTER THIRTY-FIVE

As the hours, the days, as the weeks went by, Sara was feeling more and more unnerved. Although the shaking happened less and then less often, her heart seemed to pound harder when it did happen. When she thought she ought to be feeling safer, once again, she was not, at all. She dreaded being home alone and was afraid to go out, then to come home to an empty house, especially at night.

In less than a minute, the place she had always felt most secure, the place she loved to be in that held her memories and her dreams, had become a place of horror. The cracks on her walls seemed to widen before her eyes, the sound of a slight wind outside, a truck going by her window would trigger an immense fear of it happening again.

On the outside she tried to act much more casual about what happened than she was feeling inside. As she tried to calm the nerves of her daughter, who immediately wanted to move out of California, Sara cried herself to sleep at night, wanting someone to calm her own fears. But in actuality, they were fears that could not be calmed by anyone else. Did it help to know that so many others were feeling the same thing, that this fierce anxiety was normal? No! She wanted someone to tell her it could never, never ever happen again. But no one could.

One day while talking to a friend who lived miles away in town, the woman interrupted the conversation with, "Oh, oh... here comes another one," and Sara's heart dropped as she braced herself for yet another hated tremor to reach her in Santa Monica. And it did. And she thought she might throw-up.

Eventually, the pressure of the earth's erratic movements consumed her to the point that she thought she might be going quite insane. She couldn't sleep. She couldn't eat. Her life, like most Angelenos, had become one of waiting, one of never knowing, one of the ultimate knowledge of being out of control.

Sara watched her television in a hypnotic stupor, mesmerized by the city's destruction. Days after the quake, when some stations finally went back to regular programming, one had a small window at the bottom corner of the screen that had the now famous 'seismograph' registering every shock, no matter how large or small. And she found her eyes glued to it, waiting to feel it herself, when the little gage started zigging and zagging, ignoring the relief of a laugh she might get from her favorite sitcom.

She went out on her patio, thinking she would try and fix it up, then thought better of it. A few flowers she had finally planted in terra cotta pots had died when they had crashed off their ledges. Why plant now, when it could happen again, she thought, as she picked up the broken pieces of pottery? Why do anything, why live, when you might die?

Finally, she dragged herself back to work, dreading what she knew she would find there, thousands of books on the floor. At least she didn't own a liquor store, she thought, trying to laugh, but unable to do so.

What she found at her precious Book, Nook and Crannies, her labor of love, was not half as bad as she had envisioned. Malibu, not being on the fault line that had exploded its power, sustained much less damage than other areas. Within days her shop was back in order, but without customers. At a tragic time such as this, buying great literature, buying anything not related to quake repairs, was not foremost on people's minds. But Sara pushed herself to go into work everyday, desperate to bring some kind of normalcy back into her life.

Her phone remained quiet, except for a few business calls from out of town book reps who had become friends, now calling to see if she was alright, if she was still on their list of buyers. And so she told her story over and over again, thinking if she kept talking about the earthquake, it would seem less real, like nothing more than a good story.

Although constantly talking about it did help to make Sara feel better and not so alone in her misery, it made Rebecca feel worse. How differently, Sara thought, people reacted to the same situation. Even though most moments she felt like she was going completely out of her own mind, she continued to try and quell the fears of her child, because that is what a mother does. And she hated to admit this was hard to do, because besides Rebecca not having felt the quake half as much as she had, the child at least had Thomas, her husband, whereas she had no one.

Who was there to hold her and comfort her? Who would tell her she was alive and had a place to live and should consider herself lucky? Who would dry her tears or whisk her away to a safe place, away from nature's southern California's wrath? And she cursed the fact she was alone. Never before had she hated it the way she hated it now. Never before did she ever feel so desperate in her life, so sick in her body and her soul. She felt she would take any companionship now, anyone, just not to have to spend one more scary, endless night alone.

She was jealous of Carol and Dan, that Carol hadn't been in town when it had struck. Then she hated herself for her selfish thoughts. All she wanted was to feel safe again, in her own home, in the world. She did not and she wondered if she ever would again. She wanted the healing process to finally begin, but it did not. She now even wanted Peter to call her, but he did not and she could not bring herself to call him, because she knew deep down, it was the wrong thing to do. Even in her desperate situation it would be wrong. And so she lived, day after day, in this zombie state, wondering if she would ever feel like a whole human being, again.

One day she and Carol took a walk, their favorite walk down the tree-lined San Vicente Boulevard. Neither had ventured down this main road since the quake hit and they were aghast at the sight. Not only was every other apartment house 'Red-Tagged,' but there was rubble from the brick buildings, everywhere. Crumbled chimneys laid in heaps by the side of what was left of houses. Hundreds of cars were parked on the grassy medium between the east and west traffic lanes, where happy, energetic joggers used to exercise. Moving vans stood double-parked as workers emptied the contents of homes still able to be entered. Deep crevasses were evident on the formally smooth sidewalks.

What had started out as a healing walk, a time to talk with a close friend and temporarily forget the recent mayhem, quickly turned into yet another horrific reminder of the city's ruin.

"I have to get away from here, Carol," said Sara, as they made their way down a small street that held a spectacular view of the Santa Monica Canyon and the ocean. "I can't stay here, anymore."

"You mean move away?" asked Carol, alarmed at her friends fears and words.

The thought was an inviting one, although Sara knew she never really would  This was her home, where she had lived her whole life.  How could she leave the place where her roots went so deep?  And where would she go, anyway?

"No," Sara answered, "just for a little while. I have to make some sense of all this, in my mind. I can't seem to do it here.  Yesterday, I was actually sick to my stomach, threw-up, you know after those two four-pointers. I can't stand it anymore."

That is what life had been reduced to, guessing the magnitude of aftershocks. In any store, after a tremor, someone would say, 'That was a three point five.'  Then someone else would pipe in with, 'No, more like a three-nine.'  Then the radio would be quickly turned on to see who was closest. Had it paid, the game would have been more popular than playing the lottery.

"Where will you go?" Carol asked.

"I don't know.  Maybe back to the island."

"The island?  But Christina won't be there."

"I know, but Jane will.  I want to see Jane, again."

Carol smiled at the thought of the old Crone and their adventure that had led them to her.

"Oh, Sara, I want to go with you!"

"Really?" Sara said, feeling excitement for the first time in weeks. "That would be great!. Could you really get away?"

"Why not? Dan probably won't even miss me. He's completely involved with damage control on houses he's built, plus a new job. And Jonas is going back down to San Diego to find an apartment. I offered to go with him and help, but he wanted to do it, himself.

Carol's casual voice belied her continuing depression at learning Jonas had, in fact, gotten the animation job.

"So, how are you with that?" asked Sara.

"Oh, back and forth. I know it's the best thing that could happen for him, but I'm still not sure *I'm* ready. He is, but I'm not. But I've never seen him so happy. He's like a different person, like overnight he grew up."

"Yeah, I know what you mean. Even though Rebecca lives ten, fifteen minutes from me, that's how I felt when she got married. Ah, the old empty nest, huh?"

The two women continued their walk, now in silence, lost in their own thoughts of individual loss.

By the time they got back to Carol's house, they had planned their whole trip. The more they planned and talked about it, the more they couldn't wait to get back to the woods, to the river they had canoed on. They couldn't wait to sit outside at night and gaze at the moon and the stars they had come to know so well. They couldn't wait to get back to their earth and their Goddess. No matter how hard they had tried for it not to happen, they had lost sight of Her. They wanted Her back in their life in Her full glory. They wanted to sit and talk with old Jane and learn how to weave baskets. And most of all, they wanted to again feel the peace that was so hard to find, and once found, so easy to lose.

# CHAPTER THIRTY-SIX

Dan was unhappy with what was happening. Even though he didn't admit it to Carol, he was also worried about his son moving away. He wondered if he had given Jonas all the tools he would need to be able to deal with the world at large, on his own. He knew how hard it was to be a man, these days.

Years ago, when Dan was growing up, life was much more cut and dry. A man knew what a man was supposed to do, what was expected of him. He was supposed to be strong. He was supposed to be the bread-winner. He was supposed to always keep his emotions in check, except his anger. That, at least, was what his father had taught him, That was what all his friends had also been taught. What was a man, anyway, if not all those things?

He had done everything right, everything expected of him and look where it got him, a son who hated sports, instead going off by himself to paint or scribble, as he saw it, and a wife who never seemed happy. And now she wanted to go and get herself a career! Then she told him she was going back to that place. She hadn't even asked him. She had told him! And now she was gone. What the hell was this world, his world coming to, anyway? He was getting too old for all these changes.

And when had she changed, so dramatically? Why was she continuing to do these things so unlike the way she used to be? He liked it better when she had simply been miserable with all those damn menopausal symptoms. At least then, she hadn't had all these cockamamie ideas. He could deal better with all her whining, than this. Why was she no longer happy, the way he thought she had always been, with all he had given her. Security. A beautiful home. Luxuries any woman would die for.

Hadn't he indulged her, letting her go on that retreat? Hadn't he? And where had it gotten him? Now she was into all this Goddess crap, reading all those books that bad-rapped everything men did. Was this the thanks he deserved for being so understanding?

Dan walked through his empty house, ending up in the kitchen. He made himself a cup of coffee and took a Danish off a plate she had left for him, then sat down at the kitchen table. His son was in San Diego and his wife was on her way up north with her single friend, for what he did not know. Dan looked around the spotlessly clean kitchen with Carol's touches so evident and suddenly felt very alone.

Hundred of miles away, Carol and Sara stepped off their plane after a thankfully smooth ride, got into their rental car and headed north toward their island. Already Sara felt better than she had in weeks. As her feet had touched the Washington earth, a peace came over her. But it would still take her a while to accept the fact that she was safe, far away from the fear that had plagued her every waking hour since the great quake.

As the two friends drove away from the city and the scenery outside their car became more and more rustic, they chatted, endlessly. All the heavy feelings that had gripped their hearts started to slowly lift and by the time they reached the Sound, they both already felt they had been gone far longer than half a day.

As they slowly drove their car onto the ferry and it finally started its ride over the clear, blue water, they knew they were home, back in the fold of the Great Mother. Now, standing on the ferry's deck, they breathed in the fresh air, gazing at the beauty that surrounded them. They were again one with the world. How could they have ever forgotten this feeling of freedom, of being so a part of the earth? How could they have let this vision, this feeling escape from their beings, they wondered, as they passed through the mists that for a few minutes inhibited their view of the little island? Then as suddenly as it appeared, the mist vanished and their eyes again saw the sacred place where they knew the Goddess dwelled... their own sweet, sweet Avalon.

After the ferry docked, they drove a short way to their beloved retreat. They stood outside their car and listened to the wind whisper her secrets through the trees. And they thought they heard Christina's voice, reminding them of their womanhood, their aging womanhood.

*'The Great Mother lives within me. Again, after so many long and barren years, today She is resurfacing, to experience with and in and on. And I shall listen to Her heartbeat, because it is my heartbeat. And I shall weep Her tears for all the injustices She has endured, for they are my tears. And I shall celebrate the blades of grass and sweet smelling flowers She brings forth, because they are my children. Through the history of woman's worship, through the pain She has suffered from the destruction hurled against Her, and through the exuberance of Her fertile soil, I shall find my own sacredness. I shall continue to look to the Great Mother, the Great Goddess... to explore Her mysteries... to become one with her.'* So spoke Christina.

It surprised the women to see the retreat now filled with the laughter of little children. They scrambled back and forth, playing rope-tug and hide and seek and games of ball.

Although a shock for them to see this once serene place now a summer camp, they felt it fitting. On the land where a few months before Crones-to-be, women at the beginning of their descending years had walked, now in the soil were the footprints of little ones, just starting on their journey of life.

And Carol and Sara watched the innocents for a short while as they played and leaped and rejoiced as only children can, oblivious to everything except their own immediate needs and desires.

At the tiny general store they bought food and water and then in the public rest room changed into their hiking clothes. After renting a canoe at the old boat house, they were on their way.

Securing life jackets around their bodies, they suddenly wondered if they really knew what they were doing. Could they handle the river again, if it got rough? Would they even be able to find the little cabin in the woods where Jane lived? And most of all, how would they do all this without their beloved guide, Sophie?

"Are we out of our minds doing this?" asked Carol of herself as much as of Sara.

Remembering what a therapist had once told her many years before, Sara answered with a question. "What's the worst thing that could happen?"

Carol laughed, "Are you kidding? We could get lost! We could capsize! We could die out here and it could take weeks for anyone to find us!"

"Well, if that happens, at least we won't know about it! And we'll die happy, won't we?" laughed back Sara.

"Very funny," said Carol, as they loaded their belongings and supplies into the canoe.

But as they pushed off onto the river, they knew in their hearts that the decision to come here was better than a good thing to do. And this was realized moments later as they began to row their oars, back and forth, back and forth, through the velvety water.

They were indeed home, so quickly comfortable again in this environment, as if there was nothing unusual about boating like this to get to where one needed to go. This time as Sara and Carol made their way up the river, they were not first-time explorers from the city, they were just women living on the land that had given them life.

Everything looked so familiar, the trees, the rocks, the lush ferns growing on the banks they now rowed smoothly past. This time when they reached the area where the river got rowdy, almost magically, they steered their canoe with confidence, never losing control. They saw themselves as primitive women transformed back to a time of years gone by, a time now forgotten, when women feared not nature's elements, when women feared not man's anger and violence toward them, because it didn't exist. They were Amazons, fearless women, strong in thought and deed.

A while later they docked and secured their canoe at the very spot in the forest they knew would lead them to the cabin of the treasured oldest Crone, and they felt empowered and engulfed by the sacredness and the beauty of that which was the Mother.

Heavy backpacks on their shoulders, hiking up the path, they were silent, listening to the sounds around them, to the birds sending messages of greetings, to the small creatures who scurried through the brush on their daily errands. And they listened to the wind, the wind which had been there from the beginning of time, the wind that had seen and heard it all.

For Sara, especially, it was such a welcome relief to once again experience the land and the power of nature, not in fear, but in awe and grace and love. And out here in the wilderness, a million miles from civilization where danger could be anywhere, she felt safe and alive, again.

"There it is!" called out Carol, who was striding ahead of Sara. "We found it!"

The two women then quickened their steps until they were at the bottom of the porch of Jane's cabin.

"What if she doesn't remember us?" asked Carol, suddenly nervous.

"Oh," said a thoughtful Sara. "You know, I never even considered that. Well we'll just have to remind her, then."

Sara walked up the rickety old wood steps to the front door and knocked. As she did this the door, that had no lock, pushed open. She peeked into the cozy home.

"Jane? Jane, are you there?"

There was no answer and this distressed Carol. "You don't think she moved away, do you? You don't think we came all this way for nothing? You don't think…"

"No, all her things are in there. She's probably just out in the forest, napping." Sara said.

The remembrance of their first sighting of the old woman brought forth laughter from the two.

"What're you girls laughin' at?"

The two whipped around to see their spunky elder. She was carrying a basket filled with wild flowers.

"Jane! It's us! Carol and Sara! Remember us?" asked an excited Sara.

"Of course I remember. I was expecting you."

Sara and Carol looked at each other, then at Jane, again.

"What'd you mean? How could you?" asked Carol. "We only just decided ourselves to come up here for a few days."

"Oh, I knew you'd be back to learn how to weave baskets," said Jane simply. There was a twinkle in her old, wise eyes. "Don't *you* remember?"

The youngin's laughed.

"Well, you're here, so come on in and have some home-made lemonade." Jane said as she hobbled up the steps and into her home.

Sara and Carol followed close behind her, already delighted to be in Jane's presence, once again.

# CHAPTER THIRTY-SEVEN

"Now girls, why don't you settle in.  Go and put your things away in that bedroom, the one on the left, there.  It ain't big, but it has two beds and clean sheets," the mother ordered the children.

The two women looked surprised.

"You mean you want us to stay here, with you?" Carol asked, delighted inside.

"Where else were you going to stay?  Isn't that what you wanted?" Jane asked simply, while she poured three glasses of the lemon drink.

"Oh, well... Ah, we just thought we'd stay at the inn near the ferry dock." stammered Sara.

"No, no, you didn't.  You want to stay here with me. So it's settled."

Sara and Carol looked at each other and smiled, a little embarrassed. The truth was they hadn't made any real plans to stay anywhere. Oddly, it just hadn't seemed important, even for the two normally organized, obsessives that they both were. They would have slept in the forest with leaves as their blankets, if need be. All that had seemed important was to be there. Somehow they had had faith everything else would work out, feeling this spur-of-the-moment adventure was somehow powered by some kind of destiny. After all, hadn't the boat-house man stated before they shoved off, "Have fun. See you in a few days," even though neither of them remembered telling him when they'd be back with his boat. Oddly, he hadn't seemed concerned. But then, maybe that's the way things were up here. Trusting. They hadn't even needed to leave him a deposit or show him identification. How nice, how strange to be in a place of such friendliness and faith.

And stranger still was their distinct impression that somehow Jane actually did know they were coming.

Since they got on the island, both Sara and Carol felt as if they had entered an unreal world. They certainly knew they were there, but where was there? Without the retreat, without Christina, the aura of the island seemed different, even more dream-like than before. It was as if they had gone into another dimension, to a place that had no time, no reality. They had had the sensation of almost floating through the minutes, the hours it had taken them to get to this magical place, this warm and secure home of Jane's. They had come here because they knew they had to, although they did not know exactly why.

They were quiet as they unpacked the few clothes they had brought with them, putting them into the empty dresser drawers that seemed to be waiting to be filled with their belongings, alone.

By the time they came out of the bedroom, their bedroom, Jane had set up on her wood table the necessary things needed for basket weaving.

"Sit, children. We are going to use grape vines to begin with, because they are soft and bendable and your hands are not yet strong."

The women then sat themselves down and began to learn the intricate skill their foremothers had performed thousands and thousands of years before.

"No, no, Dear," Jane told Carol, putting her old, rough, arthritic hands over Carol's soft, long tapered fingers, helping her to tighten her weave. "You see, like this... That's right, child."

There was something so healing, so primitive in this work. Sara was taken back in her mind to the Seventies, when she had learned to macramé. She smiled to herself, fondly remembering all the plant hangings she had made back then, the colored beads she had strung onto the jute, then how proud she had been as she carefully placed plants into them for the first time. Back then, she had also made, by her own hand, a wood-framed loom. Over and under she wove. Over and under, making colorful designs on her little loom while listening to Jackson Brown and the Eagles and Janice Ian on her stereo. Then she had the woven wool backed and filled and make into pillows she gave as gifts.

And now, over a quarter of a century later, here she was, doing much the same thing. Over and under. How could she have forgotten the peace this kind of craft work brought?

As they silently worked, helped out now and again by old Jane, there was no such thing as time or even place. They were far away. They were tribal women making baskets that would hold food that would feed their daughters and sons, making baskets that would hold sacred objects they would bring to their Goddess shrine as offerings for a spring that would yield from Her soil all they would need to survive.

When had the clouds appeared, masking the light of the sun, as it headed west toward the horizon, plunging the island into darkness? When had the wind starting blowing, the trees started rustling, loudly?

"Dinner time!" Jane's crackled voice broke the quiet of their thoughts. "You did well, girls. We can do more tomorrow if you like."

Carol and Sara looked at their work. It certainly wasn't close to the perfection of their mentor's, but it mattered not. They had made a basket out of grape vines, out of nothing man-made. They proudly looked at their handiwork before cleaning off the table that would soon be filled with fresh fruits and vegetables from Jane's garden.

After the natural feast, Jane retired for the night, leaving her wards to fend for themselves.

"What'd you think?" asked Sara, as the two women sat near the fire and candle lit living room.

"Nothing," said Carol. "Isn't it fantastic. Well, it is for me... to think of absolutely nothing. Just to be. I'm exhausted and feel peaceful and sort of charged up all at the same time. It's funny, I feel like I'm learning so much, just by being here, although I'm not sure what it is I'm learning."

Sara agreed. "I know, but I'm too tired to analyze it. What a day, huh?"

"Yeah, what a day."

That night they slept on two single beds, something neither had done since they were children, living at home with their parents. But as soon as their heads had hit their soft pillows, they were out. They didn't hear the wise old owl hooting in the moonlight. They didn't hear the rain as it tapped on the roof, overhead. And when they woke the next morning, they didn't remember if they had dreamed or not through the night.

"Lazy girls," Jane told them when they finally appeared the next morning. "Eat your breakfast. You have gardening to do. Then later I'm going to take you somewhere. Don't ask me where. Now, come and eat."

And they were children again, obeying their mother.

It all seemed so natural. So normal and right. It was as if this was their life, living here with Jane. They belonged and had not been here a mere day, but a lifetime.

And so it was that they spent the morning picking tomatoes and zucchini, digging up carrots from the earth. They collected eggs from Jane's chickens and found wood for the night's fire.

Later, after a light lunch, when Jane took a little nap, the women wondered if she was feeling alright. This time she hadn't spoken of her children or her grandchildren. She seemed more quiet, more frail than when they had first met her, such a short time ago. Hardly a hint of the feistiness they had remembered, had gotten such a kick out of.

And as they looked at the old and yellowed photographs of her when she was young and breathtakingly beautiful, they worried about her. In her plucky way she was so wise, so knowing. How many miles her now swollen, veined legs had walked. How many things those old, crooked hands of hers had touched. Her now tearing eyes, surrounded by deep wrinkles had seen so many things. She was ageless, they thought. Ageless.

"How old do you think she really is?" asked Carol, gently touching the faded image of who Jane once was.

"I don't know," said Sara in a soft whisper. "Eighty-six, eighty-seven?"

"I'm ninety-seven!". Jane's voice filled the room. "I'm ninety–seven and I feel just fine! So! Are you ready for your surprise?"

Jane then picked up her hand-carved walking sick and led the way out of her cabin into the sunshine, yet again amazing the women.

After walking a while on what could hardly even be considered a path, the three women came upon a wondrous sight. Before them was a waterfall that flowed over a cliff, emptying itself into a glorious pool. The water then swept itself into the island's streams and rivers, eventually making its way to the Sound.

The women 'ooh'd' and 'ahh'd' at the magnificent sight, as Jane sat her old bones down on a rock over-looking the pool.

Nature, nature. Beautiful nature. But while the youngsters saw it as amazing, the old Crone saw it as yet another constant in the earth's evolution of life. It fills itself up, while emptying itself out, only to fill itself up, once again.

"Whatever She does you must accept, because it's the way it must be."

For a moment Carol and Sara were sure it was Christina who spoke, not Jane, not the spirited old soul they knew her to be. And they were sure she would then say, "I am Goddess." But, she didn't.

"It never ceases to amaze me, how a woman life's so parallels the earth," said Sara, half to herself.

"The earth is smarter." Jane laughed with a cackle.

It was there as they watched the waterfall's endless flow that they saw such a continuity to their lives, as mothers, as children, as womenfolk living on the Mother who had conceived them. And that knowledge comforted them. Birth, death, rebirth, never ending, if only in memories of those still living.

The women, even Jane could have sat there in silence for many more hours, just looking at the great falls, listening to the rush of the water, but the sun was moving to the west, lowering in the sky as it went. It was time to go home.

They stayed a few more days with Jane, working side by side, tilling the land, harvesting the food, wandering the woods. The night before they were to leave, a full moon rose in the sky. On the porch in the dark, the three women sat. Watching over them a blanket of stars, holding mysteries they had still yet to discover.

Then out of the silent night came Jane's voice, gentle and tired sounding from the day's work, from a life's work.

"I know I am old, my children. And it will soon be my time to return to the earth."

These words, so unexpected, shook the younger one's sensibilities as they denied out loud it could well be the truth.

"No, it is true. Do not mourn me, though. Just remember me. Remember my existence in this world."

They did not want to hear this. No matter how old this wonderful woman was, she couldn't die. She somehow was going to live forever. Why was she saying these things, now? Had she some kind of premonition? Had she seen something they could not see? She seemed to be in fine health, albeit very old, yes, now frail and fragile, but that didn't mean she was going to die. They would not accept it!

And then what? Out here, living in the loving arms of the Great Mother, amongst Her most exalted creations, with life at its most vibrant, death seemed so far away. And yet it was all around them, but in such a natural harmony it was hardly noticed, simply a part of the scheme of things, the way it was supposed to be. A plant died, only to have another take its place. A mother animal breathed her last breath, only to live on through her children and then her children's children. Out here death seemed only another aspect of life. Not to be mourned, but to be rejoiced in the immense cycle of life, to be treasured for what it brought to the earth while it lived. The old in the forest were not cast aside, as they were in the cities. Was the ancient tree with her massive twisted trunk not the favorite of the squirrels, to romp up and down on? So many more limbs to climb? So many more leaves to find shade and protection under? No wonder Jane had decided to live and grow old out here, away from the cruel, judgmental eyes of the human species.

Slowly, yet suddenly, the women, during these days in the wild, realized they had never in their real lives had a greater sense of themselves. They had heard all the wisdom of Christina's words. But words alone could not give them the serenity they craved. Now, with Jane, they had begun to experience what these words had meant. And this clarity of who they were came in the silence of the doing, in the silence of the living. They saw, they felt, they experienced, not needing to speak of it. The knowledge they absorbed transcended any kind of verbal teaching, anything that could be written by the most intellectual, even spiritual minds.

And the next morning, as they bid their loving fond farewell to their old friend that had so touched their lives, their thoughts were not on the fact that she may soon be gone, but rather that she had been here. And they would keep their minds and hearts on that truth.

By mid-morning they were back at the shore of the river where their canoe awaited, like a chariot, to carry them home. They were ready now to face whatever the future would bring them.

As they took their duffle bags off their backs and began to again load them into their water carriage, along with the treats Jane had packed for their journey, they screamed in unison.

There in the canoe, a large snake lay sleeping.

Their peaceful feeling was abruptly broken.

"What're we going to do?" cried out Sara, who hated snakes more than life itself.

"Maybe if we poke at it, it will just go away." This from the also scared out of her wits, Carol.

And then before their frightened eyes, the snake awoke and looked at both of them. It was not a threatening look, just a look. It then slowly started to move, to stretch, always keeping its eyes on the women who stood paralyzed in fear on the grassy shore.

The snake then slithered right past them and into the woods.

To say the women were relieved would have been a gigantic understatement, as they breathed sighs of relief, as they hustled into the boat and started paddling faster than they had ever paddled in their lives.

Once they were away from shore, out of what they perceived to be imminent danger, they remembered Christina's words, telling them the snake represented the feminine wisdom, that the shedding of her skin was her transformation, a sort of death, then a rebirth, another chance to live again, in a new skin.

Carol happened to look at her feet and on the floor of the canoe, not noticed before, was the old, dried-out skin of the snake.

In awe and wonder at the immensity of the symbolism, they rowed the rest of the way back saying not a word to each other.

# CHAPTER THIRTY-EIGHT

Carol came home to find all the cracks caused by the earthquake fixed. The city had been told to wait at least two months before repairing even minor damage, because of the regions instability, but Dan had gone ahead, anyway. He could no longer stand to look at his home's imperfections.

Jolted by the mere fact of being back in the hustle and bustle of city life, yet still in a place in her mind still so absorbed in nature's harmony, Carol could have cared less what her walls looked like. This, in itself, was so unlike her. But it simply did not matter to her, anymore.

The first few days home she drifted through her chores, hardly aware of her husband, his needs, or his frame of mind. Whereas when she had returned from the retreat, she had felt desperate to keep that peaceful feeling she had temporarily acquired, now she was enveloped in tranquility.

And like the mother bird, she was now ready to let her son leave the nest and fly free, to seek out his own happiness and all the possibilities that life, his life had to offer, be they her choices for him or not. When the thought, the acceptance of his leaving swept over, she did not know. Seeing his enthusiasm, what could she be if not excited for him.

Suddenly, he had purpose in his life and no matter her sadness in his leaving, she knew she had done her job. She had nurtured him well, as well as she had known how. As much as she wanted to always be there if he fell, to support him so he would not fall, she surrendered to the knowledge that he would now have to depend on, to stand, on his own two legs. And if he wobbled at first, she knew he would eventually find his strength. Her answers, Dan's answers, could no longer be his answers. It was a painful awareness to come to terms with, but one she would have to accept.

"I love you, Mom," Jonas said to her as he began the hard, yet exciting task of packing up a life that had been the only one he had known. "You both were right," he told her. "I've lived off you and Dad. I haven't carried my own weight around here and I apologize. But I don't think I can grow up, living here. You make it too easy for me to remain a child."

How could he have become so wise in such a short time?  He was right, she thought, as tears of truth filled her eyes.  She, herself, had said it to him before, not sure, though, she believed it.  But she was almost sure she believed it now.

"Oh, come on, Mom, don't cry.  I'll be fine.  I think this job could really lead somewhere.  And my apartment is great!  Wait 'til you and Dad see it!"

"I can't wait, Honey."  Carol noted he hadn't asked her for any help with it.

"But I don't want you coming down until I've fixed it all up, okay?

"Okay," she agreed.

Wrenched in two directions, she was extremely proud of her boy, who was no longer a boy.  Yet she felt the pain that another part of her life was ending. Empty womb. Empty nest.

A few days later Jonas waved a good-bye to his parents, on his way, finally to chart his own map, his own destiny.

After many hugs, even a surprising one from his father, Jonas took off down this new street in his life, his car pulling a U Haul filled with his furniture and too many odds and ends Carol had insisted he take.

"Wear your seat belt.  Drive safe," she called after him, as she always did.

As mother and father walked back into their now less full house, Carol swore she saw an inkling of tears in Dan's eyes.

"He'll be fine," she assured him.

Quickly gaining his manly composure, he said, "I tried to tell him about the bank and his tenants insurance and to re-register his car with the DMV and..."

"Dan! He'll be fine. He'll figure it all out. He's not stupid."

"I know he isn't! But I've always taken care of all that stuff for him," Dan replied with worry in his voice.

"And if he screws up, he'll learn from his mistakes."

"I don't want him making any mistakes," said Dan.

"But he will and you can't help it from happening."

Was this really she saying all these things, or had some sane, mature, knowing woman taken over her body? She laughed out loud.

"What's so funny?" asked Dan. He saw nothing funny about the situation. Didn't she care, anymore, what happened to their son, that he had left home for the first time in his life, even if it was long in coming? Was she now so selfishly involved in her own little life, doing all these new things that she didn't give a damn about anything but herself, not even about her son?

She looked at this husband of hers, the man who tried so hard not to let emotions affect him and was surprised at the love she felt for him at the moment.

"It's time to let go of him, Dan. It's past time."

"You're awfully casual about this, Car. I was sure you'd be a complete basket case, today."

"I'm not casual about anything. It was just inevitable, that's all. It was time for him to go on, just like it's time for us."

What did she mean by that, Dan wondered, but instead of asking her, he went into his garage to spend the afternoon rearranging his tools.

With Carol's outward strength, it wasn't until she ventured into Jonas' empty bedroom that the full extent of her loss hit her. There, where his bed had stood a few hours before, she sat on the area of the rugged floor that was so many shades lighter than where his feet had trampled back and forth for years. And she wept alone for a good long while.

The next few days Carol and Dan kept themselves busy, he at work and she digging into her required reading for her coming school semester. She wanted to read every book on her list. She wanted to be more than prepared before classes started. She was both scared and excited as she began her studying, highlighting what she thought to be important sentences, until noticing she had yellowed complete page after page.

But she was already driven to be the best, knowing her classmates, her eventual competition would be kids close to thirty years her junior. She had her work cut out for her and she knew it. But the more she read, the stronger was her conviction she had made the right choice for her future.

Surprisingly, Dan now didn't fight her decision. She was so busy, so self-involved, she, in fact, hardly noticed that when he was home he moped around, his eyes sad, not unlike that of a neglected puppy.

One night he dragged her out of her room and took her to an eatery, a countrified restaurant in Topanga Canyon. It was a warm, balmy evening, as they sat outside, sipping white wine at a table covered with a red and white checkered cloth, lit by a candle.

They hadn't gone out for dinner in a long time and Carol was touched that Dan had made reservations at this, her favorite spot. It was right out of the sixties with a menu of all natural foods and waiters and waitresses who looked like hippies from days gone by. An adjoining shop sold incense and crystals and New Age books and music. A little stream gurgled as it ran over rocks below where they sat. Roosters and cats meandered around their feet, friends, never thinking of fighting with each other.

"Do you hate all men?" asked Dan, seemingly out of nowhere, after their fresh, home-made broccoli soup arrived.

The question certainly took Carol by surprise, even more so because there was no malice in his voice. She had to think before answering.

"I don't know.  Not really, I guess.  I do hate what they've, in general, done, what they've been taught to do."

"You don't mean 'they, do you?  You mean me."

He didn't give her a chance to answer, going quickly on.  "Well, I guess if I were a woman, I'd be pissed, too.  I think I'd be less generous than you," Dan said, his voice soft.

For the first time in quite a while, Carol really looked at her husband.  Where, she had to wonder, was this coming from?  She saw no anger in his face, only a somberness she had never remembered seeing before.

"I wonder why it's always been such a struggle between men and women?" he said, almost asking himself to think of the reason.

A naïve question, thought Carol.

"It hasn't, Dan!  Before you men took the power away from us, everyone lived in relative peace.  I know you never want to hear about it, but when the Goddess was worshipped, life was so much different.   It's an oversimplification, but men eventually couldn't stand it!"

Carol braced herself for a philosophical and historical fight.

"Yeah, the Goddess.  But was it so wrong for men to want something powerful of their own?"

"You're damn right!" she said, her voice immediately raise.  "Especially if it meant the only way they could get it was to annihilate everything women had stood for, for eons! Why did they have to destroy a whole sex, just to feel better about themselves? I know that sounds simplistic and it's much more complicated, but it's basically true."

"I know."

Carol stopped cold. She stared hard at Dan. 'He knows?'

"You know?"

Dan suddenly looked embarrassed. "Okay, okay. While you were gone, I, I, well, I was just looking over some of your books. Okay? I admit it. Are you mad I went into your room?"

"Mad? No! I'm speechless. I'm delighted. Really. But what made you do that?"

"I don't know. I guess I was curious to see all this stuff you've been into. I didn't touch anything, I promise. Well, okay, I shook that rattle a couple of times."

Carol laughed. "Wow."

"There's some interesting stuff. Yeah."

"You sure didn't think so before, when I tried to explain some of it to you."

"A guy can change, can't he?"

Carol smiled, still not quite understanding this turn of events, but more than willing to accept them. She continued to listen to the now thoughtful Dan.

"Okay, so from what I read, and I don't agree with everything, but I guess some of it makes sense, has some truth."

"Some? Look how we've been treated, Dan. You wouldn't stand for a moment of such disrespect! Disrespect? Hell, men tried and succeeded in taking all of our rights away, making us into what they want us to be, housekeepers or sex objects, second class citizens! Why should we even have to fight so hard for things that should have been ours to begin with? We've finally fought back and some things have changed, but, truthfully, not as much as should have!"

"So, you don't think men have any redeeming qualities?

"It's not that they don't, it's just that for so long they haven't seen that women do."

"But men love women," Dan tried to argue, getting the impression he was way over his head, here.

"Oh, yes, they love beautiful, skinny women. Don't you see that we've spent lifetimes trying to be exactly the way you want us to be? Men control what they want us to be and look like and act like. And when we fight back, when we want equal pay or the right to control our own bodies or anything, it all goes back to what's morally right, as far as men are concerned, starting back with the Bible that *man*dated what we could and could not do!"

And so began a different kind of communication between two people who had lived together more than half their lives, but had grown so far apart because they had followed predestined roles that had been decided by others who had gone before them, roles that shaped behaviors of those willing or not.

By the time their pie and coffee arrived, they had run the gambit from the Goddess to God, from women to men.

"Tell me the truth, Dan," asked Carol, "what really, really happened that made you interested in all this, now?"

"The truth? I guess I've sort of felt left out. You've been doing all these things, going away, holing up in your room, now going back to school. It's all been so unlike you. You changed and I guess I didn't like it."

"I have changed, Dan. And you know what? I like myself a hell of a lot better, now."

"Yes. I can see that. I guess I started out feeling angry at you. But lately, it's been more like, I don't know, like jealous and I'll admit I've sort of felt threatened by all you've been doing. You're always with your friend, Sara. And you never tell me anything, anymore." Dan sounded so sad.

"Come on. You made it quite clear you weren't interested," she said, wondering if this was really her Dan she was having this discussion with. "I kept telling you how hard everything was for me, the menopause, all the changes my body was going through. I felt like I was so empty, like I was drowning. And then you had this, what, macho attitude, always telling me it was all in my head, like something was wrong with me and I should just buck up like a man. Truthfully, I just decided to stop telling you anything."

There was a long pause as Dan just looked at his wife.

"I'm sorry, Car. I really am. I didn't understand. I'm still not sure I do, but I'm really, really sorry. I've been an insensitive bastard, haven't I?"

Carol smiled and simply said, "Yes, you have."

"Well, I'm going to try and change, Honey. I will. I want to learn more, about... everything. I don't like the way things have been with us. Help me learn." he said emotionally, as they got up to leave.

"Okay. Okay," Carol softly answered him.

And as they walked to where their car was parked, he took her hand. She wasn't hoping for a miracle, not an instant epiphany, but perhaps this was a beginning.

Later that night they made love with a passion neither of them had felt for each other in a very long time. Afterwards, as she was curled up next to him, his arms around her, holding her tightly, he whispered, "I've missed you."

"I've missed you, too, Dan. But I'm not who I used to be."

"Then I won't be, either."

How odd, thought Carol, as she drifted off to sleep, still encircled by her husband's body. When she had yelled and screamed, trying to change him, trying to make him understand her, she had been powerless. But now, by the simple fact of her changing, sticking to what she knew was right for herself, her own growth stemming from the truths she was learning, Dan seemed to be beginning to change, too.

For the first time in so long, she fell asleep with her lips curled into a smile, as he snored softly by her side.

# CHAPTER THIRTY-NINE

Sara had just spent hundreds of dollars on plants. Finally fixing up her patio was her way of taking back her home, her space, her life. She told herself that after spending all this money and after doing all this work, a large earthquake could not happen again. And it was with this thought she lived and it somehow got her through the days and nights.

She dug her hands in the soil, weeding, fertilizing, planting, then finally watering. She hung wrought iron baskets on her high wood fence and filled them with colorful flowers she did not know the names of. And as she planted she talked to the new residents of her home, telling them how the sun and water would be their nourishment, how during the cool nights they must rest and replenish themselves for the next day's light.

She replaced the broken pots and filled her small plot of earth with a mixture of flowers until it resembled an English garden. Then she bought identifying wood markers that said things like, 'flowers,' 'marigolds,' 'weeds,' and 'I don't know.'

In a large barrel shaped planter she stuck a wood sunflower. Night blooming jasmine finally went into the ground, as did vine-type plants she hoped would eventually climb their way up the wood fence. In the shaded part of her patio, she hung ferns and ivy.

She worked obsessively. No matter how much she bought, she felt she needed more, until the small area was so crowded with new growth she hardly had room for a chair to sun herself on.

Then she tackled the terraces off her bedroom and office. There she planted sweet smelling gardenia bushes and carnations and fuchsias.

The piece de resistance was the Garden Goddess she found which she lovingly placed on the wood-slated floor of her now blooming downstairs piazza, between two planters filled with morning glories. And when she was all finished, she went from patio to patio to patio to view what her labor had brought forth.

What she had not counted on was how long it daily took to keep up her handiwork in the heat of the summer. But the routine gave her pleasure, calming her, as she misted every morning and watered every night.

But Sara was not done. She then decided to fill the empty spaces in her home where she had lost things to the quake. Most everything she bought related to the Goddess. A large ceramic woman's form called 'Dreaming Sister,' who was adorned with beads and shells. A framed photograph of old women, Crones kicking up their heels, entitled, 'Dancers Of The Third Age.' More candles, rose quartz stones, another drum she put near her fireplace and more Goddess figures to put in every room, including her bathroom.

And if it were true or not, she felt protected in her house, now. It was becoming her sanctuary, again, a place she loved to return to at the end of a long day at work

And when it happened, when the earth swayed, as it still sometimes did, she took it more in her stride, now just a bit less fearful. She had made the choice to no longer live in fear and she was trying her damnedest not to.

And then finally, finally she was done. No! She was not done, after all. Feeling so good in her home, surrounded by all her sacred items, inexpensive as they were, yet still sacred to her, Sara decided to start carrying some of these objects at her bookshop. And so her fun continued, as she ordered Goddess jewelry, Goddess figurines, Goddess stamps with purple ink pads, purple being the color of the Goddess and even T shirts representing The Maiden, The Mother and The Crone.

And she talked about them and they sold like hot-cakes. Women told other women and the awareness continued to grow. The jewelry sold best, women wanting to wear around their necks a symbol of their own, this from women who had never heard of the Goddess, before. And it was then, as they fingered their necklaces, that they asked to learn more about Her and were quickly accommodated as Sara brought forth book after book on her favorite subject.

As much as she loved this new financial windfall, what was more important to her was that the message of the Goddess was being discovered. Rediscovered.

Out of her display case she took one of her favorites, a silver Goddess Spirit Healer and put it around her neck. Then she gifted her dearest friend, Carol, with one, also. How empowered they felt everyday they wore it. How protected and how at peace.

As the days went by, women came in droves, thirsty for knowledge of a time when they had been important, when women were cherished, powerful and respected... a time when women's bodies were honored for what they brought forth into the world, instead of being seen only as a vessel for a man's happiness.

Sara's Goddess books began to sell as never before. Was it because of her enthusiasm on the subject, or the desperation that had also come to so many other women with the earth's shaking? Whatever it was, she felt the beginning of real change in the air. She was now more committed than ever to charge that change with her energy and her new-found knowledge.

She decided the time was right to start a women's group, a women's circle. It would begin small. She would invite a few friends and she would ask Carol to do the same. It would be a group of women sitting around, talking about their lives, their problems and their dreams, discussing whatever they wanted to discuss.

Sara closed her eyes and imagined millions of these groups springing up across the country, maybe even the world. And they would talk about the earth and the Goddess and what went wrong with the world and how they could take it back and make it their own, again... how they would build their own ladders instead of trying to climb up man's. And they would talk of getting older and how it did not have to be terrible at all, how instead, this could be the best years of women's lives, just as she had learned from Christina... and of course from old Jane.

Sara's mind raced, ideas tumbling out of her very core. Perhaps she could get speakers to talk at her circles, maybe even Christina. And Sara thought about starting a newsletter, networking, finding out about other groups already established and what they were doing. She didn't see any of this to be on the fringe, wacky women trying to start up their own society. No, the whole point was to integrate what she knew to be true into this society and to make it better. This was her dream. Her elaborate dream.

Her excitement grew as she looked over her calendar to see when she might plan her first meeting. And then she saw it. Her birthday, her fiftieth birthday was now only a few short weeks away. Had she let it slip her mind? Fifty! She had lived half a century. How could that be? It seemed impossible to comprehend.

How do you rate a life? How could she rate hers? Six, on a scale of ten? Seven? Nine? Some years, a two? She had raised a daughter. Been married. Twice. She had had assorted lovers. Owned her own business. Had her share of pain. And she had loved, oh, how she had loved. It was a life and now that life was far more than half over. What did she have, at best, twenty-five, thirty-five or so more years, left? And at worst...? She didn't want to think of that.

She was alive today. More alive than she had felt in ages. Of course, it was easy to think positive thoughts when one was feeling good. And today Sara was feeling good.

The idea of forty-nine had been tough. It was so close to fifty it had been depressing, but now it seemed just to be another number. And at that grand moment, at seven-forty three A.M. she would not be a year older, hell, no, she would just be a day, just a minute older than she had been. That's the way she

331

decided to think about it. You see, she thought, it was just in one's mind. And today her mind said it was alright.

"You look great, Mom."

Sara and Rebecca were strolling around an outdoor mall.

"Thanks, Honey."

"Something's different about you." Then Rebecca's face dropped. "Oh, no! You're not seeing Peter again, are you? Tell me he hasn't wormed his way back into your life, again."

"Becca! He hasn't. I only make mistakes twice with the same person."

"Three, Mom. What about when you went together when you were young?"

"Young? Thanks, kid. And the first time it was good, very… wonderful"

"Sorry. But why do you look so good? Are you in love with someone else you haven't told me about? What are you hiding from me?" the child asked.

"I'm not in love with anyone, Rebecca! Can't a person feel and look good when they're alone?"

Rebecca could hardly consider it, but then she was in love.

"I'm so glad you found out about him when you did, Mom. I always said he was a creep."

"Enough, child! I don't want to talk about Peter, anymore. Ever! Okay?"

"Okay, but don't worry. You'll find someone wonderful one of these days."

The kid never gives up, thought Sara. "You always say that. And for your information, I'm not worried about it."

Rebecca stopped in front of a children's clothing store and started to drool.

"Oh, look, Mama. Look at all those teeny, tiny clothes. They're so adorable, aren't they?"

Sara also looked. Was it really twenty-five years before that her daughter had been that small? Her heart swelled as she remembered giving birth to her, counting her little fingers and toes for the first time, sitting in her rocking chair, singing her to sleep. Where had the years gone?

Rebecca saw the yearning look in her mother's eyes. "Mama? Would you like to have another baby?"

"Me!? I think not!"

"No, really, you could adopt. Women your age are doing it."

"No, no!" Sara said, laughing. "I couldn't imagine having to deal with having a teenager when I'm sixty-five! It was terrible enough when I was in my thirties."

"Thanks a million, Mother!"

"No, my time has past. Now it's your turn."

"Okay!" Rebecca had a big grin on her face.

Sara studied her daughter long and hard. "Okay, what? What?"

Her daughter's grin got even wider.

"Rebecca? Are you? You are, aren't you? You're pregnant! You're pregnant, aren't you?! Oh my Goddess!"

Sara's voice had gotten louder and Rebecca looked around embarrassed, but happily glowing.

"Maaa, shhh! The whole world doesn't have to know!"

"Why not! I don't care!"

She hugged her daughter tightly and started laughing and crying at the same time. "My baby's having a baby! I'm going to be a Grammy!"

Women passing by stared at them and smiled.

"Mom! C'mon, you're really embarrassing me."

"Oh, Honey, when did you find out? How far along are you? When's it due? Are you feeling alright? Why didn't you tell me right away?" Sara questions went on and on.

"Mom, calm down. Yesterday. A few weeks. Next May and I'm feeling fine! Does that answer all your questions?"

Now Rebecca, Sara's little girl, was also laughing and she looked at her daughter in awe.

"Oh, Darling, I'm so happy for you. Is Thomas? Of course he is. Oh, this is so exciting!" And Sara hugged Rebecca, again and again.

"This is the best birthday gift I could have asked for."

"Well, see, I planned it this way!"

Then Sara started to drag Rebecca into the children's clothing store.

334

"Come on. I want to get her something."

"Who said I was having a girl?"

"No one, but that's what I think you're having. Of course, I'd love a little boy, just as much, but girls, oh, little girls are the best. But then again, if you have a boy you could teach him to be an enlightened thinker about women. Oh, the things I will teach him. No, have a girl first, then a boy…"

"Maaa…!"

Once inside the store, Sara bought her soon-to-be grandchild an adorable, white infant outfit, a soft and cuddly doll, because just in case it was a boy, he should know it's okay to play with them… and a yellow rubber ducky for its bath.

## CHAPTER FORTY

A week later, Carol and Sara received the same letter in the mail. It was from Jane's doctor daughter, regretting to tell them that her dear and loving mother had died, a few days before. The letter told how she had held her hand as Jane had passed over, peacefully in her sleep, a smile on her old and wrinkled face. She had had no pain at all. She had simply laid down in her bed, the same bed where she had bore all her children and had gently slipped away. The letter went on to say how before she had left this world, Jane had told her daughter how much their visit had meant to her.

Carol and Sara later met and took a somber walk on the beach, at sunset. And it was there that they remembered her words.

"I know I am old, children. And it will soon be my time to return to the earth. Do not mourn me, though. Just remember my existence in the world."

And so the two women's thoughts would not remain on the fact that she was no longer, but rather that she had been here and that she had touched the earth, touched their hearts and they shed their tears for her. No, they would never, ever forget the old one who had taught them so much, who had allowed them into her life and her world, who had laid her hand on theirs as she taught them how to weave baskets, baskets that now sat with honor next to each of the women's bedsides, always as a reminder of their dear, dear Jane.

It was late summer and the earth was starting its slow decent toward autumn, then toward winter, the season when flowers no longer bloomed, when the soil ceased to yield its fruit, when the chilling, bone-numbing wind blows fierce through the land, except, of course, in Southern California.

It was the time when the old Crones tried to make peace with themselves before death, wondering if they would live to see another spring, when the frozen earth would thaw, once again.

But it was not yet the season of cold for Sara. There was still much life to be lived and celebrated. There would still be many more springs for her to see, she hoped. There would be a new child upon the earth for her to throw with joy into the air, for her to love.

Carol was acting very mysteriously, Sara thought. She had only been told that her friend was taking her away for a birthday surprise.

How strange it was to drive to the airport with no idea what her destination would be. When she finally learned it would be San Francisco, Sara became excited. How long had it been since she had strolled in Golden Gate Park, or wandered around Fisherman's Wharf?

But when Carol rented a car and started driving away from the city, Sara was confused.

"So, just when are you intending to tell me where we're going?" Sara asked for the umpteenth time.

Carol laughed to herself, thoroughly enjoying keeping Sara in the dark.

"You're driving me nuts, woman!" she said. "Oh, okay, I'll tell you this much. We're going camping."

"Camping? You're kidding. Don't you think to celebrate my fifty years on this damn earth I deserve room service and a mint on my pillow, not sleeping in the dirt in a tent?"

Now Carol laughed out loud. "Don't worry, my *old* friend. I've rented us a deluxe tent!"

Even Sara had to laugh at this.

Carol finally turned off the main highway onto a rural back road, seemingly in the middle of nowhere. She then stopped the car and checked her directions, saying nothing, as Sara nervously waited while her friend studied a hand drawn map of who knows where.

"It's pretty out here, isn't it?" Carol said as she took off, again.

"Yeah... wherever here is." said Sara sarcastically.

"Oh, will you relax and enjoy the scenery, old woman. Hey, look over there. A cow!"

"Old woman? That's easy for you to say," Sara teased. "Just wait a year or so when you'll be old, too." Let's see how you'll feel then, Crone.""

"Yeah, but I'll always be younger than you." Carol teased back.

Finally Carol slowed down, double checked her map, again, pulled off the road and stopped the car.

"What're you stopping for, Carol? Don't tell me you weren't kidding and we are going camping. So, where are we? I didn't see any camp ground signs."

Carol ignored Sara's yammering on and on, as she reached into her purse, pulling out a red and white bandanna.

"Now, remain calm, old woman, and don't get pissed off, but I have to cover your eyes for this."

"For what? For what? No! You can't!"

"What'd ya mean, I can't," Carol was now laughing, quite uncontrollably.

"Ah... It doesn't match my outfit!"

Carol continued to laugh as she tied the scarf around Sara's head. "Hold still, already!"

"My god... and I use the term, loosely. You're really doing it! Is this so I won't see all the bears?"

Just leave it on, Sara and don't give me any more lip! And promise me you'll keep it on and not peek."

"Fine, I promise, but I'm gonna get you for this."

Carol then quickly got out of the car and ran around to Sara's side, opening the door, then helping her temporarily blind friend out. She then guided the tripping, laughing Sara down a path and through a small grove of trees.

"What the hell have you planned for me?"

"Sara! This is the last time I'm telling you this! Shut up and enjoy!"

Carol continued to walk Sara past the grove and into a small meadow. She could hardly contain her excitement and laughter at what she had actually accomplished.

"Okay? Ready?"

"For what?" Sara said as she tried to will her ears to hear something her eyes could not see.

Carol then whipped off the bandanna, as shrieks of the word, "Surprise!" were screamed out.

And there before the birthday girl stood all her bunk-mates from the retreat. Beth, Penny, Annie, Elaine and Victoria.

Sara was dumb-struck, absolutely speechless, this an incredible feat for the always verbal Sara, as all the women surrounded her with warm hugs and laughter and greetings.

When she finally found her voice, she still couldn't put into words what she was feeling. As when she found out about the impending birth of Rebecca's child, again she found herself laughing and crying, all at the same time.

"Oh, Carol, this is more than fantastic," and she gave her friend a warm and wonderful hug.

After many more minutes of the excited reunion, Sara said, "Now, will someone tell me where the hell we are?"

Everyone started to laugh, again, as Victoria explained it to her. "At my cabin. Remember I told you about it and how I'd hoped we could all meet again, here? And now, look! It's happened!. It's a good thing you're having a birthday, otherwise who knows if we'd ever really gotten together."

Sara was amazed at all that had transpired without her knowledge, all the planning this must have taken on Carol's part. And she was so happy and grateful.

"Yeah, and the bitch complained the whole way up here," Carol feigned disgust.

"The bitch? The bitch? I did not. I was just… inquiring," countered Sara. Then she stopped her joking. "What a birthday present to see all of you, again. Look at you. Everyone looks so wonderful."

Eventually, the troop made its way back to Victoria's house to talk and really catch up with each other, to make a dinner feast and for Sara, even more surprises to come.

At dinner, everyone wanted to hear about the earthquake, but Sara was more interested in hearing about her friends and what had happened in their lives since they had last all been together.

Just as Sara and Carol had, most of the women had also struggled in their search for continuing inner peace. Elaine had all but given up her passion for the tabloids and was putting her energy into something real, volunteering full-time at a battered woman's shelter.

Beth still thought about her late husband on a daily basis and had started keeping a journal of her life with him. She had also taken to writing poetry, some of which had been published in her local paper. She still gave massages and life wasn't bad.

Annie had met a man. She didn't know where it would lead, but he was a good man and it gave her faith that there were a few of them out there. She had also rescued a puppy from certain death, from the pound. Now, besides having a dog of her own, she worked at the pound a few times a week, helping to find homes for other unfortunate furry creatures.

Penny had finally put her foot down to her loving husband and demanded more equality in her house. She no longer wanted to be treated like a porcelain doll and had finally convinced him to take her out fishing with him.

And Victoria had made the most dramatic change of all of them. She had left her husband, finally having enough of his philandering ways. And although she was scared to be on her own, at her age, she knew she had made the right decision. Having no money woes, she was deciding what she should do with the rest of her life. She was also working hard at trying to reestablish a relationship with her grown children, thus far, not one hundred percent a success, but she was hopeful.

It was such a warming feeling for all of them to realize how the enlightenment of the retreat they had shared had begun to change all of their lives. Of course, there would still be pain as they grew older, as they walked a step closer toward that uncharted territory, but what they learned of most value, was that there was always hope and what they had started out thinking was an end, was in truth, a beginning.

"I just wish every woman, especially women our age could experience what we did," said a passionate Sara. "Maybe Christina should hold those retreats for Maidens and Mothers, too, so they will understand the beauty of their womanhood early on in their lives. I just wish all women knew what we know, what we are learning, now."

Fingering the Spirit Healer necklace Sara had given to her, Carol quietly said, "One Goddess necklace at a time, my friend."

# CHAPTER FORTY-ONE

After their fine feast of a dinner, the women all sat down on the braided rug in front of the fireplace. Beautiful Celtic music played in the background. Each woman, except for Sara, held an unlit candle. And in the center of their circle were six empty candle holders, in the middle of which was one lit candle, representing Sara, the birthday woman, whose flame still burned bright.

Beth spoke first, explaining to Sara what was about to happen.

"When I turned fifty, what seems like a very long time ago, some friends of mine gave me a Candle Wish Ceremony. It was a sure wonderful beginning of that year and this third stage of my life, although then I didn't think of it in that way. So, tonight, Sara, we've decided to do that same thing for you."

Sara was so filled with love and excitement, she could only shake her head in happiness.

Off of the lit candle in the center, Big Mama Beth lit her own.

"My wish for you, Sara, baby, is that you have the ability to take each day as it comes and live each of those days, not as if it might be your last, Honey, but instead, as if it was your first... with that kind of excitement and anticipation."

Sara mouthed a warm 'thank you' to Beth.

Then the large woman turned to Annie, who sat besides her and lit her candle, then placed her own into one of the empty candle holders next to the one that represented Sara.

"Okay, here goes," began Annie. "I wish you very few wrinkles, as little cellulite as possible..."

"Too late for that, my friend," laughed Sara, along with the others.

"... and no osteoporosis. And that you always keep your own teeth! And that you never experience incontinence! In short, may you always look and feel as healthy and as beautiful as you are, today."

"From your mouth to the Goddess's ear," laughed Sara, again.

Next was Penny, who was obviously nervous. After her candle was lit by Annie, she began, shyly.

"I hope I remember what I wanted to say. Well, Sara, my wish for you is that you'll always have someone in your life to talk to and to share with, who really understands you."

Sara smiled, her mind for a split second thinking of Peter and of Sean and even of David. Maybe someday, she thought. Maybe someday.

Next was Victoria's turn.

"I hope... I wish for you on this your fiftieth birthday, that you never forget how to laugh. I did. And I now believe that when we lose that ability, we die inside, way before our time."

Sara smiled warmly at Victoria and blew her a kiss.

Elaine, who was next, started laughing. "Hey, I wish... I wish I was fifty, again!"

This brought about laughter from everyone else, also.

"No, seriously, I wish you a wonderful life, Sara. And now that your daughter is going to bear a new life, I wish that she gives you a granddaughter..."

"...I told her that very thing," interrupted Sara.

"Absolutely," went on Elaine. "So the tradition will live on. Think of it. Then in your family you will have the three Goddesses, the Maiden, however small at first, the Mother and the Crone."

"So, this is it, huh? I'm finally stepping over that great line into Cronehood?" asked Sara.

Carol's candle was lit by Elaine's, as she started to speak.

"Not quite, my dear friend. Since you haven't started your total descent, yet, my wish for you is an easy journey, easier than mine has been, through this jungled web of menopause. I wish for you no hot flashes, no bloating, no headaches, no dizzy spells, no uncontrollable crying jags and no manic behavior! But, since you'll never be that lucky..." Carol then reached behind her and grabbed a paper bag. She continued her wish as she took things out of the bag, one by one.

"... Here is aspirin for the headaches, tissues for all the crying you can expect to do, water pills for the bloating and if you don't like drugs, some asparagus, a natural diuretic. Now here's a list of women therapists, for when you think you're going out of your mind and I'm sick of hearing you complain, and last, but certainly not least, here is a fan for your hot flashes!"

By now the women were hysterical, Sara laughing the hardest.

"But wait! I have one more wish," continued Carol. "and that is that we remain friends, forever."

The laughter quickly turned into sentimental 'ahhhs'.

Then Carol placed her candle in the last empty holder making the center of the circle resemble a lit birthday cake.

"Alright, Birthday Woman," Mama Beth said, "it's your turn to make your own wish and then blow out your candles, Darlin'."

Sara thought for a moment as she raised herself up on her knees. What eloquent words could she possibly come up with that could even come close to expressing how she was feeling at that moment?

"What can I say? I am so overwhelmed by all of this and all of you. I can't even think what to say."

"Ah oh! That's the first sign of your descent!" joked Carol.

"Probably," Sara laughed along with the rest of them.

"Well... I want to thank all of you for what I have to say is the best birthday I think I have ever had. And you know what? Suddenly I'm glad I'm this age. Right this minute it feels just fine. Terrific, in fact. So, my wish is that if I'm only lucky enough to have half of all your wishes for me come true, then I'll still consider myself a very lucky and blessed woman. Thank you, everyone... so much."

Sara couldn't help but to beam, as she looked around the room at her friends. And then she closed her eyes and took a deep breath, and in one fell-swoop, blew out her candles.

After the women toasted her with wine and ate some real birthday cake, they went outside to watch the moon, as it regally sat high in the sky, watching over them.

The women searched the dark, clear vastness and picked out constellations, the Dippers, Orion's Belt, the North Star, the Great Bear, as they twinkled in the heavens.

And as the music from the house filtered out into the otherwise quiet night, the women began to sway back and forth, getting closer together, their graceful, rhythmic movement in harmony.

And they all felt peaceful and proud and powerful and unified as they swayed. They were All Women, moving together to the music. They were One Woman. They were Goddesses. And there were Crones among them.

# EPILOGUE

## (2011)

Eighteen years had passed and the Great Mother felt as if She were dying. So very sadly, hate, not love was being preached from some pulpits and in the highest halls of government. Pain and suffering of Her people was accelerated. There was famine and disease. Wars continued to rage. The rich got richer, the poor, poorer. The middle class had all but disappeared. Worker's rights were in great jeopardy. The great Katrina hurricane quite nearly destroyed New Orleans and surrounding areas. Oil spewed into the Gulf and decimated the land and the sea, the birds and the fish. Greedy banks rendered good people homeless. Fracking and endless drilling deep into the Great Mother's soul was poisoning the environment and the people. And more and more money was made for the very, very few.

A black man was elected to the highest office in the land and suddenly there was hope. But it was short-lived, for prejudice in its ugliest form took root, although for a very long time it was denied, by those who spit out their hate, night after night on TV and on the radio and by those who had political ambitions of their own. The other side, the side that could not bear the fact that a man named Barack Hussein Obama was president, admitted their one goal was to see him fail. And again, forefront in the news was the intolerance of other's beliefs. Whose god is better? Mine! Mine! Mine! And so the license to kill was acceptable. And yes, as had always been the case, most wars happened because of that religious intolerance and hatred. Whose god would win? Mine! Mine! Mine!

And what of the women folk? Whatever strides women had made in the past, they seemed to systematically be reversed. Unbelievably, there was now a concerted effort in this country, to once again take away a woman's right to decided what went on in her body. Abortion doctors were being murdered. These people cared more about the fetus than the child, once it was born. Could this actually be happening in this country?

Sara, Carol and millions more women were outraged beyond belief, yet seemingly impotent to fight against the old, white men in Congress and the

351

robed men who sat in judgment on the highest court of the land. And worst of all were the women, the TV blond Barbie dolls or the new crop of political women looking like happy homemakers of the 50's, who were quite ecstatic to help take women back to medieval days of yore, because of their personal religious and political beliefs, those which were so intertwined.

Young female starlets thought showing their feminism was to exhibit their naked bodies, going panty-less, knowing male photographers watered at the mouth as they stalked, then shot them with their long lenses. Bikini-clad girls with overly huge fake breasts served leering men coffee at drive-thru fast food joints. Sexist ads on billboards and on TV were the norm. Sitcoms were filled with boorish husbands making sexists jokes to and about their beautiful young TV wives. Did our society actually forget what the true meaning of feminism really means? It seemed to be the case and Sara thought, 'I sure as hell didn't burn the bra I never needed to wear, back in the 70's, for this!'

Women of every age were out of control, pumping up their lips and sucking here, adding there, becoming unrecognizable, thinking they were holding on to their youth while they filled their once beautiful faces with Botox and the like.

Women in different countries were still being raped by men at alarming rates. In too many countries women continued to have no rights, couldn't drive, couldn't vote, had to cover their bodies and faces with heavy clothing, Berkas, a word most had never heard of until that illegal war, filled with lies, had begun in Iraq.

And as they fought, it was the great Mother Earth who suffered the most. And She wept for what was happening to Her, what was happening to Her children... by Her children. Yes, Her ice caps were melting at an alarming rate. Her insides now sucked even dryer of Her life's blood, oil. And for what? For money, for power, for greed. It seemed leaders of too many countries cared not for the people, nor for the land, but only for themselves. Young soldiers continued dying for nothing. Innocents, men, women and children, in the line of fire, were shot down, dead. For what? For nothing. Fear was the name of the game, getting otherwise reasonable people to do and think unreasonable things. It seemed the world had gone quite mad.

And, yes, the Great Mother was so distraught, so angry, so enraged, Her wrath was evident in the destruction She wrought over the lands. She had done it before, for that was Her nature, but now it seemed everyday She screamed out in horrific pain, causing more and more earthquakes and hurricanes, floods and tornados, monsoons, waves from Her oceans rising so high and fierce and powerful, they covered the earth, destroying entire communities, devastating entire countries.

Would Her children never learn? Would they never remember past lessons? And now She felt

Herself dying, really dying and if something didn't change soon, She would take them all with Her. She would be ignored no longer. And interestingly, or perhaps not, when these natural disasters came to pass, it was She who was blamed, yet when Her children happened to survive Her rage, it was God who was thanked.

Yes, the Great Goddess was dying. Who would save Her and Her children before it was too late? But truthfully, the way some of them were behaving, were they worth saving, at all?

For Sara, these depressing thoughts were never far from her mind She did not like the world these days, at all. She was outraged at the changes that had happened in the last number of years. But, new president or not, black president or not, hope and change were hard to come by. In fact, in the first two years of his presidency, things seemed to be getting worse, what with his opposition blocking every move he made.

Sara sat behind her desk, making out her monthly check to her Medicare supplemental care and adding her Social Security funds into her check book. And now the Republicans wanted to basically obliterate both Medicare and Social Security. But there were now, some signs that the people were beginning to rebel. That's what we need, she thought, a revolution! But she finally decided to stop thinking politically, if only for a little while and instead wondered how the years had passed so quickly by.

Out to lunch with an old, high school friend, he remarked, "Sara, can you believe in a couple of years we'll be seventy!" Seventy!! How could that possibly be happening to her? She didn't feel it. She didn't think she looked it. And didn't it seem only yesterday that she had celebrated her fiftieth birthday with all those wonderful women she had met so long ago on that island beyond the mists. And she thought of them all. Through the years they had stayed in touch, now mainly through emails, the new way of communicating Sara wasn't that fond of. Youngin's, their fingers flying over their now more sophisticated, ever smaller computers or texting on their cells phones their most intimate of feelings through the air, actually thinking this was the way to have substantial relationships. Sara, more than not, still wrote letters and cards, delivered the old fashioned way, by snail mail. Such a funny word to her.

And what of her old bunkmates at that delicious, week-long retreat where Crones roamed?

Country-girl Penny was still married to good, old Sam, and now was the grandmother of five. She made it a point to go fishing a number of times a year.

Elaine started her own shelter for homeless and battered women and was living a fulfilled life. It was only now and again that she would peek at the cover of some tabloid while waiting to be checked out at the market. She was living a life, not reading about other's lives, now.

After a number of relationships, Annie ended up marrying a younger man and got back into the clothing business on a smaller scale, designing clothes for older women who still wanted to look attractive, even trendy, but still their age. She sold them to local boutiques and even to some chain clothing stores. And she was happy.

Victoria, who was now almost seventy-seven ended up back with her husband, who one day decided it was she whom he still loved, that it was his own fear of getting older that led him to stray with younger women, thinking that would keep him young, too. Quite ill with cancer, she tended to him with love and compassion, making the most of the time they had left, together. She never forgot, but somewhere in her heart, she was able to forgive.

With the greatest of sadness Sara learned that big, beautiful Mama Beth had died a few years before, of a stroke. The thought of this woman with the twinkle in her eye and that raucous laugh of hers was now gone, brought pain to Sara's heart. And she remembered Mama Beth's words about her dead husband, "… And one of these days we're gonna see each other again and laugh about what a grand time we had…" Sara hoped they were together now, laughing, as Beth regaled him with, "… what the hell I've been doing all this time."

And then, of course, there was Carol. As it turned out Dan had read and studied and learned his lessons well, from Carol's extensive women's library, in her private room, that wasn't so private, anymore.  And she was thrilled.  It didn't happen overnight, but he eventually became a man of real sensitivity, to the point his men friends all but walked away when he started talking on and on about men and women and the Goddess.

Years before, Carol and Dan gave up their beautiful home in Santa Monica and moved back to the South, to her childhood place of birth, where he was also raised and built another house surrounded by acres of land which included a small lake with woods behind it.

Carol had gotten her degree in psychology and now had many clients who adored her.  Jonas was doing well, still cartooning, had finally married and Carol never gave up hope he would soon give her a grandchild, continuing the circle of life.

Although Sara and Carol didn't talk often, they stayed in touch by letters and yes, emails, always remembering each other's birthdays and knowing no matter how many miles separated them, they would always remain friends, dear, dear friends.

And what of Sara?  By now Rebecca had given her three grandbabies.  The first being a boy.  The second being a boy.  And finally, finally a little girl.  Mother and daughter were close as ever, that tie even strengthening as the years went by, if that was possible.

Book, Nook and Crannies still stood in the Malibu plaza and had its regular customers and tourists who came looking for young celebrities who lived in the area, but of late, Sara wondered how long she could keep her beloved shop open. The big, corporate bookstores with their discounted prices made it harder, year by year, for an independent to survive. But what would she do then, she wondered? This, she didn't know.

What she did know was that she was alone, still alone.

"Ma, I can't believe you haven't had a date in what, almost twenty years? This is ridiculous. You're still young, you're still cute and smart and…"

"What, Rebecca, you want me to start hanging out at trendy bars in five inch heels and skin-tight pants to meet guys?"

"No, but…"

The funny thing was Sara didn't really mind living alone. Used to it, she certainly was. Set in her ways? Possibly. But still, that gnawing thought of growing old, really old all alone, she didn't like. But she dismissed all thoughts of that, for now. No, she would not think about aging alone. She would not think about politics. She would not think about anything of a negative nature. Not today. Not now. Instead, she bounded up her stairs to pack for her trip.

In the rustic amphitheater, around a great bonfire, nineteen women sat on wooden benches, excited with anticipation, yet nervous of what this week would bring. They were of all sizes, colors and faiths. They were all women. All women inching closer to older age. They had come for as many reasons as one might laugh or cry in any given day's time.

Sitting in a wheelchair in front of the fire was this beautiful, beautiful woman, this over eighty year old beautiful woman named Christina. She was probably the most beautiful woman any of them had ever seen. She, with her long, unruly silver-white hair. She, who was clothed in a flowing Indian madras dress and high-laced leather moccasins. She, who was adorned with silver and turquoise necklaces around her now very wrinkled swan-like neck, bracelets wrapped around her wrists, feathered earrings hanging to her shoulders and silver and stone rings on her slender, yet arthritic fingers. Next to her sat her two regal German Shepard dogs.

In her still strong and lyrical voice Christina spoke.

"Welcome, welcome, my women. I see you have met my children, Buddha and Luna. Luna, of course, is the moon, that which shines down on us during the night, watching, always watching over us, keeping us safe until the sun rises to warm us. And Buddha, of course, was the Enlightened One, something I hope you shall find during this next week. Enlightenment."

The still twinkle in her eye and the melody of her voice was infectious, spreading throughout the women. What magic did this old, old woman hold, the soon to be Crone women thought?

Christina spoke a little longer and then...

"I now want to introduce you to a Crone Supreme. This is Sara."

Sara, dressed in jeans and a sweatshirt with a large peace sign on it, came and stood beside her beloved mentor, first bending down to kiss Christina on the cheek. Christina continued.

"I am still young in spirit, my women, but older in my bones and now, my Sara will take you to places I can no longer go, climb mountains I can no longer climb…"

The next morning, on the great plateau that overlooked the Sound, where sail boats looked like toys from the height the women stood and down below were small rivers and streams winding their way through the dense woods, where a huge eagle majestically soared, as if on cue, in the cloudless, azure sky, Sara looked at the already exhausted women and smiled.

"We are no longer young, my friends. But our soaring days are far from over. Mark my words, this week you will learn to celebrate. Celebrate yourselves. Celebrate your soul. Celebrate your knowledge and your strength and your courage and all that you have accomplished. It is time to celebrate becoming a Crone. It is time to celebrate your life, my women… what you started out as and what you have become! Every new line on your face, like every new ring inside the trunk of the great ancient oak will become an affirmation of your knowledge and your wisdom from living on this earth. For this, my children, is the Crone. Like the earth itself, you are to be revered and respected for all the days and nights you have roamed this land. Her land. And so welcome to the beginning of this magical journey toward this third portion of your life. You might not believe it today, but you are all Goddesses. Yes. You are. And as this week passes, as you really look inside yourselves, you will see it. You *are* all Goddesses. Each and every one of you... Goddesses! So celebrate, my women. It is time to celebrate! For there are Crones among us and believe me when I tell you, that's a very, very good thing."

CPSIA information can be obtained
at www.ICGtesting.com
Printed in the USA
FSOW04n0735190917
38934FS